When an organised crime gang takes over the peaceful fishing village of Karumba it sets off a chain reaction of murder and kidnapping along the wilderness coast of the Gulf of Carpentaria, the domain of crocodiles.

Detective Sergeant Bill Madsen is transferred by the Queensland Police Service to bring law and order to the Crocodile Coast, but first he must survive the hostilities of the criminal element that have taken control of the sleepy fishing village.

Out in the wilds people are murdered in their fishing camps as the criminals assert a grip of terror along the Crocodile Coast where they rule with fear and intimidation. The ultimate showdown takes place on the Mitchell River, when the "Barramundi Mafia" dares to challenge the might of the authorities.

© 2022 Richard (Dick) Victor Eussen

ISBN: 978-0-6453511-5-6

Proof reading/Editing: Brad Connors

Cover design: James Barron

Cover photograph: Ann Leighton

Typeset in 12/16 Bembo

THE CROCODILE COAST

DICK EUSSEN

Also by Dick Eussen

Australia's Gulf Country

Fishing Kakadu National Park

Duck Hunting Australia

Barramundi and Tropical Freshwater Fishes

Complete Book of Barramundi Fishing

The Savannah Way – Cairns to Broome

The Fishing and Camping Guide to the Top End

Author's Note

This action-packed adventure novel is set in Australia's remote Gulf country, where the small Gulf coastal fishing village of Karumba and the lawless coast is ruled by man-eating crocodiles, but there is another evil that pales in comparison.

In the wilderness that fringes the tropical Gulf of Carpentaria commercial and recreational fishermen are under siege from a drug cartel that has made the wilderness its own. People vanish, never to be heard of again, while Karumba is controlled by criminals who have no respect for human life. Following the brutal murder of a deep cover detective, the Queensland Criminal Investigation Branch sends Police Sergeant Bill Madsen to the Gulf to infiltrate the cartel. He is in danger at every turn as he fights the criminal coalition putting his own life and others in dire straits. He meets the love of his life, Julie a widow and a local schoolteacher.

Together they face the onslaught of the Gulf country's unpredictable dry and wet seasons, the tyranny of distance, its isolation and the greed of those who rule the crocodile coast and kill anyone who gets in their way. Madsen connects with boar hunters and an army patrol who help him to eliminate the crime boss and his cartel at an exciting climax in the mangrove wilderness of the Mitchell River delta.

Terror on the Crocodile Coast is an adventure novel about love and a lifestyle in a remote tropical community where a way of life, that has been lost elsewhere, has endured. This is under siege from a powerful and evil drug lord who has made the town his own. Here in Australia's wild north life is raw with danger at every turn as man and the elements battle for supremacy.

Dick Eussen, 2022

To all my good mates, may you enjoy the read and share the adventure.

Chapter 1
THE COMPOUND

Don "Wog" Marotsi poured himself another wine. He checked the bottle's contents before placing it back onto the table with a loud belch. The heavy, monotonous electronic drum like beat of the "doof doof" music assaulted his ears. Lucky the compound was far enough out of Karumba that it would not bother anyone, or the coppers would shut it down, he thought. The town folks called it the "Gulf Barra Club," as it was only open to invited people and the staff of the Gulf Barramundi Company who lived in the fenced compound in demountable accommodation units or "dongas".

Wog loved the place. It had been his brainchild to house staff and business visitors away from the prying eyes of the town. Besides a well-stocked bar, it had a small conference room and kitchen area and was surrounded by an inner fence where guard dogs roamed free, but that bloody music was something that he could do without.

Having been brought up in Mount Isa and its country music culture, Wog hated the nightclub beat, but told himself that it was what the crowd wanted. Some forty odd people, mostly men, were gathered under the open hangarlike shed. A few women were sitting away from the main crowd, drinking wine, though a couple were dancing with each other on the concrete floor, shaking their butts and boobs to the beat to attract attention from the men.

'The blonde will have her tits fall out soon,' Wog thought as he savoured the blood red wine.

He reflected that life was good as he again topped the glass. Who would have thought that a hard rock miner would one day have what he had achieved? Mount Isa had been good to him though, he mused, taking another long nip from the glass, rolling the wine in his mouth before swallowing and enjoying its sweet flavour.

After leaving school he had undertaken an apprenticeship with Mount Isa Mines as a diesel fitter. When he had done his time, he had gone underground on contract mining where he slaved for ten years before walking away in search of space and freedom from bosses. Twelve years had since passed, he mused.

If there was one thing that Wog loved more than anything else, it was fishing. He had spent most of his spare time fishing the Australian tropics between Cairns and Broome. For those who knew him, it was no surprise that when he walked away from the mines, he purchased a commercial barramundi fishing licence in the Gulf of Carpentaria and settled at Karumba, a small fishing village on the mouth of the Norman River in Australia's Gulf country. His work mates called him the unkind nickname of "Wog" because of his Sicilian background and dark looks. No matter how hard he tried to shed the name it stuck like glue, and he had reluctantly accepted it as being part of life. His father, a hard rock miner, had told him that when he was two years old, they had migrated to Australia, and ended up in the mining city. Both his parents were dead. He missed them.

Wog was tall for a southern European and had inherited his striking good looks from his mother. He had never married, not that it bothered him as he was seldom seen without a woman at his side. None lasted too long as he would "bush" any who displeased him. The blonde with the big boobs, who was dancing on the concrete pad, was his latest acquisition, but he knew that she would not be with him for long as a new "package" was arriving on the next shipment. He had done a deal for her on his latest Thailand trip, and she would be on the next boat to arrive from Indonesia. Just the thought of her had him rubbing his crotch.

'Thinking about rubbing those big tits tonight, Boss?'

Wog recognised the big wheezing voice and replied without turning around.

'None of your business, Bull,' he replied. 'though I don't mind admitting that there is some truth in what you are saying. Grab a seat, about time you got here.'

He turned, kicked out a chair and looked at his lieutenant. "Fuck," he thought. 'Bull would have to be the ugliest man I know.'

Indeed, Bull Atinus was ugly. He was almost two metres tall, and wide across the shoulders. He had no neck, his head just appearing to rise from his massive beefy shoulders. They sprouted a set of thick hairy arms that hung down to his knees, that along with a massive chest and an overlapping beer gut, gave him the appearance of a hulking gorilla that Wog had seen in the Singapore zoo. As always, he wore a green singlet, rugger shorts and a pair of thongs – his usual dress mode. Wog knew that Bull's real name was Shirley, a cruel hoax that his parents had bestowed on him. Due to his first name his work mates had named him "Bull," which suited him well.

'Hell,' Wog thought' 'Bull would be a bigger attraction in any zoo than a monkey, especially to Asians who know what one looks like.' He laughed aloud at the thought.

'Something funny Boss?'

'No mate, just looking at those two trying to attract attention,' Wog grimaced nodding to the gyrating women. 'Fuck, I hate that music. You want a wine?'

'No thanks Boss. Weed is getting me a green can from the bar. Here he comes now.'

Wog was in a good mood, and he laughed as he saw the small man limping over, carrying a couple of VB cans of beer in stubby holders. Weed was Bull's best mate. He was five feet tall and as skinny as a rake, though all of it was muscle and sinew. He had formerly been a jockey and had done well in numerous country races in his time before taking up with Bull as his first mate on a barramundi fishing boat.

Weed's limp was a legacy of a crocodile attack when he had seen part of his left leg ripped away. The croc only let go when Bull shot it with his .44 Magnum revolver. Weed was dressed in a pair of stubby shorts and a black T-shirt, embossed with a Karumba logo. He wore a battered hat that had seen better days. But unlike Bull, he was always in bare feet and as far as anyone knew he did not own a pair of shoes.

An unusual pair, Wog thought, but they were the best of mates and reliable. The locals called them Jekyll and Heckle, though never to their faces as both were hard men and not to be crossed. Bull had put several men in hospital who had been foolish enough to fight him or had been unlucky enough to be in the vicinity of his rage. It was common knowledge that Weed was handy with a knife in the dark, though the police had never been able to prove anything against him.

'Hey, that sounds like the boys coming down the track,' Wog grunted. 'Fuck, those Harleys make a fucking roar, they will drown the music out when they pull up. Does the gate know to let them in?'

'They do, I fixed it when Weed and I came through,' Bull replied.

The roar of thirty odd Harley Davison bikes drowned the music as the bikers rode through the gates and into the compound, the rising dust almost engulfing them. They parked their bikes with lots of noise and engine revving before walking out of the dust into the bright lights of the open shed – dusty, leather clad men, most with long beards and long hair. There were a handful of women with them, easily recognised when they took their helmets off and shook their hair loose.

Everyone knew each other and there were handshakes and hugs. The noise of people talking increased tenfold. The newcomers jostled and crowded about the bar for a drink. A big biker strolled out from the throng and looked about. He nodded towards Wog and walked up, a beer can in his hand.

'G'day Wog, Bull, Weed,' he said as he shook hands with the three men.

'Axel, how the fuck are they hanging?' greeted Wog as he took the firm grip. Stan "Axel" Shute was a big man in his mid-forties.

He had long reddish-blond hair, and an even longer beard, flecked with grey, that set off his steely blue eyes. He wore gold ear and eyebrow rings, which Wog thought looked ridiculous for a grown man, but he knew that no man would ever tell Shute that because it was well known that dead men lay under his tracks. Wog did not doubt it.

There was a lot of small talk as it had been several months since the men had met. The Gulf Rats, as the bikers called themselves, were stationed on the Gold Coast and had affiliated branches in all the capitals and larger cities. They were of interest to the police, though few ever got into trouble, unlike some of their better-known affiliated club members. Three, sometimes four times a year, they rode north to Karumba to relax and for the fishing. It was a cover; Wog knew the real motive was the expected arrival of the ship and its cargo.

He reflected to a time when Tony Broggetti had come into his life almost seven years ago. He had never heard of him, though Broggetti knew all about him. He was a short man of thickset stature who wore horn-rimmed glasses and was in an advanced state of baldness.

'I am your cousin,' he informed Wog. 'Like you, I came to Australia from Sicily with my parents, but I was ten years old. You may not know this, but your real parents were assassinated in a Mafia dispute. Your true mother was my mother's sister. It was your uncle and aunty on your father's side who adopted you and saved your life. You and I would have been killed if they had not taken us away from the vendetta. The way of the Sicilian Cosa Nostra families is to kill everyone so that they can't come back and kill you later. I am proud to inform you that the family was avenged, and the family honour was restored.'

Wog had been spellbound by the tale of his forebears. He now knew why his "dad" and "mum" had been so secretive and never talked about the mother country. He told Broggetti about it.

'That would be right,' he replied. 'Uncle Alfonse and Aunty Maria vanished after arriving in Australia. My parents thought the mob must have got them. But it was by chance that I saw your photo in a commercial fishing magazine about your Gulf fishing business and recognised the remarkable family resemblance, though I was unlucky and took after my father in looks,' Broggetti added ruefully.

'I had a private investigator investigate you and the picture came together. Now I have a proposition for you that will make you rich beyond your dreams. I will tell you now that it is illegal, but from what I know about you that is a minor problem.'

Wog had laughed.

'Oh, you're talking about my poaching exploits of illegal barramundi fishing, crocodile skin poaching and "hooch" growing? It's not a big thing, and I have never been caught.'

'No, but the reason that you have not been caught is because you are ahead of them. I think that is because of the family genes. Both our families have been involved in such matters since records began. I am the head of a large Australian syndicate with overseas connections, and I would like you to join us. I guarantee it will be rewarding and adventurous. My syndicate is in the business of exporting and importing, matters little what, providing we make money, lots of it.'

They had talked long into the night, enjoying a meal of succulent mud crab entrée and barramundi fillets with a salad side dish that was savoured with a couple of bottles of the best wine that Wog had ever tasted. Broggetti told him of the syndicate's grand plan to buy every cattle property between Karumba and the Mitchell River, fishing licenses, and of boats arriving loaded with contraband – drugs, guns, people and whatever else that could be turned into cash money by the syndicate.

'But what about the commercial barramundi fishers that operate in these waters, or the hundreds of recreational fishers that roam the coast in the dry season?' Wog had asked. 'And what about the Navy and

14

Custom's border security patrol vessels and planes, and the police?'

'Again, that is not a problem. They don't matter, we will buy those who want to sell and scare the others out of the country. There are ways of doing this. For instance, our Asian boat is the same as the local seagoing trawlers. They just blend in with the prawning fleet once they enter the Gulf. As Plan B we have people in Indonesia that flood the entire northern coastline with illegal fishing boats when we have big shipments. Border security is busy elsewhere when our ship comes down from the north. As for the police we have our own people in the force, and at a high level I may add, so the local coppers and fishing inspectors leave us be.'

Wog sipped on his wine in deep silence, thinking the worst. What would happen to him if he ended up in jail, the worst thing for an outdoorsman like himself.

'Are you in?' Broggetti had asked sharply, holding out his hand.

Wog hesitated for a moment before he shook hands and agreed to be part of the smuggling operation. He regretted it in the morning but was wise enough to know that if he decided to pull out, he would be killed because he now knew too much – family connections or not.

The rest was history: The huge amount of money that flooded in, the investment by the syndicate in the purchase of cattle stations and barramundi licenses. They put Wog in charge of the Gulf Barramundi Company (GBC) as the syndicate named it and from there, he worked his way up into the marketing and distribution of the products. In fact, he was the brains behind many ventures, something that Broggetti appreciated.

He had wanted Wog to come south to control the business from the city, but Wog would have none of it. The Gulf country was in his blood, and it was his home. All his business was done with a laptop from his boat, via the Internet.

Wog had picked his men with care; most, like many others in the fishing village had no name but aliases and were on the run, either from the law, criminals, or wives. They worked on the GBC fishing boats that plied the Gulf. It was Bull Antinus who had chosen the bulk of them. Bull was the instrument that made it all possible thought Wog as he looked at the ugly man with affection.

The GBC now owned six fifteen metre purpose build fishing vessels that could roam far out to sea in all but cyclonic conditions to meet ships arriving with contraband from the north. When not engaged in illegal activity, the boats and their crews were fishing for barramundi, pelagics and reef fish, because things had to look good so as not to raise the suspicions of the authorities. Besides, there was big money in fishing and the income helped to launder some of the illegal money back into the system.

Wog, as company CEO, had splurged his money on a new twenty metre cruise vessel that was used for supervising both the illegal and legal activities of the fishing fleet. The ship was his home. All that in less than seven years. Wog reckoned he was a lucky man.

'Looks as if the Big Boss has arrived,' Weed noted in his raspy voice, indicating with a nod towards the gate house lights where three dust-covered black Range Rovers were waved in by the security guard.

'Fuck, the prime minister doesn't have as much security as this bloke,' Shute swore.

'No, but then again the whole bloody police force and every two-bit crook in the land is not after him or his job either,' Bull replied. 'I would hate to try and get close to him without being invited. That bodyguard of his are hard core, born fucking killers; ex-SAS troops kicked out of the army for misconduct, or similar. And of course, there is all that loot. If certain people knew how much money was in those boxes in the 4WDs they would hijack his convoy, no matter what the cost.'

Wog got up, walked the short distance to the first Range Rover and opened the front passenger door.

'Welcome Tony,' he greeted.

'Fuck Don, how did you know I was in the front seat?' Broggetti asked as he stepped out and hugged Wog.

'Because you are a creature of habit and always lead,' Wog said. 'Last time you were also driving the front car. Be careful that your enemies don't twig to it.'

'Don, I hear you, you are a wise man. Come, we will have a drink and some fine seafood as we talk. You boys put the boxes into the safe room and ensure that it is locked down tight and guarded. Weed will assist you. Come Don, let us drink to your health.'

He put his hand on Wog's shoulder and the men walked to the conference room, closely followed by Bull.

'So, who is still to come?' Broggetti asked as he sat down in one of the comfortable chairs.

'Well, the Russian Mafia and Asian Triad people are here, so is Shute, the west coast biker's representative, and two Middle East characters. I have told them we will see them one by one after dinner. The cook is heating up the barbeque now and dinner will be ready soon.'

'Good, I hope they have the money,' Broggetti replied. 'The problem with the Asian syndicate is they want forty per cent up front before delivering. They initially wanted fifty per cent, but we have whittled them down. If we don't have upfront money from our clients, it makes it too expensive and risky for the next shipment.'

Broggetti paused before turning to Antinus.

'Bull, how is the fishing? The returns are looking good. You know, we could go legit on fishing and the income from our cattle stations alone. It pays for all our expenses and more. It is good business and keeps the law looking the other way.'

After dinner Wog and Broggetti talked to the clients separately and took their money, the Russians had Asian women for prostitution, and guns awaiting shipment; the bikers and the West Coast syndicate wanted more drugs and handguns. The Asians had narcotics waiting for shipment. The Middle East men were new customers and said they wanted to smuggle undeclared cargo and relatives into the country, family members unable to get visas from the Australian Government.

Broggetti said he would talk to the syndicate about it, and that their concerns would be shared. When the man put a case containing a million dollars in cash as payment on the table, Broggetti made a captain's call and said the people would be brought in on the next ship, provided they were in a remote Indonesian island port for shipment.

After the meetings, Wog said he was worried about the Russian Mafia bringing in weapons that could be used by right-wing and religious terrorists, but Broggetti told him that it was not his concern, their money was as good as anyone else's so Wog, having no choice, dropped the matter.

'We have a little cash flow crisis at the moment,' Broggetti informed him. 'This extra money will enable us to buy an enormous number of raw products for our own drug factories and enable us to distribute drugs over a much wider area than we have ever done before. There is a call for more women also from both sides of the continent because they have a high turnover. You know we have millions of dollars in those boxes, but we must get it into Asia for laundering before we can get it back and use it. With those dollars we can buy more products and goods.'

There was a knock on the door. It was Shute, who looked visibly upset.

'Look, one of my boys reckoned that you fellows have a spy on board. It's a bloke called Shep. He is a CIB detective who served on the Gold Coast last year.'

'Do you know of this Shep?' Broggetti asked, looking hard at Wog.

'Yes, I do. Bull gave him a job about six weeks ago. He is working on the Estuary Queen.'

'Okay, you have a problem, get rid of it, but first find out what he knows,' Broggetti ordered.

'At least he hasn't been on one of our expeditions, so his knowledge is limited,' Wog replied.

'Let me know how it goes in the morning,' Broggetti grunted as he stood up. 'It's been a long night. Bull, will you tell my men I'm ready to go home to Blood Gulley.'

Wog leaned over and whispered in Bull's ear.

'Bull, you'll take care of that little matter for me, won't you?'

'Yeah, sure Boss,' Bull panted as he made a huge effort to stand up from the comfortable chair.

'I will take care of the fucking copper myself. I gave him the job because he looked and sounded like an ex-crim, though come to think about it he did not say much about himself.'

The men walked outside to where Broggetti's bodyguards were waiting at the vehicles. They had eaten but, having avoided the free-flowing alcohol, they were keen to get on the road for the long drive to Blood Gulley Station. Bull watched as the Range Rovers departed, the dogs barking madly.

'Bring the fucking dogs on and let's have a fight,' someone cried.

There was a roar of approval. Soon there was a circular fence erected in the middle of the concrete floor where minutes before couples had been swinging to the 'doof doof' beat of the music. A big ringer, who worked on one of the company stations, dragged out a huge mixed Alsatian-great dane cross dog from a cage on the back of a Toyota Hilux 4WD. The dog's size was matched by a black and white dog that showed signs of pit bull in its breeding. It was controlled by his owner wielding an electric cattle prod. The crowd roared approval as the two men entered the cage and waited for instructions from the referee, the dogs snarling at each other viciously, fangs drooling with saliva dripping down their barred fangs.

Weed was taking bets and collecting money in his hat or stuffing it down his singlet for safe keeping. There was a sudden roar as the dogs were released in the cage. In seconds they were covered in saliva and blood as they tore at each other trying to get a kill grip. The owners and the spectators screamed at the animals to harass them even more into tearing each other to pieces. At last, the pit bull grabbed the other dog's throat and the snarling of the animal turned into painful whining. The owner yelled at someone to stop the fight, but it was too late as the pit bull ripped out his opponent's throat with a powerful tug that scattered blood and mucus over the spectators. Women screamed, and men swore as they attempted to wipe the offending slime off.

The dogs were removed, the ring hosed out and another pair entered the stage as the next fight ensued to keep the blood lust of the spectators at a high level. Wog walked away, dog fights did not do much for him, even less for Broggetti – the reason he had left early.

Bull noted that the man called Shep was part of the group. He and the crew of the Estuary King were staying in the quarters, so there was little chance of the man going anywhere. Wog stood alongside him.

'It's okay Boss, Weed and I will take him for a drive after the dog fights are over,' Bull said.

'Weed loves this shit and there is no way he will want to get away from it now until the bets are off.'

The busty blonde was sitting with another woman away from the fight ring. Both were pissed to the eyeballs and happy to see him. The blonde gave Wog a big slobbering hug that reminded him of the dogs. The other woman was a little younger. He did not know, or care, who she was and when he asked her if she wished to join them for a threesome she jumped up and hugged him saying she would love a good fuck. Wog nodded to the smirking Bull and drove out of the compound to the GBC wharf where he parked the Landcruiser. The tender, a six metre custom built Stabicraft fitted with a 250 hp Yamaha motor started at the turn of the key. Wog turned the boat and headed out across the river to where the dim lights of the Italia were visible. Wog knew it was going to be a good night.

Chapter 2
MURDER IN THE MANGROVES.

Bull watched Wog depart and shook his head in disbelief at the man's luck in taking two good looking women to his den, as Wog called the boat's bedroom. Weed came up, looking sad.

'Fuck mate, my luck turned sour after the first fight, and I lost the lot. I reckon some of those dogs were nobbled as they couldn't fight for shit.'

'Don't worry about it,' Bull replied. 'we have a job to do. Get Shep and tell him we need him to help us. I'll be in the car park, at the Toyota.'

'Why Shep?'

'Because I said so,' Bull retorted sharply. 'Just tell him it's overtime or something. Okay?'

Weed stumbled off, mumbling under his breath about bossy bastards, as Bull walked toward the car park. It was still full because people from the stations and the boats normally crashed in their swags under the hangar roof, instead of heading home and risking a police breathalyser test. Those who lived in the compound often shared their rooms with others who spread their swags on the floors. The few single women, living in the compound, seldom slept alone.

Bull found a length of rope in the back of a Toyota tray back company vehicle based in the compound. He heard Weed and Shep walk up.

'About bloody time you bloody pricks got here. Hurry up we need to shift one of the boats before the tide takes it into the mangroves. Some fucking arsehole moored it in the wrong spot, and we must move it, as he is too pissed. Sorry about this Shep, but you are about the only one sober enough to help me.'

'That's okay Bull, I don't mind,' Shep replied as he walked past Bull and opened the vehicle door. Bull turned and king hit him with a powerful right fist. Shep was unconscious before the hit the ground.

'Fuck Bull, why did you do that?' Weed cried in alarm.

'Because he is a fucking cop. Give me a hand to tie him up and toss him in the back. And keep an eye open to make sure no one sees us.'

They tied the man up. Bull stuffed a dirty oily rag into Shep's mouth, tossed the unconscious man in the tray back, and threw a tarpaulin over him. The security guard opened the gate and waved them through, cursing at the barking guard dogs. A little later, Bull turned the Toyota onto a track that headed upriver.

'Tell me Bull, what the fuck is this cop shit,' Weed pleaded. 'Shep is not a bad bloke. The boys like him.'

'Well one of Axle's boys recognised him as a cop who served on the Gold Coast. Wog told me to find out what he knows and to get rid of him. I reckon we'll take him up to the High Banks and toss him in the river after we finish with him.'

Bull slammed on the brakes as a wallaby, dashing across the track, paused in the full glare of the powerful driving lights. There was no time to stop and the force of the bulbar killed it.

Bull pulled up and cursed: 'Fuck it! Might as well pick it up and toss it in the back for the dogs.'

Weed leaped out and heaved the carcase into the tray on top of Shep, who moved away from the animal.

'So, you are fucking awake copper? I'll deal with you later,' Weed shouted as he jumped back into the cab.

They drove through a locked gate until an opening in the scrub highlighted a small clearing where the remains of a rusty 4WD, all that remained of an old fishing camp, lay under a huge mango tree. Ahead, the track was covered by an incoming tide from the river a hundred metres away. There was some lightning across the river, an early summer storm.

'Fuck it! I forgot that we had a spring tide tonight. We must work fast before the storm hits us. It's too late to go back, so we must do it here, as daylight is not that far away,' Bull swore as he parked alongside the big tree.

Shep was pulled from the trayback and dumped onto the ground. He moaned with pain as they dragged him under the tree, tossed a rope over a thick branch, tied it about his wrists and hauled him up, where he hung in the glare of the Toyota's driving lights, his mouth bleeding and his nose broken from Bull's brutal king hit.

'What do you know about our operation, Shep?' Bull asked, in an almost gentle tone.

'What operation? Why are you doing this to me?' Shep moaned.

'I'm asking the questions. I know you're a copper. All I need to know, is what you are doing here. Tell me and I might consider letting you go.'

'Pig's arse, I'll never leave here, and you know it. I'll die first, but before you kill me let me tell you that you, and your bunch of arseholes, are on notice and it's only a matter of time before we will get you all.'

'You got guts, but what good will that do you?' Bull replied, admiration in his voice. 'Your bosses don't give a rat's arse. You would have been better off with us. We could have used you, but I reckon I'll let Weed cut you up a bit first before we finish you off. He is good at that sort of thing. Got your knife, Weed?

'Never get out of bed without it,' Weed snarled as he stood alongside Bull holding a thin strip of skin he had cut from the wallaby.

His hands were bloody, the folding Buck belt knife dripping with it. Bull stepped aside as Weed handed the skin strip to him before cutting away Shep's shirt, his methods none too gentle, the keen blade cutting the policeman. He bled profusely, the blood dripping from his feet.

23

Weed cut away the shorts and the jocks, teasing the cringing naked man with the blade by rubbing it across his penis and testicles.

Thunder rumbled closer as the sky flared with lightning, flickering across the river. A bull crocodile roared nearby letting the females know that it was time to mate. Shep screamed in fear as the blade cut him across his stomach. He had visions of his bowels dropping out in front of him. His tormented cry drifted across the river and the flood plain, but there was no one in the whole wide world to hear it.

Bull leaned back against the Toyota's bulbar and said nothing, being content to watch Weed's surgical work with the sharp blade as he cut deeper to increase the bleeding.

'Talk, you copper bastard,' Weed cried. 'Tell us what you fucking know, and I might cut your throat and end your miserable fucking life quickly.'

In reply, Shep spat a mouthful of blood over Weed. It enraged the little man to a point where Bull stepped in and grabbed his arm.

'Steady little mate, don't let him get off too easy.'

'You're right, sorry Bull.'

'Where is that fucking wallaby strip? Thanks Bull, old mate. Can you get me a length of log or something heavy to use for this?'

'New trick, eh, Weed? Will do, I'll have a look around and see what I can come up with. You never cease to amaze with your skills.'

As Bull wandered away into the darkness, Weed cut a slot in the end of the strip and made a little lasso that he looped about Shep's testicles and pulled it tight. Shep winced in pain and moaned causing Weed to tug even harder on the lasso. Bull returned with a rusty car axle and dumped it under Shep's feet.

'Fucking beauty, mate,' Weed exclaimed 'Give me a hand to lift him up a bit more for this to be effective.'

The two men grunted as they hauled Shep higher, the ropes cutting into his wrist and shutting off the circulation. Next, they placed the axle near his feet and tied the end of the skin strip tightly to it.

'You got to give him a little knee room so that he can stand on the axle and pull his own nuts off when he can no longer bear the pain,' Weed said gleefully. 'If they ever find him, they will be reluctant to send another fucking cop to spy on us.'

'Okay mate, let's leave, I'm done,' Bull grunted. 'There is no fucking need to kill him, no one ever comes here anymore since the gate has been locked. Let the bastard suffer.'

In the east a rosy glow indicated that daylight was near. The storm hit in a crescendo of noise and fury driving dust clouds in front of it before the rain belted down and washed away the tracks of the Toyota as it headed back to the compound. A day and a night passed and Shep was alone in the wilderness, close to death. The rain had been a blessing that washed away the blood, though the hot sun burned the skin from him, even in the shade of the mango tree.

But it was the shrinking, of the greenhide strip as it dried, pulling out the testicles from his stomach, that caused the most pain. The cutting of the blood circulation, and the onset of gangrene, had turned his testicles black, the same colour as his tied hands. Most of the time the man was conscious and aware of the flocks of crows and kite hawks gathering for the feast. But they kept their distance if there were any signs of movement. The crows were the worst, black feathered heathens that dropped sticks on the man and watched for movement and signs of life.

By midmorning, the end was near as the man regained consciousness for a brief period. For some reason, his mind was clear as death neared him. In a superhuman effort, he managed to place his feet up on the axle before jerking his body up and pulling the rotten testicles from his groin. The carrion eaters flapped away in fright as the man's last breath cried out an eerie tortured scream that sounded like neither man nor beast as the life blood gushed from his body. Then the crows moved in, pecking out his eyes and feasting on him.

Tom "Crabby" Dunn had departed the Town site boat ramp at

Karumba, at daylight. He was busy setting his crab pots downstream from the clearing on the river when the inhuman scream cut like a cold, chilling knife blade through the hot humid air of the mangrove-fringed Norman River. Dunn almost dropped the crab pot he was baiting with a fish frame.

'What the fuck was that?' he swore aloud, his hand trembling.

There were no more sounds, and he dropped the baited pot in the water before starting the outboard motor and turning the dinghy upstream to where kite hawks were circling overhead. The carking of crows in the big solitary mango tree was loud and clear. It was not only the birds that aroused his curiosity, but the memory of that inhuman scream and the humanlike object hanging under the dense shadow of the lower branches.

He nosed the boat to the bank and leaped out dropping the anchor behind him in the mud. As he neared the tree, he paused at the sight of the man hanging under its deep shadows. Dunn was not a religious man, but he could not help himself.

'Holy Mother of Jesus, who the fuck would do a thing like this?' he cursed aloud, his face white and his knees trembling. Dunn, a veteran bushman and long-term former soldier had seen many things in his life, including the Vietnam war.

The horror of the scene that confronted him suddenly took him back to a humid, dense jungle far away. But he quickly composed himself and checked for signs of life in the still body. He thought for a second and considered cutting it down, but he paused knowing that the police would want to see the body like it was. The horror was clear to him, and he shuddered, looking about in fear in case the perpetrators of this evil act were about and looking for more victims.

He hurried back to his dinghy and took the mobile phone from the waterproof Plano marine box before walking back to the tree where the raucous crows and the hawks were gathering in ever increasing numbers. The phone was well in range of the town, and he dialled 000 and asked for the Karumba Police Station. The girl on the other end recognised the alarm in his voice.

'Are you alright sir?'

'Of course,' he snapped back curtly. 'just put me through now.'

The phone rang and was picked up.

'Karumba Police, Constable Bridges speaking. Can I help you?'

'Jack, this is Crabby Dunn, I am at the end of the High Banks track at the old fishing camp. There is a man hanging from the mango tree and he is dead. Get over here as fast as you can before the fucking crows eat him.'

'Bloody hell, Tom, I'll get the Sergeant and we will be over right now. Don't touch anything.'

'Fuck off, just get here now,' Dunn cursed, as he ended the call. 'Fucking cops and their fucking advice, they think everyone is fucking stupid.'

An hour passed by as Dunn waited near the dead man, chasing hungry crows away that wanted to get at the body, before the sound of an approaching vehicle indicated the arrival of the police.

Sergeant Barry Johnson, a veteran outback copper, had seen many dead people but when he saw the dead man hanging from the thick tree branch, he was sick alongside the police 4WD. Bridges was made of sterner stuff though, unlike Johnson, he was not suffering from a boozy hangover either.

'G'day Crabby, shit mate, what the fuck happened to this poor bastard? No one deserves to die like this.' He walked around the body before starting to untie a rope.

'You better leave that, Jack,' Dunn advised. 'forensics might want to do that.'

'You're right, I forgot, not every day you see something like this. You okay Sarge?'

'Yeah, I am now. Too much fucking 4X Gold last night. Jack, get on the phone and call the CIB and see how they want us to handle this.

Hell of a thing for a man to see Tom, especially at your age.'

'Age has nothing to do with it, Barry, I have seen worse in my time. The Viet Cong used to skin our boys alive and drive bamboo sticks under finger and toenails, though I must admit the bloke who did this knew his stuff.'

Bridges ended the call and informed Johnson that forensics could not get here until the next day.

'They said to take plenty of photos before taking the body down and to take it to the morgue in Normanton. They also want us to look for tracks, anything that can help. Oh yes, they want us to identify the body if possible.'

'Fucking great,' Constable Johnson swore, wiping sweat from his brow. 'Now we are doing Forensics' job. No worry about tracks though. There are none. The rain from that storm the other night washed them out. Fuck, that means this poor bastard has been out here since. He hasn't been dead long, or the fucking crows would have eaten him by now.'

'He died a little over an hour ago,' Dunn informed them. 'I heard the most inhuman cry I have ever experienced when I was setting a crab pot. Only after I passed by and noticed the crows and kites did I investigate that nightmarish scream. Hell, I still got shivers down my spine from that cry.'

'Jesus, that means the poor bastard was alive all that time. No one comes down here anymore since the GBC put locks on their gate, except to dump things like this fucking axle someone tied onto his nuts with fucking greenhide of all things. As it dried, it shrunk and stopped the blood flow to his balls. In the end the pain got him, and he managed to stand on the axel and pull his own nuts out so he could die. Jack, get the camera and take the required photos. Don't fuck them up like you did at that car accident last month, okay?'

'Yeah, right Sarge, I had no training with it then. I know how to use it now. Besides, I joined the force to be a copper, not a fucking photographer.'

Dunn laughed.

'Look boys, I'll be in later for a statement if that's okay with you. I have work to do and still must put a few pots in otherwise I won't eat tomorrow.'

'No worries, Crabby, you know what to do if you get too many muddies. The police station is always in need,' Johnson appealed.

Three days passed before the coroner identified the body as that of John Henry Sheppard, a detective in the State's Criminal Investigation Branch. It sent the CIB into panic mode and for the first time they became involved in the investigations by raiding the compound, the last known sightings of Sheppard, or Shep as he was known.

But in the days ahead they found nothing or had any suspects. They tested vehicles for blood but again there was nothing, or they did not look hard enough according to the know-all "bar fly's" and the conspiracy theorists. The only thing the police knew was the motive, Sheppard had got too close in his deep cover role to penetrate the GBC.

Chapter 3
BARRAMUNDI COUNTRY

Below the Robinson R44 helicopter the Gulf country and its savannah landscape spread out to far horizons, its surface dyed brown under the onslaught of the dry season sun and the persistent southeast trade winds. Beyond the flat tidal plains, the Gulf of Carpentaria came in sight, an endless expanse of blue water that vanished under the atmospheric haze that had no horizon or sky.

Ian Johnston thought that the scenery was bleak and forbidding, but his new bride Tina was excited and pointed out many features to him. Thinking back, he knew he had no option but to go along with her choice of a honeymoon escape because of their love of fishing and the outdoors.

'We both love fishing,' she had stated in a determined voice. 'so why not a fishing honeymoon? It's not that we want to stay indoors all the time screwing each other stupid. We have been doing that since we moved in together two years ago. This way we can enjoy the great outdoors and the fishing also. You always wanted to catch a wild barramundi, don't you?'

He had admitted that he did as fishing for the big barra in the stocked water impoundment of local manmade lakes was tame. They both had read about fishing the wilds of the Gulf country and crocodiles – a wilderness that was like nowhere else. In the end, she had booked them in a remote fishing lodge located on the Staaten River, 260 km east of Kurumba, the nearest settlement. Being Brisbane born and bred, it seemed incredulous to him that there were places so far away from anywhere.

They flew into Cairns from Brisbane the day after they got married and spent a few days exploring the region, the Daintree Rainforest, Cape Tribulation, the Great Barrier Reef and Port Douglas before catching a Gulf Air flight to Normanton, from where they were transferred by helicopter to the Remote Island Fishing Lodge. After leaving Cairns and the lush green belt of coastal rainforest behind, they saw the country change to a rustic brown. A fellow passenger told them that this part of the Australian tropics only had rain for about four months of the year and that the dry season was well advanced.

They both enjoyed the hour-long flight in the Robinson R44 helicopter. It reminded them of being inside a little dragon fly that flitted across a surreal land. They were excited when they saw the lodge. It was located on a large billabong and surrounded by tidal streams, lagoons and freshwater billabongs. It had all the hallmarks of barramundi country.

When the dust cleared after landing, they were met by a woman who introduced herself as Mary McCarthy, the manager, and wife of the chief fishing guide. After putting their baggage in one of the spacious airconditioned units, she led them to the lodge restaurant for afternoon tea. Later, they watched as the pilot lifted the copter into the sky and vanish behind the tree line. Even though they were both tired, they sat on their unit veranda watching waterfowl frolicking in the fringing billabong.

'Oh shit! That is a crocodile,' Tina suddenly exclaimed. 'Over there, see it?'

'Yes, I do, which I suppose is why they have a spa bath out the back, and signs warning people not to swim in the local water holes. Look, there is another one and there are more towards the end.'

Mary walked up to see if there was anything they needed. They asked her about the crocodiles in the billabong.

'Yes, those are freshwater or Johnstone's crocodiles, but the odd saltwater croc also lives in the billabong,' she informed them. 'By the way there will be a couple of other guests joining us tonight. They should be arriving by road soon. They are friends of the owner. One bloke is Vic Hawkins. You may have heard of him. He is a well-known outdoor YouTube presenter, adventure magazine writer and author.'

'Yes, I think I may have seen and read some of his stuff,' Ian mused. 'He is pretty famous and spends all his time fishing and hunting from what I know.'

'Yes, he does. Hello that sounds like a vehicle coming from the west. That will be my husband Mick, coming back from servicing the boat. We leave it in the water in the estuary. You are lucky to have the lodge to yourself this week as no one else booked in, though we are full next week.'

Mick turned out to be a jovial fellow that they both liked instantly. He told them that the fishing was great.

'Big barra over a metre tomorrow for both of you, I'll promise you that. The warm weather makes them hungry,' he stated. 'But excuse me for now. I have some work to catch up on and will see you both later. Not many anglers about now, too hot for most. We were full up last week. The staff have taken time off and headed to town.'

'Town, you mean Normanton?' Tina asked.

'No, Cairns. That is town for most of us in this part of the country. See you folks later.'

It was almost dark when a dusty 4WD Toyota Landcruiser wagon towing a trailer holding a boat pulled into the parking bay of the unit next door. Mick came over to meet the new arrivals. Ian saw them unloading their gear from where he and Tina were enjoying predinner drinks at the restaurant bar. He noted the gun cases and pointed them out to her with concern in his voice.

'Oh, don't worry about it, silly, this is the bush. Dad told me that everyone in the Gulf country carries guns to shoot wild pigs. It's part of the lifestyle and for many a work tool.'

The men came in later to the bar, clean and showered and smelling of soap and Old Spice aftershave. They were introduced by Mick as Vic Hawkins and Jim King. Ian had expected a younger man than Hawkins, who looked like he was in is mid-sixties, a tall man of slim muscular built and by appearance fit for his age. His mate, Jim King was some ten years younger, but he was half a head shorter, and showed signs of a developing beer belly.

'So, you're both here to catch a barramundi? No doubt you are after a meteri, as we call barra over a one hundred centimetre long,' Hawkins stated. 'The big ones are all females. All barra are born as males, but they change sex when they are about eighty centimetres long. Mick will get you a big one, he is a great guide. Take my word, there is no one better. Where are you people from?'

'Brisbane, we are on our honeymoon,' Tina replied.

'Well, you would be the first couple I have met who took a barra fishing honeymoon. Congratulations. You have your priorities right.'

Later over a delicious evening meal of fresh prawns and barbequed barramundi fillets they were entertained by rousing tales of big barra, black jewfish, and threadfin salmon, huge crocodiles, wild boars and charging scrub bulls. There was no doubt in their mind that this was adventure country, with all of it backed up on the photo board in the small library. Ian asked about crocodiles, but Mick assured him that they were not a problem.

'The commercial fishermen kill many in their gill nets,' he said bitterly. 'gill nets kill everything in the rivers, crocs, dugong, dolphins, sawfish, and more. It is high time that the Government does what they did in the Northern Territory years ago by closing selected river systems off to gill netting. It restores the natural balance.'

The talk led to big crocodiles and attacks on humans. Hawkins told them that a mate of his was killed by a crocodile in the Northern Territory years ago.

'But in all there are few cases that are not caused by human error,' he stated. 'People do stupid things, especially so when full of grog.'

He informed them of a large croc that lived in the river.

'It's close to seven or more metres in length and it may even match the one shot by the late Kris Pawlowski on the Norman Bank of the Norman River back in 1957. That brute was 8.3 metres long, one of the largest ever recorded and indeed the biggest ever shot by a woman. There is a replica of it at the Carpentaria Shire Council office at Normanton.'

Tina shivered, big man-eating crocodiles were far from her mind when she had planned and booked the trip. Hawkins noted it.

'Don't worry too much about it, the local crocs have a healthy respect for boats and people. Most carry lead from encounters with idiots that shoot at anything that moves, including protected species.'

'You are right,' Ian scowled, looking hard at Hawkins. 'guns should be banned. There is no need for anyone to have a gun in this country for self-protection, that is what police are paid for.'

Hawkins gave him a sharp look and his voice had changed to a harsh tone as he replied.

'You sound like a copper I know. He has the same sentiments. Yes, it would be nice if the police could protect us from drug induced crazies, robbers, thieves, and murderers, but the records more than prove they can't. Besides, my guns and those belonging to thousands of other licensed shooters, are used for target shooting, hunting, and for pest destruction like wild pigs, not for self-protection.'

'Yes,' Ian argued. 'but guns are also used for crime.'

'No argument from me,' Hawkins replied. 'so are cars. The only thing that gun control does is to make extra work for police and of course more revenue for hungry governments. But now we have a thriving black market for guns that never existed before.'

'Ian is a police officer Vic,' Tina informed Hawking to change the subject. 'and so was my dad. But he is now the police minister, and he is on your side if you are interested. Dad used to be the inspector for northwest Queensland. I was born in Mount Isa. We used to go fishing and hunting in the Gulf and Channel countries a lot. You might know dad. He used to mention you, his name is Roger Waters.'

'Yes, I do, I met him a couple of times and probably you also years ago on the Gregory River and the Lawn Hill Gorges. I remember a little girl of about four years old. That must have been you.'

'Wow, I don't remember that, but those camping days are the reason that I love the outdoor life so much. It's so much in my DNA.'

They talked about the old days as Hawkins had worked in the mines at Mount Isa and knew many people. Ian felt that he was left out of it and turned to Jim King who had not said much. However, as Ian discovered, he knew all about barramundi fishing and he felt inspired by the man who assured him that tomorrow would be the day that his dreams of catching a metre or more of wild saltwater barramundi would come true. Breakfast was served at daylight as the sun forced some weak rays through the trees.

With the vehicle loaded they headed out to the boat ramp. The drive across the flood plains and salt pans was delightful and Ian began to relax and enjoy the wildlife that the sharp eyes of Tina picked out amongst the stunted coolabah trees – bustards, emus, cranes, finches, doves, and a herd of wild pigs that rushed away from a drying swamp, as they passed.

'They better hide, because Vic and Jim are not far behind us,' Mick laughed. 'Both are coming with us, but not to fish. We will be dropping them off on a small delta island that they clean out of feral pigs each year to protect turtle breeding sites.'

The tide was high when they stopped at the boat ramp at track's end. A dinghy lay on the bank and a 6.5 metre plate boat was moored in the middle of the tidal arm. Mick pushed the dinghy into the water and rowed out to the boat. He climbed on board, started the 250 hp Suzuki outboard and headed to the ramp, leaving the dinghy tied to the mooring. Ian handed him their gear, while Tina climbed into the boat.

Hawkins and King pulled up and handed a couple of daypacks, water bottles and two cased rifles to Mick who stored them away before everyone boarded the vessel. Mick reversed the boat out, turned it upriver, and pushed the throttle down, the boat coming up onto the plane in seconds. The morning air was warm and humid, the breeze created by the boat's speed more than welcome.

'It's going to be a bloody hot day,' he cried to no one in particular. 'make sure you put heaps of sunscreen on and wear your hats.'

Tina pointed to a couple of big birds that were feeding on molluscs on a mud bank.

'Great billed herons, one of the world's largest herons,' Hawkins informed her. 'Hello, here come the resident sea eagles. They are magnificent birds and in total control of the sky.'

The water was calm and clear and everywhere there were birds – herons, egrets, plovers, eagles, hawks, while flocks of brolgas and sarus cranes passed overhead with loud trumpeting. Tina grabbed hold of Ian's hand tightly.

'What a magnificent place, darling, the wildlife and this beautiful river. Oh, look a big croc, over there. It's huge.'

She pointed to where a four-metre crocodile rushed off the bank and splashed into the water, its basking disturbed by the passing boat. Mick slowed the boat some distance down the river and turned the bow towards the bank before pushing the nose into a sandy spot. Hawkins and King climbed out. Mick handed them their gear. They both uncased the rifles and handed the cases back to Mick. Ian noted that both rifles were fitted with scopes and appeared well cared for, almost like new guns. Hawkins noted his interest.

'This is a .270 Weatherby Magnum,' he said, patting the rifle's stock. 'Jim has a Winchester Model 70 in .308 calibre. Both rifles are over 20 years old. I'll give you a few shots before you go and take you both boar hunting if you are interested.'

'Yes, I would love too,' Tina said. 'we will, won't we darling?'

'Okay, but later in the week if that is okay with you, Vic.'

'No worries, it will be done. Thanks Mick, we'll see you about lunchtime at the usual spot,' replied Hawkins. 'You guys enjoy the day and best of luck with the fishing.'

They vanished over the bank and into the low scrub as Mick instructed the couple on how to use the rods and what lure to put on the line before backing the boat into midstream for the first trolling run. They trolled less than one hundred metres when Tina cried out "strike" as her rod tip buckled down. Forty metres away a metre or more of silver barramundi rose like a Polaris missile from the water and hung in mid-air for a split second before slamming back under the surface leaving a hole the size of a 200-litre drum in the water.

'Get your line in Ian, quick. It's a meteri for sure,' Mick cried as he dropped the motor into reverse and backed up to the fish. Again, she rose to the surface and tail walked for a few metres before diving under. Twice more she came out in fear-stricken panic trying to dislodge the cruel hooks before Tina wrestled her alongside the boat. Mick was ready and slipped the landing net under the fish before heaving her inside the boat for all to admire, a beautiful barramundi that measured one hundred and twelve centimetres. Some hurried photos and Mick held her over the side, pushing her back and forward to force water into her gills. The barra bit hard on his fingers, and he released her, watching with a big grin on his face as she vanished below the surface.

'Wow, thank you Mick,' Tina exclaimed. 'What an adrenalin rush that was. Your turn, darling. See if you can get a bigger one.'

Again, the lures bobbed behind the wake of the boat, and again it was Tina's lure that was slammed by a big fish. She held the rod grimly, winding on the line as the stubborn barra pulled hard on the end of it. But it was not to be as the hooks pulled out of the hard mouth when the big fish neared the boat and made a last-ditch jump.

Thirty minutes passed before the next hit on a Rapala XRap lure. This time it was Ian's turn and he pulled up hard on the rod tip to set the hooks. Some ten minutes passed before the stubborn barra came to the net. It was a fish of one hundred and eight centimetres that brought a cry of joy from Tina.

'Mine is still the biggest, darling. You will have to try harder.'

'I will. Mick promised me a horse, didn't you Mick?'

'I did, and it will happen. We have made a great start so far to the day. Hello, the boys must have got onto some pigs by the sound of those shots.'

Several rifle shots broke the torpor of the plains in quick succession, the concussions harsh in the humid atmosphere. Mick explained that the shots were a long way off as they resumed trolling the lures.

The scenery was pleasant, and he reminded himself that someone had to do his job as he watched with interest as Tina discarded her clothing to reveal a firm well-tanned model-like body that fully filled the skimpy bikini she wore. She was beautiful Mick admitted to himself, feeling a little jealous towards Ian.

'Lucky bastard,' he mused. 'Wonder what he's got to score a beauty like this?'

His attention was drawn to a large boat that came in sight from the bend upriver.

'Bloody GBC barra boat,' he swore aloud. 'they are stuffing these waters with their gill nets. This being a declared wild river and all, yet the Government still allow vandals like that to net it. It's beyond me.'

'Will they net this rock bar?' Ian asked.

'Probably not while we are here as it is too deep for their nets, which are hung on floats, but poaching with submerged nets is ongoing. We will keep on fishing, they know about the bar, so there is no sense in pretending it doesn't exist.'

They continued to troll, catching another barra while the barra boat dropped anchor on the downstream end of the rock bar in a deep hole.

The path of the troll took them within fifty metres of it. The sight of Tina in her tiny bikini attracted several wolf whistles and rude calls from the four men on board the vessel. It prompted her to put her shirt on; a shame admitted Mick to himself. He had been enjoying her body.

He recognised the boat, the Raider, as one belonging to a syndicate that had moved into the Gulf waters some years back and purchased several fishing licenses. He thought it odd that the fifteen-metre vessel had four men on board, as it was manned by a crew of only two or three at most, but his thoughts were interrupted as Ian called out: "Fish on."

It was another huge female barramundi, the largest of the day at one hundred and twenty centimetres. After photographing the couple with it, Mick swam it in the river, flushing the gills with water and welcomed the bite from the toothless mouth on his hand, the signal to release the fish.

'Okay, time for lunch. We'll moor on the bank over there and have a bite to eat. I'll put the canopy up, that will give use some respite from the sun. Vic and Jim should be along soon.'

As Mick broke open the lunch packs that Mary had prepared, he noticed that a dinghy from the Raider was heading towards them. There were two men on board. The dinghy slipped up alongside them and the man in the bow grabbed the railing and pulled the dinghy up against the boat. He waved a part empty rum bottle in his hand.

'G'day, how the fuck are you all,' he shouted, his voice slurred. 'Trevor is the name and my mate, Red and I have come over to give you blokes a drink, providing you let us fuck your bitch.'

They both roared with drunken laughter, the big man called Red wracking deep in his chest as if he had a bad cough. Mick noted that there was a short-barrelled shotgun on the boat's floor. He reached over and pushed the man's hand away from the boat rail. His action has an instant reaction from Red, who roared with rage as he suddenly pulled out a .22 rimfire pistol from his belt.

'You bloody mongrel, you're fucking dead,' he roared in angry voice.

'Don't touch me, arsehole.'

He fired once, the bullet striking Mick in the right upper shoulder before turning the gun on Ian who was on his feet. The bullet slammed him back against the seat. He sat there holding his left breast, looking at the blood that was gushing between his fingers onto the floor of the boat. Tina screamed in fear as she tried to support him.

The man, who called himself Trevor, attempted to climb in the boat, but he fell back in the dinghy laughing in a drunken fit. As he pulled himself up for another attempt, he stared towards the shore where two figures were silhouetted against the sky on the rim of the high bank.

'What is going on?' cried someone in loud angry voice. Red looked up and saw the two men. He raised the pistol and fired a snapshot. One of the men stumbled and fell. But before he could swing the pistol on the other man, he was swept back by an unseen force that smashed into him and propelled him over the side of the dinghy into the water with a huge splash even before the report of the shot reached the boats.

Trevor stood up in the dinghy, raising the shotgun in his hand. But again, the report of the big rifle sounded before he could swing the weapon to its target. His chest exploded, blood and bone splattered the boat. The shotgun dropped from his lifeless hands. He fell back against the gunnel and into the water, vanishing under its green blood-spattered surface as Red had done seconds before.

Tina was screaming, laying across Ian to protect his body with her own, the loud concussion of the rifle shots ringing in her ears. Somewhere in the distance came the sound of another shot and she heard the bullet whining over and slamming into the bank above her with a loud thud. A split second later the big rifle on the bank roared in return, followed by another quick shot.

She heard the diesel motor of the barra boat roar into life as another shot from the bank abused her eardrums. Someone moved near the boat, but she was unable to open her eyes and look up, fearing she would be the next target.

'Tina, it's all right. You are safe now, what the hell happened?'

She recognized the voice of Hawkins and looked up in his concerned face, a wild look like she had never seen before on any man in his eyes. It made her shiver in fear, but his look changed to one of concern as he saw the wounded men.

'Tina, you must be brave. You and I are the only people that can save their lives. Jim is also wounded, hit in the upper leg. He is looking after it. We must stop the bleeding. There has to be a medicine kit here somewhere.'

'Under the seat,' Mick moaned. He had remained conscious throughout the shooting. 'It's under my seat, Vic. Help Ian first. I can wait.'

Hawkins located the first aid kit and unpacked it, his hands shaking. He looked at Tina.

'Pull his shirt away from the wound, girl. I must stop the bleeding.'

Tina tried to pull the shirt away but was unable to do so. Hawkins handed her his hunting knife.

'Here, use this and cut it away from the wound.'

She managed to cut the shirt away from the chest wound, exposing a small red hole bubbling with air.

'He has a bloody lung shot. I should have guessed,' Hawkins swore as he pulled a plastic bag from the kit and handed it to her.

'Here Tina, hold this over the wound. I must tape it to stop the air from bubbling out.'

'Will he be all right, Vic?'

'I don't know, Tina, because I never have treated bullet wounds. There that should do the trick until we can get the flying doctor out. Now Mick, let me look at you.'

Mick moaned in pain as Hawkins cut away the shirt and applied a pressure bandage on the wound to stop the bleeding.

'There that was easy. Now for Jim. He needs help to get down the bank. I won't be long. Now where is the Sat phone? Must be under the console. Yes, here it is. Okay Tina, ring the flying doctor while I attend to Jim. The number is on the box. Let them know where we are and to meet us at the lodge airstrip ASAP. Also, tell them to inform the police and give them the number that is on the phone for the police to ring back. Tell them everything that happened here and that we need urgent medical help. Reckon you can do that?'

Hawkins climbed up the bank with the first aid kit. Tina noticed that the rifle was hung over his shoulder as she told the Flying Doctor base at Cairns that three men had been shot and needed urgent attention. The woman on the other end was calm and businesslike and promised that help would be waiting at the lodge when they arrived there.

'The doctor is doing his weekly clinic at Kowanyama,' Tina said. 'They won't take long to get to the island. Yes, I will inform the police and give them your number so that they can contact you. Stand by the phone, the doctor may be in touch to give you instructions for the wounded.'

A few minutes later the phone rang and a police officer at Cairns wanted to know what the problem was. Tina told him in a few words what had happened.

'Okay, stay calm and get the wounded to an airstrip. I believe the flying doctor is on his way. I will contact the Normanton Police Station. Officers from there will be on the scene as soon as they can. We will also dispatch our Rapid Response Team as a matter of urgency.'

Hawkins was back, supporting King, who had a tourniquet and much blood on his leg, his face ash grey. Hawkins had both rifles and the day packs slung across his shoulder. Tina ended the call and helped King on board before making him comfortable in one of the seats.

'He has an upper leg wound and he stopped the bleeding by using his belt, but when I released the pressure, the wound started bleeding again. The pressure bandage should stop it. Thank Christ that mongrel only had a .22 rimfire pistol. Just push down on this, Jim while I get the boat under way.'

After ensuring everyone was as comfortable as possible, Hawkins started the motor. Mick was conscious, but Ian was not. It worried Hawkins as he pointed the bow upstream and pushed the throttle down. In seconds, the boat was on full plane. Less than fifteen minutes later, he nudged the bow onto the boat ramp. In the next few minutes, he and Tina helped the wounded into the vehicles.

'You drive my Landcruiser, with Ian and Mick in it. They will be okay. Take it easy, watch the bumps, and head out now. Just follow the track. I'll take Jim with me in the Troopie. I'll be along as soon as I secure the boat on the mooring. It will only take me a few minutes. Now you go, Tina, and stay brave.'

The track across the saltpan plains appeared endless but at last Tina entered the monsoon forest, knowing it was only short distance to the lodge. A glance in the mirror revealed that Hawkins was following behind her, just close enough to keep out of the dust. Her heart skipped a beat of relief as she noted a plane circling ahead. It had just finished taxiing when she drove across the cattle grid and onto the airstrip and stopped alongside the plane. Hawkins pulled up beside her, opening vehicle doors and shouting instructions to the doctor and his nurse who rushed over.

'Here, look at this bloke first, the others are okay and will live, but this bloke has a bullet in his lung,' he shouted standing aside to allow the doctor access to Ian.

Mary had rushed over on a quad bike and was comforting Mick, while King leaned back against the front seat of the Troopie.

Soon the wounded were stabilised and loaded on the plane, including Tina who insisted on coming along. There was no room for Mary. Hawkins leaned back against his 4WD, his hands trembling and his body shaking. He stared at Mary who was standing nearby looking at the plane that already was climbing high into the sky. He walked over and hugged her, the tears flowing down her face.

'Come Mary, let's get out of this hot sun. I need a coffee before the cops arrive. My guess is that they won't be long. Don't worry about Mick. He will be back in a week. He is a tough bastard. I'll talk to the boss and get him to fly you into Cairns so that you can be with him if you want too.'

'Yes, Vic that would be fine, but we will be hosting a large section of the Queensland Police Force tonight and they must eat, so I will stay. They called in earlier. What the hell happened?'

On the shady veranda Hawkins sat back and told Mary about the gunfight.

'I'd like to know why they attacked the boat,' he mused. 'I know that some remote area commercial fishers think they are a law unto themselves, but this sort of stuff is unheard of. Hello, that sounds like a helicopter. I'll bet it's the Normanton cops. Better put the kettle on again, they will want a coffee. I'll go and meet them.'

Chapter 4
THE RAIDER

Hawkins watched as the Jet Ranger helicopter did several fly overs before it settled down some 80 metres away from his vehicle. Three armed police officers jumped out, rifles cocked and ready.

'Fuck, I should have thought of that,' Hawkins thought. 'They think they have a siege situation. Don't blame them, can't be too careful. Not after today.'

He walked out to meet the men his arms held out wide from his body. They had spread out and were walking towards him, Ruger Mini14 rifles held in combat position. Hawkins stopped and raised his hands at shoulder height.

'Put those fucking guns down. It's all over. I'm Vic Hawkins,' he called out.

'Sorry Mister Hawkins, we are just following procedure. What is the problem here? We have a garbled message from Cairns that someone was shooting the place up, something along those lines anyway.'

'It's all over. Come over to the lodge, I'll tell you all about it over a cuppa coffee,' Hawkins replied. 'Mary has coffee or tea and scones waiting. What about the pilot, is he coming along?'

'Yes, we may need him later, though we are packed to stay the night if we have too. By the way I am Senior Sergeant Matt Gland, this is Constable Luke Hodges, Constable Jarrod O'Donnell, and our pilot, Bob McGill.'

At the lodge, Gland requested McGill have his coffee with Mary as he interviewed Hawkins, who told him about the attack on the sport fishing boat by the Raider crew.

'No idea why it happened, Sergeant. Jim and I walked over the bank and below us we saw Ian and Mick get shot before we could help. When Jim yelled out the bloke with the pistol turned on him and shot him in the leg. He then swung his pistol on me, but I was faster. The other bloke came up with a sawn-off shotgun, but he was also too bloody slow. I shot both. Next, we came under fire from the Raider. I missed the shooter with the first shot, but I think that I put a bullet in him before he could get another shot away. The other bloke ran into the cabin, lifted the anchor and motored away in a real hurry.'

'Fuck, Vic. That sort of stuff is unheard of. Do you think you killed the man that fired at you from the boat?' Sergeant Gland asked, pausing in his notes.

'I seldom miss. Hunting bullets are designed to kill game instantly, so there is no doubt the job was done,' Vic replied thoughtfully.

'Look, it is not up to me, but you could be in a lot of trouble for this, Vic. However, I can't see any problems as it appears to be self-defence. But I suggest that you should contact a good lawyer before we go any further on this.'

'Suspected as much, but I suppose when the cards are on the table it will all be in the hands of a jury. By the way, we were told that a taskforce team is en route from Cairns. Any idea when they will get here and how many people are there as Mary needs to know the numbers for tea.'

As if on cue, the police sergeant's sat phone rang. He answered it and walked some distance away into the open. When he came back, he looked grim.

'Vic, why didn't you tell me who the guests were? That was the

46

commissioner who told me to look after you and ensure you get treated well. He said that the young man you saved was one of ours and that his wife is the daughter of the police minister. Did you know that?'

'I did but it should not make any difference to what happened.'

'I know, but it does. Anyway, we are on our own. The task team is stranded at Chillagoe due to a mechanical fault with the plane and they won't be here until the morning. In the meantime, I have been instructed to take the chopper up and look for the Raider. Interested in coming along? There is room for all.'

'Yes, I am. But I better let Mary know what we are doing so she can plan dinner.'

'Think she will be okay by herself?'

'Yes, she is the daughter of a professional kangaroo shooter and the most capable bush woman I know.'

Mary was on the phone and looked relieved. She hung up as Vic entered the kitchen.

'Wonderful news, Vic. That was Mick. He and Jim are okay He said Ian will make it. They are all in the Cairns Base Hospital. Mick said not to bother for me coming to see him, as he will sign himself out tomorrow and catch a plane home. Isn't that wonderful?'

She gave him a hug, tears in her eyes. He held her tight before letting her go.

'That is great Mary. Have you told the boss?'

'Yes, he arrives tomorrow after seeing the men in hospital. He said that he would bring Mick home if he is discharged.'

'Good, now you reckon you will be okay for a while? We are taking the chopper up to look for the Raider. The taskforce team is stranded in Chillagoe and won't be here until morning. So, there are only us people to cater for.'

'You know I will be, Vic. My double barrel snake gun is loaded and behind the kitchen door if anyone turns up, I don't like. See you later.'

The helicopter rotors were whirling when Vic climbed aboard, a pair of powerful binoculars and a camera around his neck. He shoved a cased rifle under the rear seats before climbing in. Gland gave him a strange look but said nothing. Soon they were over the junction, the tinnie and the fishing boat looking forlorn in the saltwater arm at the river junction. A big crocodile, basking on a muddy bank near the junction panicked and hit the water creating a large bow wave as the helicopter flew over it.

'Fuck,' Constable Hodges exclaimed. 'If we have engine failure put her down on the grass. I'd rather take a chance with hard ground than with one of those monsters in the river. Shit, there is another one. He is as big as Kris.'

Hawkins guided the pilot over the site where the shooting had taken place and took some photos before Gland ordered McGill to land in a nearby grassy spot. They walked to the bank where Hawkins pointed out where he and King were when the shooting started. The remains of King's bloodied pants leg lay in the grass and dried blood caked the ground. Hawkins picked up three shells and pocketed them. Hodges found another.

'Better give them to me Vic, they might be needed for evidence,' Gland requested. The shells were handed over.

'Fucking big case, no wonder those arseholes died,' he said as he inspected the cases. 'Do you reload?'

'Yes, I do, that is why I want the cases back. They cost a couple of bucks each,' Hawkins replied, as he took some pictures overlooking the bank.

'We better keep an eye open for bodies,' Gland noted thoughtfully. 'Though after seeing those big crocs in the river, I reckon we won't find much. Not too sure how that would go for you Vic. No bodies, no case to answer as far as I am concerned,' he added with a laugh.

Back in the air again the pilot turned the helicopter downstream to the river mouth. Near it they saw a drifting net dinghy being carried out on an outgoing tide. There was no one in it, though Hawkins said he could see a shotgun laying on the floor when they hovered over it and said it appeared the same one used by the shooter. He handed the glasses over to Gland, who confirmed the sawn-off shotgun.

'It's a gun alright and what appears to be lots of dried blood splattered over insides of the boat. Anyway, there is no way we can recover it, unless we land on the bank and have someone volunteers to swim out to it. Any takers?'

'No way boss,' replied the two constables in unison.

'I'm only joking, men. There is no way I would put anyone in this river,' the sergeant replied with a laugh.

The pilot turned the helicopter out to sea and turned north, climbing to eight hundred metres before levelling the craft. Now they had a bird's eye view of the Gulf, the coast stretching out to where it vanished into the sea haze to the north where no horizon existed as both sea and sky were as one. Long sandy beaches fringed by casuarina trees and low sand dunes were highlighted by small creek inlets, mere pen scratches on a map, that were slowly flooded by a turning tide which relentlessly inundated the mud and sand bars before spilling into the tidal estuaries. The Gulf was devoid of boats and ships.

'There, off that point, a dinghy,' Constable O'Donnell suddenly exclaimed and pointed where the reflection of the sun flashed from a boat. The pilot took the chopper down in a steep dive before levelling and holding back some five hundred metres away from the dinghy.

'Better not get too close,' the sergeant warned. 'A good shot could shoot us down and after seeing those monster crocodiles I have no wish to even put my foot in the water.'

'Turn a little so that I can see better,' Hawkins instructed the pilot, as he turned his binoculars on the dinghy. 'That is better, hold it there for a moment. It's a gillnet dinghy, and it looks like the one that was tied on the back of the Raider when it took off. Hello, there are people in it waving like mad. Try and get closer, Will. They don't have any guns.'

The pilot took the Jet Ranger nearer to the boat. Someone in the dinghy waved a fuel tank to indicate they were out of fuel.

'They are both women,' Hawkins exclaimed. 'They look in bad shape and need help and they are out of fuel by the looks of it. They can't go anywhere because there are no oars in the boat.'

They hovered over the boat and the women reached up with their hands in the air pleading for help.

'They are in bad shape, but how the fuck are we going to get them into the chopper,' Gland cried, sounding frustrated.

'Could land on the beach and take the door off and try and pull them up,' the pilot suggested. 'Its tricky stuff with a big bird like this and bloody dangerous. I don't have the proper gear either, only some tiedown ropes. Those girls might not be strong enough to hold on either. If one drops, she will become shark bait.'

'What about taking us back to the junction and I'll bring the boat up,' Hawkins spoke. 'There is plenty of fuel in it and I can get back to the ramp before dark.'

'Look, they will panic if we leave,' Constable Hodges scowled in disagreement. 'Lower me over the dinghy as close as possible and I will drop into the dinghy. Can you hold this bird long and low enough for me to do that, Will?'

'I can hold it okay, but only for a moment. Careful with the door or it will get smashed. Have someone steady it. Better drop a couple of bottles of water down also, those girls look like they need water.'

The chopper hovered above the boat. Constable O'Donnell opened the door and hung onto it, the downdraft threatening to pull it from his fingers. Hodges climbed onto the strut and dropped down onto the nets. It softened the two-metre drop. The boat rocked, and they heard the women scream in fright. Hodges gave a signal that he was okay. The helicopter pulled away, turned back over the coast and headed to the distant boat ramp.

At the ramp, Sergeant Gland directed the pilot to drop Constable O'Donnell off at the lodge and return with a vehicle before climbing into the dinghy with Hawkins. They rowed out to the mooring of the fishing boat. Both men had their rifles, something Hawkins insisted on taking along.

'This coast is no longer safe until we kill the rats that have taken over,' he said as he started the motor. 'The only laws they have are those of their own making.'

The boat roared away from its mooring, the 250 hp outboard reaching top revs as it turned into the river and headed into the setting sun.

'Fuck!' Gland exclaimed. 'how fast can this boat go?'

'I don't know, but we are sitting on eighty kilometres per hour now and I am holding it back.'

The sun dropped into the Gulf like a red orb as they blasted into the open sea and turned north. It was almost full darkness when they saw the gillnet boat ahead. In minutes Hawkins brought the boat alongside it. Constable Hodges was holding onto a young girl, her face red from sun exposure, her long hair matted and dirty. They helped her to climb over the side and made her comfortable on one of the seats. The other girl was in even worse shape and Hodges lifted her over the gunwale into the arms of Gland. She was crying, a look of relief on her face as she thanked them for helping her.

Hawkins turned the boat round and headed back to the distant river mouth, the daylight dimming. He opened the throttle and the boat rose on the plane.

'How are you going to find your way into the river?' Constable Hodges asked as darkness fell over the Gulf.

'Easy mate, we will just follow the GPS setting I recorded on the way out. Once we get into the river, we will be fine. The tide is coming in and there is plenty of water to glide over, providing we don't hit a drifting log, or a bloody big croc.'

Sergeant Gland was talking softly to one of the girls. He had wrapped her in a space blanket from the first aid kit. She looked fine under the dim cabin light, apart from the sunburn on her exposed face, arms and legs. The other was lying on the carpeted floor, and by all appearances, was sound asleep.

'Who are you and what where you both doing in the Gulf,' he asked in a gentle tone.

'My name is Jane McCarthy and I think that I have killed a man,' she blurted out in a rich Irish brogue, tears streaming down her face.

'Why do you think you might have killed someone?'

'Because I hit him with a rum bottle and there was blood all over him when I last saw him.'

'Where did it happen?'

'On a boat called the Raider. They kept us locked in a cabin for many days, but today a man called Stretch let me out. He was very drunk and bleeding from a wound in his leg that was causing him a lot of pain. He wanted me to help him and bandage it. He was drinking from a rum bottle when I tied a bandage around the wound. It looked like a big cut, almost like a knife wound, but it was very deep. He passed out at one stage. That is when I hit him over the head with the bottle to make sure he could not hurt us anymore.'

She shivered and wiped her eyes with the back of her hand.

'I let Doreen out and we ran out onto the deck and there was a dead man on it. Blood was everywhere, and he had a big hole in his chest. There was a gun near him, but we don't know anything about guns, so I pushed it over the side. We untied the dinghy, started the outboard, and got away as fast as we could. We ran out of fuel about an hour later. There was no choice but to sit it out and hope that Stretch wouldn't find us. Instead, we prayed, and God dropped a live angel in our laps to look after us until help came. Thank you so much.'

'We are entering the river now,' Hawking called, slowing down a little as he peered into the stygian darkness that was now absolute.

'Why don't you use the spotlight?' Hodges suggested.

'Because it will blind us as a million insects will be attracted to it when it is switched on. They will fly into our eyes by the hundreds. It is far better to run the night without a spotlight. The eyes adapt to these conditions if you let them. Just relax and don't strain them and you will pick up the shape of the mangroves and the banks on either side of us. I also have the GPS to direct me.'

He pushed the throttle down and again the boat planed over the water. Once they hit something soft, the object gliding under the boat.

'Crocodile,' Hawkins cried out above the outboard engine noise. 'Fair size one, but I reckon it won't survive the impact.'

There were car lights at the ramp that Hawkins used to guide him as he pushed the nose against the muddy bank to allow his passengers to disembark. After mooring the boat, he grabbed his rifle and rowed back in the dinghy. The others were ready.

'Tea is waiting,' Constable O'Donnell informed them as he put the 4WD Troopie in gear and steered it onto the dusty track. 'I don't know about you guys, but I'm bloody hungry. It's been one hell of a long day.'

On arrival at the lodge, Mary took charge of the girls and ordered the men to have a bath before they were allowed into the dining room. Gland spent the next half hour making a phone call to his superior. He was tired when he joined the others for predinner drinks. Hawkins handed him a cold beer; the bottle was almost empty when he pulled it away from his lips.

'Thanks Vic, I needed that, I really did, mate. Hell, this is turning into a nightmare. All sorts of heavies are dropping in tomorrow with police searches being planned at daylight. They have asked the Navy for help and there is a patrol boat en route from Thursday Island. I have been ordered to resume the search for the Raider at daylight, using both the chopper and the boat. Do you reckon you could drive it? My men and I don't know much about boats.'

'Yes, no worries. I will have to fuel it first though and I will take my rifle, or I don't go. I noticed that you are not too happy with me taking it.'

'No, I am happy, but regulations forbid it. But I have been called a blind bastard a few times before, so I won't see anything. I'll send Luke with you. He is a good man to have on your side. Time for another beer. Hell, I'm so hungry I could eat a horse.'

The girls were looking much better; both had showered and wore fresh clothes that Mary had provided. Their faces were covered with cream to soothe the sunburn. Hawkins noted that the one called Mary was very pretty. No beautiful, he mused to himself.

Her long flaming red hair set off her face while there was no hiding the firm, sculptured body under the loose clothing. Doreen was also attractive, and he wondered what such good-looking girls were doing on the Raider. Both were hungry and ate in silence.

'This is an amazing dinner, Mary,' Gland complimented Mary. 'Five stars, no wonder the lodge is so popular with metre long barramundi and food like this on tap.'

'Thank you, Matt,' Mary replied, blushing a little. 'Yes, the boss insists that only the best foods are served to guests and visitors. Have you all had enough? Don't forget about dessert.'

'So, Mary, you are Irish,' Hawkins stated looking at her, his voice gentle. 'Now that you are more relaxed you might tell us what you were doing on the Raider.'

'I am indeed from Ireland, Mr. Hawkins. Doreen and I are on a backpacking trip in Australia. We came to Karumba from Cairns. There were jobs advertised on a notice board at our Cairns hostel to work on fishing boats. We applied and were interviewed by a man who gave us bus tickets to Karumba. The captain of the Raider, Stretch and another man called Red, met us. They appeared very nice, and we were taken to the boat. Because it was night when the bus got there, we saw nothing of the town.'

'Yes, that worried us,' Doreen interrupted. 'Another dinghy came alongside, and two more men came on board. Both were very drunk and made lewd remarks about us. We were very frightened and asked Stretch to take us back on shore, but he laughed and said we would be okay, and that no one was going to harm us because we needed to be in good shape for the work ahead.'

'Yes,' Mary continued. 'we ate some food and had a drink before we were taken to our cabin. The door was locked behind us and soon after the engine started, and we were on our way. I think we were both too frightened to sleep as we could hear the men argue and fight all night. There was no window in the cabin, and we had had no idea where we were. Someone let us out at daylight, and we had to make breakfast for the men and ourselves. They were all very drunk and smoking 'grass' and kept touching us but Stretch said that we were to be delivered in good shape. After that we were locked up again until Stretch let me out to dress his wound.'

'Did you hear any shooting?' Sergeant Gland asked.

'Yes, we did hear some very distant shots and two shots that came from our boat,' answered Doreen. 'After that the boat motor was roaring for a long time until Stretch let Mary out.'

'Well girls, you are safe now,' Gland said. 'A police plane will take you to Cairns tomorrow where you will be asked to make statements. Just tell them what you told us, and you'll be fine.'

'What about our belongings, money and passports, sergeant?'

'Well, if it is on the ship, we will forward it to you if we find it. In the meantime, you are important witnesses, and the police service will take good care of you for now. No doubt you will be taken to a safe house until we get this thing settled.'

Mary took the girls to their unit as the men headed to theirs. Hawkins was thoughtful as he joined the police sergeant for a drink on the veranda.

'It appears to me that those girls may have been kidnapped,' he mused aloud. 'You know Matt, that may explain why attractive young women have been vanishing in North Queensland for several years. Pub talk has it that they are smuggled to Asia as sex slaves. That may be why they wanted Tina. What do you reckon?'

55

'You could be right Vic, but in my line of work nothing is proven until we have evidence. With luck we will find the Raider tomorrow and arrest Stretch, or whoever he is known by. By the way, keep a lookout for bodies when you are in the river. They should be floaters by tomorrow, unless the crocs and crabs have eaten them.'

'Hell of thing to ask a man, Matt. You might use them as evidence against me.'

'Vic, from what I have seen and heard today you will get a medal for bravery. There is no way me or anyone else will lay charges for what you did. I haven't told you, but my boss told me the shooting was on the evening news and no doubt the newspapers will have a field day in the morning editions. The press is coming tomorrow and Vic, take it from me, you're a fucking hero, and I mean that.'

Chapter 5
THE HIT

Wog Morossi slammed the cabin table with his fist in a resounding thud and cursed aloud as he looked at the big man standing across from him.

'Fuck it Bull, what the fuck was Stretch thinking about. He had orders to bring the girls direct to the Mitchell River, not the fucking Staaten.'

'Well, he reckoned it was rough and windy outside, and seeing they had plenty of time, they decided to lay up in the Staaten until the weather cleared. They were on the piss and probably smoked a few joints. They saw this guided fishing boat with a fantastic looking woman in it. According to Stretch, they planned to kill the men and take the woman to add to the cargo. But instead, someone shot Trevor and Red and opened fire on the boat, killing Lumpy and wounding Stretch.'

The big man paused and gulped down the remains of his beer. Wog was angry, as only a week ago they had planned the operation to meet the Asian smuggling trawler off the Mitchell River. It was the biggest shipment yet, and even the boss, Tony Broggetti, had attended the meeting along with Axel Shute, who presented the various biker groups, the Asian triads, the Mideast syndicate, and other interested groups, all who had boxes of cash to pay for drugs, guns, illegal immigrants, and young Asian women destined for the pleasure bars of the big cities.

The Karumba compound had been buzzing with the various delegates that wanted goods and were prepared to pay before delivery. One thing mused Wog, Broggetti was the best organizer the syndicate had. His connection with Asian crime lords and their insatiable demand for Australian dollars was responsible for setting up the biggest smuggling operation that the island continent had ever seen. Now it was in danger of being exposed due to the stupidity of a drunken skipper.

'Anyway, Stretch took off in the boat, but he said that he was bleeding badly, so he let one of the girls out to dress his wound. She hit him over the head with a bottle and both escaped in the net dinghy. That's about it, boss. Stretch wants to know what to do. He is somewhere this side of the Nassau River.'

'Well Bull, there is only one way of handling this disaster. If the cops catch him, he'll talk and blow this operation to hell. Bull, you know what to do. Get over there and take care of it. Make it look like an accident, so the cops think they were working alone. No doubt, they will come and see me later as I am the managing director of the Gulf Barramundi Company, and we own the boat. I can handle that, as I am not responsible for what a maverick captain does. Best you go now and good luck. You have a little daylight left. By the way, don't damage or destroy the ship. We will get it back when the cops are done with it. Take my boat, it's faster than yours.'

'What about the women, boss?'

'It's too late to look now. Get someone to take your boat out to sea as the tide will carry the dinghy into the Gulf, and with luck we may find them. Stay away from the shore as the cops will be searching for the Raider. If they do board the ship your man knows nothing and is mackerel fishing.'

Bull was on the water a little later, the big plate aluminium boat at full plane in seconds. The sun was almost touching the Gulf waters when he blasted out of the Mitchell River's South Arm. Almost an hour later, he saw the lights of a boat and steered towards it. It was the Raider. Stretch was leaning on the deck rails and greeted him. His leg was still bleeding from a blood-soaked bandage, while he had a deep raw cut on his forehead. The body of Lumpy was still on the deck. Bull cursed the smell of dry blood that permeated the air as he climbed on board. Without a word he pulled the body to the rear of the deck and shoved it into the water.

'Shit Bull, I was keeping him for a family funeral. He is married and has kids.'

'Stretch, you are fucking stupid. The cops are looking for this boat and the last thing we want is a dead man in it. Pull yourself together.'

'I'm trying Bull, but I can't stop fucking shaking; I need a fix, man, do you have one?'

'No, I don't, but I have this.'

Bull pulled his Ruger .44 Magnum revolver from its holster, put the barrel to Stretch's forehead and pulled the trigger. Bull flinched at the heavy concussion and pulled back as bone and blood scattered into the empty space and splattered into the water behind Stretch. Bull prevented the body from falling on the deck by pushing it over the railing and into the sea, avoiding the splash of water. Next, he pulled on a set of gloves and wiped the rails and wherever he thought he may have touched anything. He walked into the control room and removed the GPS disk from the chart plotter before starting the motor and steering the vessel east towards the dark shore. He dropped the anchor in shallow water, turned the engine off and climbed back into his own boat.

He turned the bow to the north, following this plotted GPS course back to the Mitchell River. Behind him the abandoned barra boat was anchored almost within a stone's throw from shore. Close by sharks, attracted by the smell of the decaying body and fresh blood gathered for a feast as the Gulf waters lapped the silent shore.

There was movement at the lodge as the morning slowly lit up the bush. The vestal songs of butcher birds and hoarse cries of blue wing kookaburras serenaded the men over breakfast while they discussed their plans to search for the Raider. The helicopter lifted off as the sun lit up the monsoon forests and the plains. Constable O'Donnell had been ordered to remain at the lodge with the women. Hawkins and Constable Hodges were at the ramp refuelling the boat. When done, Hawkins turned it into the river as the first of the sun's rays lit the fringing mangrove clad shores.

'How is the fuel range on this thing,' Hodges asked.

'Oh, enough to get to the Mitchell and back with some to spare,' Hawkins replied. 'We may have to yet. The Raider is fleeing north to the Mitchell River where the GBC has a base.'

As they entered the Gulf, the sat phone rang. It was Sergeant Gland.

'We have located the Raider. It is about five kilometres past the Nassau River, and some two hundred metres off the beach. It's anchored, but there is no sign of life, apart from plenty of shark activity and a couple of big saurians hanging about the area, so I am not planning to swim out. We will wait for you boys.'

Constable Hodges ended the call and passed the message to Hawkins.

'We should be there in less than an hour. It is going to be windy on the way back, though I reckon we may be bringing the Raider back and towing this boat. Be more comfortable.'

An hour later they saw the Raider and the helicopter parked behind some stunted scrub on a low sand dune. Hawkins brought the boat in as close as possible to shore, but even then, Gland was forced to walk knee deep through water to reach it, his Glock .40 S&W pistol in his hand ready to fire. Hodges stood on the casting deck; a cocked Ruger Mini 14 carbine in his hands as he scanned the water for crocodiles and sharks that were swimming about the area.

'They are feeding on something, probably a body,' Gland informed the men as he climbed on board. 'Will and I have been watching them since we landed. We picked up a few strips of clothing and a belt on the beach. There does not appear to be any life on the boat but be prepared to fire, just in case.'

The two police officers pulled themselves over the rail and onto the deck of the Raider as Hawkins held the boat alongside it. They entered the cabin, their Glock pistols ready, but they were soon back on the deck, which smelled offensively of dry blood.

'Nothing Vic, you can relax,' Gland shouted. 'Best you stay where you are. Forensics will be over this tub with a fine comb looking for fingerprints. Hello, this must be one of your bullet holes.'

He pointed at the wall of the deck, where a small hole was visible. There were no others, though the deck had plenty of bloodstains, the smell attracting blowflies. Gland made a phone call and spoke for several minutes.

'Okay, I have orders to secure the boat and the area and not to move it. We will remain behind while the helicopter heads back to the lodge to transfer police when they arrive. Forensics doesn't want anyone on the Raider. They are on their way from Cairns and are expected to arrive in about an hour's time at the lodge. Meantime we will use our boat to see what we can find in these waters.'

The helicopter lifted off, leaving the three men to scout about the sea. Apart from numerous sharks, some up to four metres long, they found little, excepting the ragged remains of what appeared to have been a pair of stubby shorts that were floating in the water. Hawkins pointed to where kite hawks and sea gulls were squabbling on the beach about a kilometre away.

'Looks like there is something dead over there, probably a fish, but we better check it out. I'll land you near it.'

He pushed the bow of the boat on the beach and the constable jumped out. He called for the sergeant to bring a plastic bag and a camera. Hawkins handed him his Nikon Z6 camera and a garbage bag and held the boat steady in the rolling waves in the knee-deep water.

'It's a whole foot and part of a leg,' Gland said when the men climbed back into the boat. 'It's fresh and doesn't stink yet. Take us back to the Raider and I'll put the bag in the freezer. Forensics will be excited by this.'

Later they dropped the anchor and erected the canopy for protection against the increased heat of the sun. Mary had prepared smoko and lunches that were kept fresh in the boat's Engel fridge, and now they sat back and relaxed enjoying the food and cold drinks.

'Shit,' the constable exclaimed. 'this must be the loneliest place on the planet. No sign of anyone, except us and that barra boat. This is so beautiful. I can see why some people work and live on these wild shores.'

'Yes, it is,' Hawkins agreed. 'I have fished these shores for half my life and never tire of it. King and I return here several times a year, and you know, we couldn't care less if we don't catch a fish or shoot a pig or feral cat. We are most happy when sitting in a shady place with a cold beer in hand, looking out across the Gulf and watching the sun set. Hello, that sounds as if we have company.'

The helicopter hovered into sight and landed on the dune, the sand swirling from under it. By the time three people got off, Hawkins was waiting with the boat on the beach. The new arrivals introduced themselves as Chief Inspector Jack Gilmore from Cairns, Sergeant Cliff Garland and Constable Lily Nicholls from forensics.

Gilmore asked questions as they slowly cruised out to the Raider riding at anchor on a slack tide. He remained in the fishing boat as the forensic team set to work. Gilmore wanted to know the fine details and recorded Hawkins on a small tape recorder as he told him about the happenings of the previous day. Gilmore shook his head and switched the pocket recorder off.

'You know, you and the others could be dead now, Vic. That was a brave thing that you did. As far as I am concerned no charges will be laid, though of course there will be an inquiry. It is something not to look forward to. And prepare yourself when you return to the lodge as the press is aware what has happened. It was all over the tube last night, and I would not be surprised if we have the dubious pleasure of their company upon return. You'd be happy to know that everyone is well, and by the way, Minister Waters sends his personal regards for saving his daughter and son in law.'

As there was little that the men could do until the forensic officers completed their work, Hawkins suggested a spot of fishing would help pass the time, something that was welcomed by the others. Using the Lowrance depth sounder, Hawkins located a hole in a tidal channel some distance away from the Raider and lowered the anchor.

'This boat has all the fishing gear we need,' he said. 'I'll net a few herrings for bait. There are plenty of rods, sinkers and hooks, and besides, with all the extra people at the lodge, Mary will need fresh fish. This should be a good spot for grunter, black jewfish, or cod.'

Baitfish were moving in under the boat for protection from the marauding and active sharks that, having run out of bodies, were now actively hunting fish by herding them up into the shallows. It was a simple task for Hawkins to drop the wide spread of the cast net over a school of herrings that were hugging the dubious safety of the boat.

'We have enough bait to last for a while,' he noted, as he dropped the baitfish in the live bait well.

The lines went down, and a few minutes passed before Gland had a bite. He hauled in a two-kilo grunter, a fine table fish. As he unhooked it, Gilmore had a run and landed its twin. For the next fifteen minutes, the bite was hot, and they landed a variety of fish before there was a lull, the men ending up with a dozen grunter.

A little later, Hodges landed a huge cod, over a metre in length. Hawkins took pictures of the men and their fish.

'Great stuff, this will make a wonderful story for one of my magazine columns. Hell, that cod has a big hard lump in his guts. I wonder what it has been eating?'

The police officers watched as Hawkins expertly killed and bled the big fish while still in the water. Hodges gave him a hand to lift the fish onto the cleaning board.

'Whatever this lump is, its bloody hard, feels like a glass float.'

He cut the gut of the big fish open and retched as he pushed at the lump with the knife and forced it partly out of the stomach. The stench of the rotten stomach contents wafted over the men.

'Fucking, Jesus Christ,' Hawkins swore loudly as he puked over the side of the boat into the Gulf, his face ash grey. He pointed at the fish. 'Shit, have a fucking look, you blokes, have a look. It's someone's head, the stink is enough for a maggot to throw up.'

The others had turned away when the stench wafted over them, but they now looked where Hawkins pointed. Part of a man's head was protruding from the fish's stomach, one eye glaring with slimy matted hair covering the other. As hardened as they were, they joined Hawkins who was still dry retching into the clear water. Holding his shirt over his nose, Hawkins started the outboard and hauled the anchor up with the electric winch. Putting the boat into gear, he turned it towards the Raider. Gilmore called out as they pulled alongside it and when the two officers came onto the deck, he pointed to the fish cleaning board over the motor.

'Now that is interesting,' Garland mused, appearing unmoved by the partly hidden head in the fish. 'It must have ripped it off a body while feeding, probably one of the boat's occupants as it looks fresh. Great catch, where did you get it? Take some photos of it, Lily before we remove it. You blokes look a bit seedy, been seasick, have you?'

He laughed aloud as Nicholl's giggled in the background.

'We have, but we'll keep the fillets for you to take home,' Hawkins joked. 'I don't think we will be eating that cod tonight, so feel free to take it.'

'No thanks,' Nicholl's laughed. 'you can toss that fish over the side after I take the head out. Not that eating it would be harmful, but the thought of what it ate is a turn off.'

She climbed on board and took a few photos before she pulled the head free and placed it in a plastic bag, appearing immune to the stench. Hawkins tossed the cod overboard, switched the wash pump on and started scrubbing the board as Nicholls climbed on board the Raider.

'We won't be long,' she declared. 'We are almost finished. You can wash the deck if you like as this blood will really reek for ever if it is not done soon.'

'What do you intend to do with the Raider, boss?' asked Sergeant Gland.

'Well, I am not too sure. What do you suggest, Matt?'

'Karumba is the nearest port, so I suppose it will have to go there. Someone will have to take it, but in the meantime, I suggest we moor it at the Staaten River boat ramp and keep someone on it until we can move it to Karumba.'

'That sounds good to me. Do we have anyone who can drive it?'

'Not me or Hodges, what about you Vic? Reckon you can handle her?'

'Probably, but not until we scrub that stinking deck. Just can't take stinks like that. Shit, my guts are still heaving. Come on young Luke, start scrubbing the deck. It will be a lot more comfortable heading back in her than in this boat. There is a nor wester coming and in an hour's time the Gulf will have white horses galloping all over it.'

After Hawkins ferried the police officers back to the beach he returned to the Raider. Behind him the helicopter rose into the sky and vanished from sight.

Hodges was busy scrubbing the deck with a hard broom, the soapy suds spilling over the side. Hawkins readied the sportfishing boat with a long rope so that it would tow properly by the big vessel. The deck was sparkling clean when he set foot on the ship. It smelled of soap. Hodges finished mopping the floor of the cabin before joining Hawkins on the bridge. Hawkins pushed the starter key and the diesel motor roared into life, belching black smoke from the twin exhausts.

'This ship is almost new. They have really looked after it,' Hawkins remarked. 'This thing can fly because the motor is overpowered for the size of the ship, something like our fishing boat, which is fitted with a

250 hp motor whereas a 200 hp motor would be fine. Hello, that's funny. The GPS is not working. Shit, there's no disk. Now that's not right. Do you think forensics removed the disk, Luke? Call your boss and ask him, this could be important. We will be cruising blind, but there is plenty of daylight left, so it's no worry, and besides I can always use the chip from our boat if I have too. They are compatible.'

Hodges called Gland on the ship's sat phone. He paused before ending the call.

'No, the disk was not removed by forensics Vic, they did note it though. However, the boss said there may have been someone else on board, as forensics reckons the head and the foot came from two different people. They said that the head shows signs of decay, and the foot does not. I wonder why someone removed the disk.'

'Well, that is obvious; they are hiding certain destinations from us. I remember, when years ago in the Northern Territory, the cops arrested a bloke on drug charges. He owned a helicopter and was a member of a local biker group. They used the GPS on the chopper to find his plantation and a lab in a remote part of Arnhem Land. I reckon this boat was involved in something like that, but there are others also. And where is Stretch? I'll bet that foot is his and the other bloke is the one I shot in the river. Stretch knew too much, and someone killed him for it. If he had been arrested, he would probably talk if a deal was offered.'

'You sound like a fucking copper, Vic, but I reckon that is exactly what happened. Anyway, it's up to forensics now to identify the remains and link them to the dead. Do you reckon you could handle a coffee? The galley is well stocked if you like a feed.'

'Coffee is fine, young Luke. The gut is not ready for food yet. Shit, it frightened the fuck out of me when that head popped out and that evil eye looked at me. I thought for a second that it had come back to haunt me.'

'Well, we get counselling for stuff like this Vic. Do you reckon you need it?'

'No Luke, I don't think so. I have never shot anyone before, but shooting those bastards was a pleasure. I hate to think what they would have done to Tina and the boys. In hindsight, I probably would be more remorseful for killing a kangaroo. Fuck, this wind is really hammering us. I'll be glad when we enter the river.'

Chapter 6
THE ASSIGMENT

Queensland Police Commissioner, Steve Farrell belched loudly as he leaned back in his chair and lit another cigarette, his fifth for the morning, and it was not even midmorning. He studied the file in front of him, slowly turning the pages and taking notes on a writing pad. The file was on Senior Sergeant William John Madsen, who at 33 years of age, had compiled a distinguished police record. Until now, Farrell noted as he read on.

Madsen had been stood down six weeks earlier after his wife Jan Dorothy Madsen, a well know police prosecutor, and another woman Mary Jennifer Olsen were killed in a car bombing. Madsen had blamed a local mafia mobster, Tony Broggetti of being responsible for the accident as Olsen was the only witness to a shooting murder that Broggetti had allegedly been involved in. Farrell lit another cigarette, noting that the ashtray was almost full. The file stated that Madsen had gone after Broggetti who had been hospitalised with broken ribs and facial injuries alleged to have been caused by Madsen, the reason for his suspension.

Had it not been for the interference of another detective Madsen could possibly have killed Broggetti. It was the only negative mark against a man who had served with distinction as a rookie constable on the Gold Coast where he received a bravery reward for talking a murderer into giving up his weapon after he had shot two people in a biker's drug heist. Of note also was his outstanding conduct in Goondiwindi during a racial riot that he stopped by arresting the ring leaders. In between he had done a brief stint at Burketown as a relieving constable and had been the investigating officer in a murder on Lawn Hill Station and latter had arrested the armed perpetrator. Madsen had joined the CIB five years ago and had been quickly promoted to the rank of senior sergeant, the youngest in the force for many years.

There were other things, his love of fishing and karate, in which he had earned a third Dan only the year before in a tournament in Hong Kong. He was also rated as the best unarmed combat instructor in the force, and during his university days had represented Australia in Rugby Union.

'This bloke is a fucking superman,' Farrell swore aloud as he picked up the phone and told his secretary to get Inspector Julian Steptoe on the line. Five minutes later, Steptoe called on his mobile phone informing him that he was out of his office.

'Julian, I need you to pick Bill Madsen up and bring him to my office.'

'Madsen, yes my best officer, but he is on suspension.'

'I know, but I want him here, including you.'

The two men were announced by his secretary two hours later. Farrell shook hands with Steptoe who introduced him to Madsen. As they sat down, Farrell studied Madsen, seeing a solid well-built man over six feet tall and probably weighed over 100 kilos. He wore an open short sleeve shirt that revealed a broad hairy chest, wide shoulders and heavily muscled arms. He had short brown hair, and needed a shave, noted Farrell being somewhat surprised that for a fighting man he sported only a few small scars about the cheeks and the left eyebrow, though somewhere along the way he had suffered a broken nose.

'Okay, the reason that I brought you here is to inform you both that as from now Madsen is back on active duty, providing he wants to. I'll make sure that all charges are dropped which will be easy as Broggetti is overseas and his return ticket is not until well after the hearing, so we will plead a no contest and that the charges are dropped due to us losing our key witness. He has political connections, but so have I and you can rest assured that mine are better. It's funny, but I can't understand why the court did not take his passport from him.'

He picked up the cigarette packet and found it empty.

'Fuck it, you blokes got a smoke? No, I'll get Sue to go down the shop and get some.' He picked up the phone and relayed the message to his secretary.

'Okay, you have both heard about Sheppard I presume. Here, Bill read his file and learn what happened to him in the Gulf country. Poor bastard, I would never have let him go if I knew this was going to happen.'

'Sorry, Sir, but I have been camping and fishing on Fraser Island and only got back yesterday,' Madsen said as he took the file and opened it.

'Drop the Sir bit and call me Steve,' Farrell offered. 'everyone else does.'

Farrell noted that Madsen had gone ashen faced as he studied the photographs of the body hung from the mango tree and the coroner's report. Slowly his face turned an angry red as he read on, a good sign thought Farrell. 'he is getting mad and that is what I want'.

'To put you into the picture Bill, we sent Sheppard on a mission to infiltrate an organization known as the Gulf Barramundi Company, or GBC. The boss is a man known as Don Marotsi, or "Wog" as he is better known. He has been in Australia since he was two years old, though we have no records that he was ever naturalised. The GBC operates barramundi fishing vessels in the Gulf of Carpentaria out of Karumba and from all accounts are doing very well. However, we believe it's a front and that they are involved in smuggling operations by meeting ships in the Gulf and bringing contraband into the country, not to mention money laundering. They purchased several barramundi fishing operations, but since they took over, they have waged war on others who refused to sell, so much in fact that most have moved to other parts of the Gulf. It is causing overfishing of the resources and conflict with those who were there first.'

Farrell talked for a long time, rumours of killings, body parts found on lonely shores by recreational fishers, who were also under harassment in the rivers ranging down from Weipa to Karumba. He mentioned the shootings on the Staaten River, the vanishing of a fisherman and his four-year-old son in the Mitchell River delta, the sinking of fishing vessels, the burning of commercial and recreational vehicles and their unmanned camps, and an unproven vendetta against the GBC by a large fishing family that had fished the area since the early 1960s and were strongly resisting the push to move or sell.

'Though they are suffering after putting up a stand with some family members dying in suspicious circumstances, one killed by a hit and run in a small Atherton Tableland town, another shot on the Sunshine coast and two missing off Cape York. We picked up the Sunshine Coast shooter. He fears to talk but had almost $20,000 in cash when he was arrested. We believe it to be hit money.'

His secretary came in with carton of smokes. Farrell tore it open with a haste that had the other men looking at each other. It did not escape Farrell.

'Yes, I know, this shit will kill me, but it and coffee are the only things that keep me sane in this fucking job. Okay, where was I? Right, as you know we also picked up suspects for the vanishing of the Mitchell River fisherman and his son. We thought we had a good case, but one witness disappeared, another, an English pack backer, refused to return to Australia because she feared for her life, and another was found shot in a toilet block in Weipa in what appears to be suicide for want of a better finding. Okay, enough of this, let's go and have lunch where we can talk some more.'

The two men were happy to escape from of the smoke-filled office.

They had lunch in a riverside café overlooking the bustling Brisbane River where Farrell informed the men of more details.

'All the major cattle stations east from Delta Downs near Karumba are now owned by a large Australian owned syndicate, Gulf Barramundi Company. They have financed other shady operations around the country as well. Now Bill, in case you haven't twigged where this is going, their CEO is one Tony Broggetti.'

'What, are you telling me that this lowlife criminal is the head of a multimillion-dollar company?' Madsen exclaimed looking at Farrell in disbelief.

'Yes, he is and while we can't prove it, his company is smuggling in illicit drugs, prostitutes, guns and explosives, illegal immigrants, and anything else that makes cash dollars. Now I know about your links with Broggetti, and I agree about your suspicion that he was directly involved in your wife's death, but if you want him, do it legally by hurting him right where it hurts most, in his pocket and get enough on him to jail him for life. That would be the best outcome.'

'So, what do you want me to do, Steve?'

'Go to Karumba, become a local by renting or buying a house and find out what the GBC does when they are not fishing. Under no circumstances join the group like Sheppard did, it may compromise you and they will kill you also if they find out you're a policeman. They have some tough hard men on their staff; the files of several are in my office. Study them and remember their faces because they will kill you if they believe you are a threat.'

The men walked back to Farrell's office where he bid them farewell. Farrell told Madsen to come back the following day to study the files and the details of the task ahead.

'Remember, tell no one, trust no one and talk only to me first. If I am not available speak to Julian. Otherwise keep your ID a secret.'

Madsen reported for duty the following day and was received by Farrell

'Look, Bill, I have thought long and hard over this. I not only want revenge for Sheppard, but I want to shut the whole operation down and jail the fucking lot, better still kill them all as the best solution. For the record you did not hear that, but I still can't sleep after seeing Shep's pictures. It will haunt me for the rest of my life. Bill, we have problems in the force, the judiciary, and on the political side as well. We have corrupt people in our camps, and they are protecting the GBC and especially Broggetti, something that you are aware of. Here are your orders, destroy them when you are familiar with the proposed operation and remember trust no one. Good luck mate and if you want help you know who to call.'

Weeks passed as Bill finalised his plans to move to the Gulf country, a task that he was looking forward too, having memories of days spent fishing in the Albert River at Burketown. On impulse he checked the real estate sites about Karumba. He found several houses for rent in the Gulf fishing town. One place looked attractive, being on a block of land that overlooked the river, and it was relatively new. Bill spoke to the real estate people at Normanton who had sole rental rights to the property. A woman informed him that the previous owners had drowned while fishing and that it was the best property in the Gulf country.

'It's for sale at a very good price in case you are interested,' she informed him. 'Much better than paying dead money in rent. It's also a great investment as holiday accommodation. I am not saying that because of the commission, but it's truly a lovely place that you would be proud to own. Sales are slow. It's a buyer's market as the mine zinc treatment plant has shut down, so you are getting the property well below what it cost to build should you decide to buy, instead of renting it. I can holiday rent it to visiting fishermen for the whole of the dry season, which makes it an excellent investment property.'

'Okay, you sold me, what are the chances of a contract with an option to buy, say in two months' time, as I want a look at it before buying. I also want to move in within a month or less.'

'Sure, we can arrange that on a term deposit. I will send the paperwork on to you by Express Mail. You should have it within two days.'

The contract arrived on cue and after taking it to a Justice of the Peace for signing, Bill posted it back. Four days later the saleswoman called to inform him that he could move in anytime he wished.

'Call in on your way through so that we can meet,' she said.

Bill had a weekend garage sale and disposed of most of Jane's belongings, something that was painful to him, but life must go on he told himself. She would not want it any other way. The removalists came in and took his furniture and other belongings away in a container for shipment to his new home. Next, he sold the house that he and Jane had shared for many happy years. The market was good, and he received a top price for it. It and the payout on Jane's life insurance gave him a sizeable bank account, though he wished that he could have shared it with her.

A day later, Bill traded his car in on a preloved Toyota Landcruiser 300 Series wagon. After collecting it two days later he headed to a boat yard and purchased a new 6.7 metre Quintrex Spirit boat, powered by a 200 hp Yamaha outboard motor. The new 'toys' made a small hole in his savings, but he shrugged it off as a minor inconvenience. Besides fuel and running costs would be paid for by the police service, he told himself. He was ready to head north a week later and received his last briefing from Farrell and Steptoe.

'Take care Bill, and trust no one,' was Farrell's last greeting as they shook hands. Steptoe was more open. 'Just send me down some fresh barramundi fillets and mud crabs,' was his farewell to Madsen.

Chapter 7
DEEP COVER

For Bill's long journey the shortest route to the Gulf country from Brisbane was via the Leichhardt Highway, west of the Great Dividing Range. It was late in the dry season, and he passed few other travellers, though there were plenty of trucks and the odd cattle train, greedy road hugging monster rigs over fifty metres long that were dangerous to overtake on the narrow strips of bitumen.

Towing the big boat with the powerful V8 Toyota Landcruiser was a joy and, in most sections, he managed to sit on the one hundred kilometres per hour speed limit. Two days after leaving Brisbane, he experienced a twinge of excitement when he turned from the highway west onto the Savannah Way and headed into the setting sun. He pulled up at the Mount Surprise service station and filled the fuel tank of the thirsty Landcruiser.

The servo claimed they were the home of the biggest hamburgers in the Gulf country. Feeling hungry he ordered one and ate it in silence and alone in the outdoor eating area. It was indeed large and tasty. By the time he finished it was dark. Soon he was back on the road, the 4WD's powerful driving lights turning night into day. Much later the lights of Georgetown fell behind. There were mobs of kangaroos and herds of Brahma cattle on the road, but very little traffic. Near Croydon, in some low hilly country, he almost hit a large brahman bull that suddenly crossed the road ahead. It gave him a start and he realized how tired he was. For some reason he was in an awful hurry, the twinge of excitement now drumming inside him. For the first time since leaving the Gulf so many years ago he realized how much he missed its vast wilderness.

He turned the Landcruiser into an empty rest stop. It was good to stop and stretch his legs, while the smell the fresh, clean night air was invigorating. The night sky was amazing, a billion twinkling lights that were clearer than he ever remembered, the Milky Way and the Southern Cross showing in bold relief. The night was alien and strange to him after living in noisy traffic-choked Brisbane for several years, the silence so absolute to the point that his ears hurt. He felt alone, like being the only living human in the world. Somewhere in the distance a barking owl called, a repeated soft "wook wook." It was a welcome to Bill as it broke the silence of the surrounding bush. He no longer felt alone.

As he tossed his swag on the ground alongside the 4WD, a dingo howled close by, its call eerily echoing away into the low rocky hills. It made the hair on the back of his neck stand up and a cold shiver run over his body. Others answered some distance away, followed by another, only a stone's throw from the vehicle. Soon the night was filled by the calls of the warrigals as they gathered to hunt down an unfortunate kangaroo or a calf. Bill took his 9 mm Glock service pistol from the 4WD console. He fitted his Surefire tactical light to it and slipped a round in the chamber from the loaded magazine. He placed the pistol within easy reach near his pillow, the nearness of the hunting dogs making him alert and wary.

He slept poorly, the marauding dingoes keeping him on edge. He welcomed the morning as a crescendo of noise from myriad birds greeted the new day – doves, honeyeaters, finches, noisy kookaburras and carking crows. He woke up hungry, wanting a cup of strong black sweet tea. He was on the road when the sun rose like a huge red orb behind him, colouring the landscape a rusty red with its cold light. He discovered that Croydon served a good breakfast at half the price of what it cost in far-off Brisbane. He lingered a little in the old town precinct enjoying the restored period buildings that dated back to the gold rush days of the 1880s, before again heading west, always west it seemed.

The Gulf lander train was pulled up at Critters Camp, a group of tourists posing in front of it, taking photos with cameras and mobile phones. He pulled over remembering the old train in its hangar at Normanton in a neglected condition years ago. From the Gulf Savannah website, he had learned that it had been restored to its former glory and that it ran a weekly trip from Normanton to Croydon, including trips to Critters Camp for tour bus groups as required.

Normanton had changed; there were more houses, motels, caravan parks and the business centre had bright facades. The old, restored Normanton Railway Station housed the district information centre and a coffee shop. The Indigenous girl working at the coffee shop was chatty and surprised that he was coming up instead of going.

'Everyone, especially the grey nomads, left weeks ago,' she informed Bill. 'They are a funny mob. They come here to fish and complain when the fish are not biting because the weather is too cold but leave when the fish are biting because when the temp gets to 30°C they reckon it's too hot.'

He stopped at the real estate agency and introduced himself. The sales lady, who sold him the property, was most helpful and said she would call in on her next trip to Karumba to ensure that he was settled in. She told him that the Karumba Post Office held the keys. When he stepped outside the airconditioned office the heat almost floored him; he had forgotten how hot the Gulf country is in October when the wet season build-up kicks in. Back in the airconditioned comfort of the 4WD, he noted that the town had indeed changed since his last visit many years ago. The purple-coloured old pub was like a smack in the face.

'Whoever came up with purple paint for a pub has no taste or they got it cheap,' he mused as he noted the huge crocodile replica in front of the Carpentaria Council Office.

Bill remembered his dad talking about the big croc that was shot on the Norman Banks in the Norman River in 1957 by a Polish born crocodile hunter, a woman, Mrs Krys Pawlowski.

His dad had worked for Harbours and Marine and had spent a few months as a relieving officer at Karumba in the late 1950s.

'It was over twenty eight feet,' his dad had said. 'I used to see it sometimes when I was fishing at the Point. It cruised by like a big submarine, with only a little bit showing, as most of its bulk was under water. People used to shoot at it with .22s and .303 rifles, but they never hit it until Krys shot it. She had a scope sighted rifle, a .270 Winchester. She was a good shot and an excellent hunter.'

Bill found it difficult to comprehend those crocodiles could grow that big as he passed "Krys" as the life-size fibreglass croc replica had been named. He turned onto the Karumba Road, noting that the tide was running out as he crossed the Norman River on the high-level bridge. In fact, he decided, everything was new or reborn. The Gulf towns, and its people were strangers to him. He smelled and inhaled the fresh clean air of the salty tidal stream. He had been away too long.

The twinge of excitement was back as he drove out of the low monsoon woodlands and onto the Norman River flood plain proper. The plain extended to far horizons, a vast shimmering lake of ebbing mirage where a few stunted trees and cattle on impossible long legs floated in an illusory sea of nothingness. Singular birds and flocks of Brolgas and Sarus cranes in their hundreds were watering at a drying waterhole along the road.

Bill pulled up and watched the thirsty birds flying in from the surrounding plains and wading into the shallow pool to drink, only to be forced out by new arrivals that bullied and jostled others out of their way in the rush for water.

For over an hour, he enjoyed the spectacle of the cranes in the coolness of the 4WD's air-conditioning, not bothering to switch off the engine. Soon he saw dozens of road signs advertising fishing tours and accommodation. Another advised him that Karumba was the 'Outback by the Sea.'

He passed the junction to the "Point" and continued past the golf club, its lawn dead and burned by the sun. Beyond it, the first houses of the "Town" commenced on both sides of the road.

Shady trees and some green watered lawns gave a surreal look to the surrounding dry drab landscape. There had been many changes about the town, though the Police Station appeared the same, a victim of successive State Governments not spending money on it he mused. As arranged, he called in at the Post Office for the keys to his new home. The Post Mistress was a pleasant, helpful, matronly woman, who had seen better days. She handed him a town map and the keys.

'Bert and Shirley James live next door and if you need anything, they'll help you. Shirley has been looking after the place, and if I know her it will be spotless,' she said.

He found the house and it was love at first sight, the cottage was set on poles over two metres high on a concrete pad. The block was on the end of a cul-de-sac and surrounded by a high fence. It had only one neighbour on one side, and bush bordering the others. It was perfect with shady trees and a patch of green lawn with a sprinkler busy cascading water onto a green grassy patch, a welcome sign. Beyond the house he noted that the Norman River estuary was a short distance, exactly as the web site had indicated.

A blue cattle dog barked and came snarling to the fence as he unlocked and opened the gate. 'Shut up, Bluey,' a woman's stern voice called from inside the house. An instant later, the door opened and a large woman in her late forties appeared on the patio.

'Sorry love,' she greeted Bill. 'Bluey reckons he owns the place; you must be Bill. I'm your neighbour. I've been looking after the house and yard. I opened it up and switched the fans on when Mrs Castling from the Post Office rang and said you were on your way. I'm Shirley.'

Bill liked her instantly, even though she kept chattering away, mostly about nothing that interested him.

'Bert, my husband, is at the Animal Bar,' she informed him as she pushed the dog away. 'Oh, sorry love, the Animal Bar is the pub in town. That is where all the men go when they have nothing to do, and a few women too,' she added with a hint. 'There is a tavern at the Point, it's more civilized, but only just. Karumba is divided by tidal flats into two areas, the Town and the Point in case you don't know. Come on I'll show you the house.'

The empty house smelled musty, though the air was clearing under the onslaught of the busy ceiling fans and open windows. Shirley showed him the rooms and, like the Post Mistress had said the house was spotless.

'I'll have to use my camping gear until my stuff gets here,' Bill informed her when she asked if he had any furniture.

'Yep, everything that was any good was taken away or sold by Joyce, Bill and Shirley's daughter,' Shirley answered. 'Strange what happened to them, they both knew the Gulf well, though mind you it's not the first time that people have vanished around here and turned up dead later. There is something terrible out there in the Gulf, a Bermuda Triangle I reckon.'

Bill agreed, though the triangle theory was new to him.

'Would you like a cold beer? I'll go over the house and get one if you like.'

'Thanks Shirley, but I have some in the car fridge. It's my shout.'

He walked outside where Bluey the dog grudgingly gave way to the territory he had claimed as his own, his tail wagging for attention. Bill patted him and by the time he backed the boat under the high stilted house, the dog was walking behind him as if he had done so all his life.

'I'll be dammed,' Shirley said as he handed her a cold 4X Gold beer from the Engel car fridge. 'he likes you, never seen him do that with anyone.'

They chatted about things in general as they sat on the stairs of the rear patio, enjoying the view and the slight sea breeze of a turning tide. Bill told her about losing his wife, his decision to quit his job as an insurance representative and to head north to escape the rat race.

'What are you going to do for living, not too many jobs about in your line of work, though you might get a job labouring on the council. They are always looking for workers and you look pretty fit. The fishing industry is another option for you, but it's only seasonal.'

'I am,' he assured her. 'I spend all my spare time outdoors, fishing, and bushwalking and I have my own gym when it turns up. As for work, I have money coming in from investments, though I might do some casual stuff later.'

'Well, I better go home and get tea ready for Bert. Would you like to join us? We haven't much on tonight, only barramundi fillets and chips.'

'No thanks, not this time Shirley. I'll catch up later.'

By the time Bill had unloaded the boat and the vehicle it was almost dark. Lights were turned on in nearby houses, the first signs that anyone lived there. Shirley had said that most people remained indoors during the heat of the day with air conditioners running and they came out mostly at night. 'or they go to the pub, like Bert does.'

After having a shower Bill drove to the Karumba Lodge & Hotel and noted that the car park area was almost full. The noise of country music, loud cries, voices, and laughter met him as he entered the infamous Animal Bar. Dozens of ceiling fans were cooling the air, and the crowd, down and it was pleasantly cool in the area. There were plenty of people milling about, the pool tables were full, and another group watched a replay of a football game between the Townsville Cowboys and the Melbourne Storm on a large TV screen.

He found a spare stool at the bar and ordered a beer and steak and vegies for one.

'Hell, this is good,' he said to himself as the amber liquid slipped effortless down his throat. He turned about pretending to watch the football, but his practiced eyes spied about the lounge checking faces and people.

There were people from all walks of life, young and old, parents with kids, retirees, and a noisy mob of young men trying to impress a couple of girls of their own age. Bill was a little disappointed, he had expected bikers, ringers, fishers, and miners, but as a collective group they were missing. His meal turned up and he ate it in silence, washing it down with another cold ale. It was one of the best steaks he had eaten in years. He ordered another beer and bumped someone with his elbow as he turned around.

'Sorry mate,' he apologised.

'No worries, mate, not your fault. It's a bit crowded in here tonight,' was the reply. The man's voice was friendly and sincere. He was as tall as Bill, though carried less weight. He was in his late sixties, one of the retirees that Bill had looked over earlier and passed by.

'Friday nights are always like this,' the man informed him. 'be worse tomorrow when the boys come back from fishing. The barra season closes at midnight, and I reckon they will be spending their cheques big time when they hit town.'

Bill studied the other man's face. There was something strangely familiar about the man. The face had seen many monsoon seasons, his skin was almost leatherlike in texture. The man wore thin glasses that made his clear blue eyes larger and highlighted the grey beard that hung onto his chest. His nose was slightly twisted, the result of a break, while scars indicate that he had collected a few cuts from hard fists in his time. Yet, the creased face indicated that he smiled and laughed a lot. Bill decided that the man had been a tough cookie in his day, and probably was not to be trifled with. Again, he felt that twinge of excitement and felt that the man also knew him.

'Drinking alone mate, are you?'

'Yes,' Bill replied. 'I only arrived today from Brisbane. I bought the Wilson's place as I love fishing.' He surprised himself by giving out so much information to a stranger.

'So, you're the bloke. The missus heard from Mrs. Castling at the post office that you had arrived. No town secrets with her. How was the trip from the big smoke?'

'Yeah, good mate, I'm Bill Madsen,' Bill responded holding out his right hand. It was firmly taken in a surprisingly strong grip.

'I'm Harry Douglas. Look, it's uncivilized for a man to drink alone in the Gulf country. Come, join us, and meet the mob. Never know they might even tell you where the fish are biting. Here Bill, can you give me hand with these beers, please.'

The mob, as Douglas had called them, were seated on the outer edge away from most of the noise. There were two women in the group. The younger woman was in her mid-thirties and strikingly beautiful but for some small lines about her eyes and mouth that spoke of past hardship, thought Bill. He noted to his disappointment that she wore a wedding ring. One bloke looked vaguely familiar, but Bill got the surprise of his life when the other man, who had his back towards the bar, turned about and faced him. He instantly recognized him as Vic Hawkins and the other fellow his fishing and hunting mate, retired SAS major, Jim King. As a police officer, Bill had taken a keen interest in the Staaten River shootings by following the police and media reports at that time.

Harry did the introduction: 'This is Bill Madsen. He bought the Wilson's place. Bill this is my wife Grace, and over there is Jim King, Julie Grant, and that ugly skinny old bastard is Vic Hawkins.'

They shook hands, the grips firm and welcoming. Grace was asking Bill questions, was he married, did he have kids, and so on. Typical small talk from a woman who could sort you out faster than any man could, thought Bill, answering her politely between gulps on his cold beer. However, the beautiful Julie appeared ill at ease and shy even though she was friendly enough.

The men asked him if he had a 4WD and a boat and what sort. What fishing gear did he have, and had he ever caught a barramundi.

Unconsciously to him they were sorting him out if he could fit in their group, how to help him catch fish, how much information they could give away and most of all could he be trusted to keep a fishing spot secret.

Bill studied Hawkins and King. According to the police reports, both men had been mates for years, though they were quite different in nature. Hawkins was fair, tall, and had a slim built with sinewy sunburned arms and broad bony shoulders. His blonde hair was thinning and his temples greying. King was short and thickset, a barrel chest matching big muscular arms, though he was showing signs of a beer gut. His head was shaved bald, and he had a walrus–style moustache that was almost grey. A small ring adorned his right ear. He knew that King had been pensioned off by the army due to war wounds he received in Iraq. He was some ten years younger than Hawkins. A highly decorated soldier, he had overseen SAS field operations in both the Iraq and Afghanistan wars. Hawkins looked about a lot and missed little. He reminded Bill of an old police partner who had a knack of picking people out and putting them into different categories. He had seldom been wrong.

Bill offered to shout the next round of drinks and Hawkins went with him to carry them back. More people were coming into the bar as the football game on the big screen reached its climax with only a point separating the two teams. The crowd roared every time a player broke away with the ball. Bill thought it odd that the game was a replay and that everyone probably knew the outcome. Still, it had an enthusiastic audience, perhaps due to boredom in Karumba.

'Bloody good game,' Hawkins shouted. 'worth seeing again.'

'Always is,' Bill shouted back. 'Bloody hell, you can't even bloody think with all this noise.'

'Same here,' Hawkins yelled. 'I'm deaf in one ear and can't hear out of the other.'

An Indigenous couple with a baby joined the table. They were introduced to Bill as Reggie and Pearl Kendall. Bill noted that both spoke in the peculiar Pidgin English known as Kriol and used throughout the

Gulf country by both Aborigines and most white ringers working on remote cattle stations. The baby received a lot of attention from the women. Bill noted that Julie had tears in her eyes when she passed the baby back to Pearl and that she was very emotional. Grace gave her a hug and said something. It appeared to settle her down a little. Bill thought she must have lost a baby or something, or she was barren. She was probably married to a council worker, or a commercial fisher, which was a shame, he mused as he studied her. He would not mind knowing her better. That surprised him as it was the first time he had taken any notice of another woman since Jan died.

'So, what are you going to do with the baby bonus, Pearl,' Harry asked. 'You reckon you might buy that motor car, ey?'

'No way Harry. 'ey you only jealous because you can't get him up anymore 'ey, you too bloody old,' she shouted gaily.

There was laughter all round and Harry pretended to hang his head in agreement. Another Indigenous couple, who were introduced as George and Sandra Gregory, joined the group. Both were in their mid-thirties. Sandra was as pretty as Julie, noted Bill as he took her hand. Harry said they were professional barra fishers and crabbers who had a fishing base up north on the Coleman River.

Rock and roll music had replaced the noisy football game and couples were dancing on a cleared space under the TV screen to a noisy rock and roll beat. The Gregorys joined the dancers. Bill surprised himself when he impulsively asked Julie for a dance. To his surprise, she accepted. Both headed for the floor where they danced to the swing of the music amidst the jostling crowd.

Suddenly there was uproar at the bar and people began to cheer two men who were attempting to flog the daylights out of each other. The word "fight, fight" erupted from the crowd as they surged forward to view the combatants. The two men serving behind the bar quickly put a stop to it by separating the men.

'It's bloody Weed,' Julie cried. 'I thought he was still out fishing in the Gulf.'

'Who is Weed,' Bill shouted, surprised at her outburst and the venom in her voice.

'That little bastard with the cap turned back to front, a real troublemaker and a fucking murderer,' she replied, her face white with anger.

Weed was wearing a green Jackie How singlet and stubby shorts. Bill vaguely remembered something about him in the police file. He was only a little bloke, thought Bill, but he had a body of sinewy steel like muscle. He had seen men like him before; most were tough bastards and generally troublemakers. Weed calmed down as the other man was pulled away by his mates.

The dance resumed and when Julie said she needed a drink they headed back to the table. She held his hand, which he found very pleasing. He had loved holding her firm taut and muscular body. She had moved with grace on the dance floor in a way that excited him very much. Back on the table, the cold beer was good as were the lies about fishing for barramundi and crocodiles.

'Oh shit!' Sandra exclaimed suddenly above the noise. 'Here is trouble.'

Bill looked up to see Weed heading towards the table, a mad, out of control look in his eyes. He stopped at the table and stared drunkenly at Hawkins.

'You fucking arsehole,' he cursed him. 'you shot my best mate. I'll fucking kill you one day when you're not looking.'

'Fuck off, you obnoxious brothel bred little piece of shit,' Hawkins said calmly. 'It will take a whole man to do that, not a little shit turd like you.'

Weed turned white at the insult and launched himself at Hawkins. He would have smashed the older man except for Bill, who on impulse suddenly blocked Weed and shoved him on his back. Bill stood up, towering above the smaller man.

'I can keep that up all day,' he said, the tone in his voice freezing Weed and surprising the others in hearing range with its venom. 'Get up and walk out or be carried out. It's your call.'

The barmen had rushed over but stood back as Harry waved them down.

'It's under control. Weed tripped over his ego and is going home.'

Weed got up slowly, trying to focus his eyes on Bill. He backed away and headed for the door before stopping and looking back at the group.

'You fucking arseholes are dead,' he screamed loud enough for everyone in the bar to hear.

Harry looked at Bill.

'Not bad for a sales rep but take note of that little prick and watch your back. He is a death adder and will stick a knife under your ribs when you're not looking.'

'Thanks for the help, Bill,' Hawkins said as he placed an empty wine bottle back on the table. 'but I would have taken care of him. I saw him coming and was ready. Come on, it's my shout. I owe you one.'

Both men and George headed to the bar where a group of new arrivals, mostly Aborigines wearing tight blue denim jeans and shirts, R.M. Williams boots and big hats, were jostling to get a drink. They smelled of dust and cow dung.

'They are ringers from Delta Downs Station,' Hawkins informed Bill. 'They have been loading cattle on a ship bound for Indonesia.'

'Hey, you blokes are late,' George greeted them. He appeared to know everyone.

'Yep, we had to load the last cattle for the season on the boat, 'ey,' said a well-built Indigenous man as he shook hands. 'How the hell are you, George?'

'G'day Vic, how did you get on with that shooting, okay?'

'Yes, I did Barney. The cops are not charging me as the coroner said it was self-defence. By the way, this is Bill Madsen. He is from Brisbane and bought the Wilson place.' They shook hands and Bill was introduced to the others.

'There is a bunch of pigs at the 21-Mile, Vic,' Barney informed Hawkins. 'you're welcome to go and shoot the bastards if you like, 'ey. They are all about the billabongs and pools. The cattle are bogging down in the bloody pig wallows where the bastards eat them alive when they can't get out. We have finished mustering there for the season, 'ey.'

'Shit yeah, mate, I was thinking about heading home after the episode with Weed tonight because if my old lady finds out about it, I'll be in even bigger trouble.'

'Weed 'ey, what the fuck was that obnoxious little piece of shit up to?' Barney asked, suddenly all ears.

'Oh, he had a go at me, but Bill here put him on his back. When he got up, he said we were all dead. Still, I would have died young years ago if I took note of blokes like him.'

'Watch him Vic, he is a fucking snake 'ey. Him and that big fucking mate of his, Bull, 'ey. You too mate, 'ey' he said turning to Bill. 'They say he knifed a bloke in Melbourne years ago and that he might have been involved in some of the killings around here also, including that poor bloody copper 'ey. Look fellows it been nice catching up, but the missus just walked in, so I better go 'ey.'

'Come and join us,' invited Hawkins. 'the more the better.'

The party dragged on until midnight. Bill was pissed, but highly pleased when everyone spilled outside. It had been months since he had been so relaxed. Before leaving, Hawkins had asked if anyone wanted to go pig hunting, but when he said it meant an early start all had declined.

Hawkins had turned to Bill.

'Looks as if you're my last hope, mate. Interested in coming along and having a go? Don't worry about a rifle. I have a spare and heaps of ammo. Got tucker also and we will be back about noon, 5.00 am start, okay?'

'Count me in, though you might have to break the door down to wake me up.'

They gathered outside, the men shaking hands, clapping each other on the shoulder, and the women hugging everyone as they bid good night.

'What about driving home and the cops,' Bill asked to no one in particular.

'Fucking cops are probably out fishing,' Harry replied. 'this is a bush town, and the local cops let things run pretty much by themselves, unless there is trouble. Just take it easy driving home and don't run over any black cats.'

As Bill drove past the harbour, he was jubilant, even though he was pissed to the eyeballs. He had made contact and had been accepted in the community.

Chapter 8
BOARS AND CROCODILES

Bill woke up to an urgent knocking and Bluey barking his head off next door. Everything was dark. He had no clue where he was. He sat up groggily on his swag that he had dumped and unrolled in the middle of the bedroom on arriving home.

'Bill, are you awake, it's me, Vic. For fuck's sake shut up, you bloody mongrel dog,' someone swore in a loud tone that he recognized vaguely as Hawkins.

Bill stood up, his memory of the previous evening flooding back to him. He stumbled to the door and located the light switch, the light painfully bright as it flooded the empty room. He made his way to the front door, lighting up the kitchen en route.

Hawkins stood on the patio, a smile on his face, showing no hints of the boozy night before, unlike Bill who felt like hell.

'Fuck mate, what fucking time is it,' he managed to ask, his head throbbing.

'Good morning, Bill,' was the cheerful reply. 'It's almost daylight and we are supposed to be on the road. I slept in myself, too much rum and coke last night. You go and get ready. I'll put the billy on for a cuppa. Fuck! You lead a frugal lifestyle.'

'Coffee, black and strong, and no sugar,' Bill mumbled as he waved him in and stumbled to the bathroom.

He turned the shower on, the water was warm and tepid, but it felt good as it washed away the weariness. By the time, he had finished and dressed the smell of strong coffee wafted through the house.

'I was going to make us some toast,' Hawkins informed him. 'but I can't find any bread. Pretty Spartan existence you live by. At least you have a camp stove to boil water.'

'Yeah, I must go shopping. I was going to do that today, but it will have to be when we get back. Hope there is a shop open somewhere.'

'Bread shop and café at the Point, always open and regular as clockwork,' Hawkins replied. 'Here is your coffee, tea man myself in the morning. I've got tucker in the Engel fridge so we will have an early smoko in case you get hungry.'

The air outside was hot and humid, and it hit Bill like a wave. There was no hint of light in the fog-like atmosphere.

'The fog is caused by a Morning Glory,' Hawkins said, as they climbed into his Toyota Landcruiser, a similar but earlier model to Bill's. 'They are late this year, a harbinger of an early Wet, but as you get older you learn not to predict the weather as it makes fools out of all who do.'

Bill had memories of the Morning Glories, large clouds that rolled horizontally inland from the Gulf of Carpentaria either in single rolls or as he once had seen at Burketown, up to seven rolls during the build-up season of the monsoon. They drove on, the tyres humming on the bitumen road, saying little, but enjoying each other's company. The fog was thick and in one section Hawkins flipped the windscreen wipers on as shower-like precipitation splattered on the windscreen. Ahead the sun rose across the misty Norman River flood plain, a huge red orb that looked as if the world was ending.

'Wouldn't be dead for all the gold in the world,' Hawkins mused aloud. 'I never get tired of seeing the sun rise over the plains, especially when a Morning Glory drops down and fogs it. Hello, someone else is up early, a set of car lights just came out of the fog behind us. He must be heading to town.'

'Town?' Bill asked.

'Oh, the Isa or Cairns, I reckon, might even be Townsville. Only locals on the road now, the grey nomads lit out weeks ago when the temperature hit 30°C. They always do, regular as clockwork they are.'

Later they turned onto a graded track and stopped at a closed gate. Bill opened and closed it after the Landcruiser drove through. He noted that the head lights were turned off as there was enough light to see as the misty cloud from the Morning Glory rolled inland and burned up under the increasing warmth of the sun.

Hawkins switched the engine off, got out and opened the rear doors of the wagon where a car fridge, toolbox, and two boxes were stored. There were also a couple of gun cases. He unlocked one and pulled a scoped Sako .308W rifle from it. Opening one of the boxes, he took a rifle bolt out of it and slipped it into the rifle. He handed the rifle to Bill along with a box of ammunition.

'I reckon you know about rifles. Load the magazine, but I would prefer that you don't put a round up the spout until it is needed. I don't trust safety catches.'

Unlocking the other case, he took out what to Bill appeared to be an expensive rifle. It was also fitted with a telescopic sight. Hawkins fitted the bolt and pushed four rounds into the magazine. They made the .308 shells look small.

'These are .270 Weatherby Magnum shells,' Hawkins said, as if reading his mind. 'I have had it for decades, and it is on its third barrel. Just got it back a couple of weeks ago. The police confiscated it after the shooting I was involved in, but it was returned after the inquiry.'

He paused and looked back toward Karumba.

'That's funny, that bloke that was behind us should have gone past by now. It could be a birdwatcher as they are the only tourists, beside anglers and pig shooters, who come to the Gulf country this time of the year.'

They drove on, the track leading past stunted coolabah and ironwood trees that rose tall amongst dry Mitchell grasses. The leaves were dripping wet and spruced up a little from the morning mist, though some were already wilting as they faced the hot day ahead. A huge brown snake suddenly appeared on the track. It lay motionless in the warming rays of the sun.

Hawkins stopped the 4WD and switched the engine off.

'Taipan,' he said quietly. 'It's a fucking big one. I'll see if I can get a photo of it.'

He stepped out and opened the rear door and grabbed a Nikon Z6 camera fitted with a 300 mm lens from a camera bag on the rear seat. Bill watched as he slowly walked up to the snake. Hawkins stopped about four metres from it, hunkered down and began taking pictures. Suddenly he jumped up and retreated from the fastmoving snake that was rapidly sliding towards him, its head held up and body coiling into striking position. Bill jumped out of the 4WD, ramming a round into his rifle's chamber.

'No, don't shoot it,' Hawkins shouted. 'He won't come any closer if we don't get into his space. I got some great shots. Let him be to enjoy the sun and peace.'

He drove around the reptile, its baleful eyes glaring at the 4WD as it passed.

'That was a bit of luck,' Hawkins said, a grin on his rugged face. 'It's been a long time since I have seen one that big. The cane toads kill most of them. Poisonous to eat they are, and snakes have no defence against it. The Taipan is the most dangerous snake we have in the tropics and said to be the second most poisonous snake in the world. Its cousin, the Fierce snake of the Channel country, is number one.'

He suddenly pulled up. 'Over there, near that dead coolabah tree is a nice boar. Take him if you want. Just put the crosshairs on his shoulder squeeze the trigger and the rifle will do the rest.'

Bill had fired many .308W rifles on the range and had carried them on duty. He got out of the 4WD, being careful not to slam the door as Hawkins instructed him. Bill had not seen the pig until it slowly moved away from where Hawkins pointed. Using a tree for a rest he picked the boar up in the scope. It looked huge, even though it was over two hundred metres away.

He did as Hawkins instructed him but was surprised when the rifle went off when he touched the trigger. He knew he had missed. Quickly slamming another round in the chamber, he sighted on the vast vanishing boar that was kicking up the dust with its heels, but he held his fire as it was too far away.

'Boom,' the report was loud and to his right. Bill saw the boar do a cartwheel and flip over in a cloud of dust. Hawkins slowly ejected the shell from his rifle and caught it before turning about and looking at Bill.

'Sorry mate, but when I saw you weren't going to shoot, I took him.'

He appeared not surprised at the long range kill on a running target from a standing position.

'Fuck, that is good shooting,' Bill exclaimed. 'I reckoned he was too far away and because I have never shot anything on the run, I did not fire. The light trigger got me on the first shot.'

'Noticed that but seeing that everything is now awake I'll put an empty can out so that you can get a feel for the rifle. But first we'll go and have a look and take a photo of the boar.'

Hawkins rolled the boar about on its stomach and held its head up before instructing Bill how to pose with it as he snapped off a couple of shots. The tusks looked mean, but Hawkins said that they were only average, and they got much bigger. He found an empty drink can in the vehicle and handed it to Bill.

'Here, you're younger than me. Place it on the ground in that little clearing over there.' He pointed to a bare patch amongst the grass about one hundred metres away.

Bill walked over and set the can on the ground, noting that the morning was rapidly heating up. Back at the 4WD, he chambered a round in the Sako and using a tree trunk for a rest he aimed at the can and slowly squeezed the trigger as Hawkins instructed him to do. The rifle jarred back into his shoulder and the can flew up into the air for about a metre.

'Good shot,' Hawkins praised him. 'try another one for luck.'

Again, Bill aimed and had the satisfaction of seeing the can spin away into grass.

'That will do,' Hawkins said. 'We don't rubbish the bush, so go and pick the can up and let's find some pigs to hunt. The 21-Mile is about ten kilometres away. It's a big creek pool, the only fresh water about for miles, a lifesaver for wildlife and stock at this time of the year.'

'Where did you learn to shoot,' Bill asked as they passed a plot of stunted paperbark trees. For all his yarns, Hawkins was a man who did not talk much about himself. He understood firearms and the bush and accepted that others knew about it also.

'When I was a kid on the old man's dairy farm,' Hawkins answered. 'I've done a lot of competitive shooting with rifles, shotguns, and handguns. Never got too serious about it and always treated it as fun. My love is pig hunting. Never lose any sleep killing pigs or feral cats either because they do so much damage to the environment and the wildlife.'

He chuckled. 'There is too much bullshit about owning a gun these days.'

A noticeable greening of vegetation appeared at the horizon.

'Walker Creek,' Hawkins said, with a sweeping hand across the plains. Nearing the creek, Bill recognised paperbarks, palms, Leichhardt and myrtle trees fringing the creek's course in almost rainforest-like stands. Hawkins parked the Landcruiser alongside a small shed sited near a set of cattle yards that were located near the creek's tree line.

'Load her up and fill your pockets full of ammo. Don't lose any shells if you can help it as I need them for reloading,' Hawkins instructed Bill as they picked the rifles up from the rear seat.

They walked and followed narrow wheel tracks under the creek's gallery forest, where under the cool shade of the big trees the smell of water and cattle dung intermingled with dust. The track ended at a large shady clearing that bordered on the cool inviting waters of a large pool. Some brahma cattle were on the opposite bank, totally unaware of the two men. Hawkins pointed to where a mob of pigs were bunched together on the opposite bank, while others were rooting amongst the water lilies.

'Barney was right; there are at least fifty or more of the black heathens. Not too much cover so we will have to take our shots from here but be careful you don't lob a round into one of those brahma bulls or it will cost you a year's wages.'

They sat on their butts in the dust, as Hawkins took some more pictures with his ever-present camera. On the way in, he had told Bill that he was a freelance author and photojournalist for several outdoor magazines and contributed movie clips to YouTube.

'I can make you famous,' he had chuckled.

Bill wasn't too sure about that as he had to remain in limbo, but for the time being he decided to go along with the older man.

'Fuck, look at that big mud gecko,' Hawkins pointed to where a long dark shape suddenly materialized in the water near the pigs. 'Fucking saltwater croc! He must be five metres or more. He is stalking the pigs. This could be the film of a lifetime.'

The huge reptile mesmerized Bill as it slowly swam towards the unsuspecting pigs that were feeding on waterlily roots and digging for freshwater mussels. When it was only a couple of metres away from the pigs it suddenly propelled itself forward in a surge of water and grabbed a large sow, it's squeal of alarm quickly smothered as the big jaws clamped about it with a fleshy resounding clunk. Water and mud splashed up as the crocodile rolled its victim in the dreaded death roll. The mob fled up on the bank with squeals and grunts of alarm. Only a big boar stood his ground for a second, tusks grinding, before rushing off to catch up to the others up the bank, his hair bristles fully erect on his back.

The saurian paused in its roll; the pig no longer struggled in the jaws. Bill noticed that Hawkins' Nikon digital camera had not stopped and even now, he waited for the croc's next move. Only when the reptile moved from the shallows into deeper water and swam away with the unfortunate pig slung between its jaws did Hawkins drop the Nikon down on his chest.

'Bloody hell!' he exclaimed, letting out his breath. 'How fucking good was that? I've waited for years to get shots like that. Thank Christ for digital cameras and flash cards. I must have shot over 100 images and video film. Ever see anything like that?'

'No,' Bill admitted. 'And I was thinking of having a swim later.'

'You have a death wish,' Hawkins admonished him, a strange look on his face. 'Never swim in pools in the Gulf country, or you will become croc shit. Fuck, those pigs have gone. What say you bring the 4WD down and we'll have a bite to eat and a drink of tea. I'll gather some firewood for the billy and start a fire. There is a track on the other side of the pool, and I reckon we will catch up with the herd at the end of it later when they settle down. There's no hurry, and they won't be far away. It's too fucking hot on the plains.'

He tossed the keys. Bill caught them and placed the Sako .308W against a log.

'Take it with you, never know when you run into a bunch of pigs around here,' Hawkins advised.

It was blazingly hot as Bill walked out of the cool shade onto the sparsely treed plain where an ebbing mirage was already formed under the heat that rose from the plain. He noted there was some dust trailing in the air on the track they had come in on, but gave it no further thought as little whirlwinds are part of the dry season.

Near the 4WD he paused in mid stride as he thought he heard a vehicle, but seeing nothing he stepped in it, started the engine and drove down to the shady place where Hawkins had piled some kindling and timber in a small clearing.

He got a lighter from the rear of the wagon and lit the fire, the smoke curling up into the leafy trees overhead. Next, he filled a billy from a water bottle before placing it on a couple of sticks downwind from the fire. They talked about the croc attack and things in general as they waited for it to boil. As they yarned, Hawkins made ham and cheese sandwiches on the tail gate, the "tailgate café" he called it. When the billy boiled, he tossed a handful of tea leaves in it and waited a little for the leaves to be forced to the top by the boiling water action before removing it from the fire and tapping it gently with a stick to settle the leaves to the bottom.

He poured the amber liquid into a pair of tin mugs and added sugar before stirring. Bill noted that his moves were almost automatic and without effort. The sandwiches satisfied their hunger. They sat on a couple of small logs, the rifles within reach, because as Hawkins said you never know when a mob of pigs will wander into camp.

The tea was strong and sweet, the best Bill had ever tasted. He had long forgotten how good billy tea was in the bush. They talked about the good time they had the previous night.

'What about Julie,' Bill asked 'is she with anyone? She wears a wedding ring, but where is her husband.'

'You might know about Julie,' Hawkins replied. 'her last name is Grant. Her husband and four-year-old son, Danny vanished under mysterious circumstance in the Mitchell River almost two years ago.'

'Fuck yes, I read about it. It was all over the news, but no trace was ever found. Wasn't there something about them being murdered?' Bill asked.

'Could be, but you as a cop would know that better than me,' was the abrupt answer. 'Look Bill, let's stop fucking around the bush. I know you're a cop. Harry recognized you. He told me last night and said you were at Burketown and involved in investigating the Lawn Hill murder. Harry worked there at the time. I have known him for years and he never forgets a face. What are you here for, trying to set me up?'

'Fuck no,' Bill replied. 'now I know why Harry looked familiar. I had a suspicion that he knew me. No, I'm not after you at all. You're in the clear as far as the Queensland Police Force is concerned. You don't know it yet, but you have been nominated for a bravery medal by the minister. No, I'm part of a sting operation and working deep cover to find out what is going on in the Gulf. Over the years people have vanished, been murdered, or were found dead with no signs of suspicious circumstances. The police reckon we have a serial killer loose in the Gulf and that he lives in Karumba. There is also the matter of police payback for Shep's murder.'

He paused to sip his tea looking keenly at the older man, who had said nothing during Bill long explanation. He spoke now looking thoughtfully at Bill.

'You blokes have got it wrong. There is no serial killer here but an organized crime gang who are engaged in smuggling drugs, people, and guns into the country, with wildlife, birds and reptiles, being smuggled out. It's big business and dangerous and if anyone finds out that you are a cop they will kill you, the same as they did to your fellow officer, Sheppard. Those bastards will stop at nothing. To them human life is cheap and expendable.'

'What about Harry, will he tell anyone about me?'

'He's good, he won't talk, and if you ever need help, he and those people you met last night will stand by you because there are mostly good people in Karumba, but the local Barra Mafia, as they are called, lord over all with intimidation and fear using thugs like Bull and Weed. There are not enough cops to be effective, while the fisheries officers see nothing because they seldom if ever patrol the coast. Their priorities are to book recreational anglers and kids for taking undersize fish and the lack of boat safety gear, not doing coastal patrols. I don't blame them as they are not allowed to carry arms, yet the Government expects them to deal with the worst scumbags in the Gulf country.'

Hawkins stood up as a bullet passed through his legs and smashed into the 4WD tyre behind him with a loud thud, a split second before a gunshot erupted the bush torpor. He hardly paused as he dropped his tea mug, grabbed the rifle and headed for the scrub with Bill hot on his heals. The flat report of another rifle shot echoed through the trees, the bullet hitting the ground near the 4WD and pinging away across the water hole. The old man was breathing heavy clutching his chest.

'Are you hit?' Bill cried in alarm.

'No mate, only fucking winded. That bullet almost took my balls off. If I had not stood up to stretch my back when I did, I'd be dead by now. Who the fuck is shooting at us? Fuck it, let's get the bastard.'

'Steady old mate, take it easy. He can't see us in this scrub. Let's outflank him. He is somewhere on the top bank where the track winds down. I saw dust and thought I heard a vehicle when I brought the 4WD down.'

The two men split up, slowly stalking to the top of the river scrub, nerves on edge and nervous fingers on rifle triggers. A wallaby bounded away into the scrub ahead and rifles came up to the shoulders. Trigger fingers froze.

Bill laughed nervously to himself; his knees were shaky. He wanted to sit down. He worried about the older man who, akin to a shadow, was moving to the left of him, but he could not see or hear him. As they neared the edge of the scrub the sound of a vehicle roaring away broke the silence. The men pushed out of the scrub only to see a dust cloud extending past the yards about four hundred metres away. They barely saw the vehicle in the bulldust that was left in its wake.

'Stuff him,' Hawkins cried angrily. 'I'll give him something to fucking hurry him up with.'

He brought the rifle to his shoulder and fired at the vehicle that was partly hidden by the dust cloud. Four times he fired, working the big bolt in rapid, practised movements as he slammed round after round into the chamber, the big rifle recoiling against his shoulder until the magazine was empty. Bill estimated that the vehicle was over five hundred metres away by then. He did not fire believing it a waste of time and against his police training.

Hawkins was shaking, the shock of the near-death bullet hitting him for the first time.

'Got to sit down, mate,' he uttered. 'This shit of getting shot at again is too much for an old prick like me. I don't fucking need it at my age.'

Bill hunkered beside him as Hawkins reloaded the Weatherby rifle with shaking hands. Five minutes passed. No one spoke until the older man stood up.

'I'm okay now, Bill, just old age. Let's look for tracks.'

He picked up the shells that were ejected in the dust.

'I wonder if he dropped his shells,' Hawkins remarked. 'Let's find out where he was.'

He found the tracks of the sniper in the dust, clearly marked by the upper damp layer of the morning's precipitation. They tracked it to where he had taken aim on them. The log that Hawkins sat on was in clear sight, with the 4WD partly visible. Bill found a shell and another about a metre from it.

'Don't touch them,' he advised Hawkins. 'I'll get a plastic bag and hand them over to forensics to check for fingerprints.'

'These are .223 Remington Magnum cases,' Hawkins stated. 'Everyone has one in this country. Bloody funny, but these bare footprints are small, not unlike a big kid or a woman, or a little man like Weed. Just look at the way one print has some drag on it. It's Weed alright,' he added thoughtfully.

'Seems plausible, but how do we prove it without blowing my cover. I note that you have a sat phone in the cruiser. I'll call the boss and see what he thinks.'

They hurried back to the Landcruiser.

'Fuck!' Hawkins swore vehemently. 'The bastard hit the rear tire. Another bloody $450 bill!'

The rear tyre was flat. A neat hole indicated where the first bullet had entered. Bill was thinking, should he report the shooting and have Weed arrested, or ignore it and let Hawkins again become a target. In answer

Hawkins handed him the sat phone, but there was no signal under the trees. Bill walked onto the plain, taking the rifle with him. The signal was good, and he talked to Farrell at length, telling him about the happenings.

'Leave it to me,' Farrell advised. 'I'll have Weed picked up and charged, providing you and Hawkins are prepared to give evidence. The bastard may even talk. It should not go against you too much. You say you have shells and possibly a bullet?'

'Yes, I have, Hawkins says they are military issue FMJs, probably surplus stuff. The projectile should be in the tyre. He has also photographed the footprints. There is nothing he has missed. He fired four shots with that cannon of his at the vehicle in the dust and could have scored a hit. He's the best shot I have ever seen.'

'Good, I'm contacting both Normanton and Karumba police to put a roadblock up and check vehicles with possible bullet holes in the rear. A 4WD you say?'

'Yes, we got a glimpse of it. Beige coloured or dust covered Toyota tray back with a couple of 200 litre fuel drums in it. I'm going back to give the old bloke a hand to change the tyre. He is a bit shaky.'

'Shaky is he, what about you?'

'I'm okay, but I think I shit myself. I'll talk to you later boss.'

Bill ended the call and headed down the track to the vehicle. The tyre was already changed. Hawking was sitting on the log drinking a 4X stubby and sweating profusely after the hard work. 'There is more in the Engel fridge,' he offered. 'How did you go?'

Bill took a beer and ripped the top from the bottle. As he drank deeply the cold amber liquid spilled down his shirt.

'Fuck, this is good,' he drooled. 'I reckon we have earned a cold beer. I talked to the Boss, and he is arranging roadblocks at either end to pick our sniper up and have him charged with attempted murder providing he has the rifle.'

'Well, I reckon I have had enough fun for the day anyway and we should head home. The pigs will be here until the first rains, so we have a few days up our sleeve. Keen to see if they pick Weed up.'

They drove out, finding the gate open. Hawkins pulled up and let Bill out while he walked some distance down to the road. After closing the gate, Bill jumped in the 4WD and drove it where the older man was taking photos of the wheel marks on the dirt track where it turned onto the bitumen. When Bill pulled up, he told him that it was his turn to drive. Before stepping in, he opened the rear of the wagon and took two more beers out of the car fridge.

'Enjoy, there are no more left,' he said as he handed one over. 'Lucky we had that little shower this morning because all the vehicle tracks are clearly imprinted in the black soil. It also showed Weed where to find us. I got good photos of his tyre tread. He is heading back to Karumba.'

Chapter 9
WEED ERADICATION

Constable Paul Warren had been transferred to Karumba two weeks before and was on callout duty for the weekend. He was catching up on some paperwork when the phone rang. He picked it up and identified himself.

'Constable Warren, this is Commissioner Farrell. Now listen carefully is Sergeant Simpson there?'

Warren stuttered a little as he replied, being more than a little nervous at the authoritarian voice of the big boss on the other end.

'I think he is home, though I will have to check. It's his day off.'

'Well no longer, there has been a shooting at Walkers Creek. You are authorized to immediately set up a roadblock at the town entrance. Stop all 4WD tray backs. We are looking for a beige dust covered Toyota tray back with fuel drums in the back. The identity of the driver is unknown but suspected of being a local fisherman known as Weed. He may be carrying a .223 calibre rifle. Therefore, I suggest that you are both armed and be prepared for any event. Now go, the vehicle left the area a few minutes ago. Talk to you later, by the way, the Normanton police are en route to assist.'

Sergeant Jack Simpson was burning garden trash in his house yard, that it shared with the police station, when Warren yelled out to him in an urgent manner saying he was required – 'now'. Warren, a man of action, opened the gun safe and tossed one of the .223 Ruger assault rifles and a couple of loaded magazines to Simpson as he burst in. He was dressed in a sweaty T-shirt, stubby shorts and wearing a pair of thongs.

'What the fuck is going on?' he asked.

Warren informed him what Farrell had ordered them to do.

'Fuck it,' Simpson swore. 'first time something happens in this town and I'm out of uniform. Let's go before he gets to the junction, otherwise we might not find him. We'll take both vehicles.'

Simpson strapped on the heavy police belt holding his holstered .40 S&W Glock pistol. He looked odd in his casual garb, and even more so as he jammed his police hat on. Grabbing the Ruger and the charged magazines, he headed after Warren who was already backing the Troopie out. Simpson leapt into the patrol car and hit the siren. He caught up and passed the slower Toyota Troop Carrier at the Golf course and had the car in position a short distance past the Point Junction before Warren arrived and did the same on the opposite side, both vehicles effectively blocking the road

There was little else to do but wait. Someone drove down from the Point and turned towards them, but Warren waved him away and the vehicle headed to town.

'If he is heading towards us, he should just about be here,' Simpson noted as he looked at his watch.

Weed was pissed off. He drove hard, but he was shaking so much he could hardly hold the steering wheel. His body was shivering and hurting. It felt as if a thousand maggots were crawling under his skin. He needed a drink, and a fix, badly.

His plan to kill Hawkins had misfired. After leaving the hotel the previous night, he had driven past the junction and pulled off the road to sleep it off. When the Morning Glory passed over the cold air had woken him.

Weed was smoking a joint when he saw Hawkins's vehicle drive past just before daylight. He recognised it as he had been stalking the man for an opportunity to kill him. On impulse he had driven after him with no clear purpose, or plan, in mind. He noted that he had forgotten to unload the two drums of petrol that were in the back of the 4WD but thought no more of it. The fog was thick. He swore when he saw taillights ahead. Weed dropped back and switched his driving lights off and followed the black strip of bitumen that led across the dry dusty plain in the strengthening light. Later he saw the lights turn off onto the plain.

'The 21-Mile, of course he is going pig shooting,' he mused, pleased by his observation.

He had another smoke at the gate, sucking in the heady fumes, when two quick shots suddenly exploded the torpor of the plain. It startled him. For the first time he realized there were two shooters as both explosions were from different calibres. He waited some more as more shots disturbed the morning's still air. He used the last of his weed to roll another smoke before he slowly drove onto the track and followed the wheel marks of the vehicle that were clear in the damp dirt.

The yards came into view, and he parked near the small shed. He got his .223 Remington slide action rifle from behind the seat and slipped a loaded ten-shot magazine into the receiver, before walking towards the forest. It was already hot and humid and by the time he reached the trees, he was sweating profusely. He saw the Landcruiser parked at the end of the track with two men walking about. They were about two hundred metres away. He lay under a shady spot for a long time watching as one man he recognised as Hawkins, boiled the billy. When the men sat down on the log and ate food, it reminded him that he was both thirsty and hungry himself.

He recognized Hawkins, but not the other man, though there was something familiar about him in his clouded memory. Hawkins was sitting on a log, facing him, almost as if he was looking directly at him. As Weed spied, the hate and anger against the man who had killed his mates slowly built up until he lost all reasoning. He pulled the slide back on the rifle and slammed a round into the chamber. He cursed the front sight because it wavered all over the place when he tried to hold it still long enough on Hawkins. The sweat in his eyes did not make it any better.

Suddenly the gun recoiled against his shoulder. He had not even been aware that he pressed the trigger. He saw Hawken's leap away, grab his rifle, and vanish in the scrub, the other man closely on his heels. Weed got another shot off but the spurt of dust at the heels of the fleeing men indicated he missed. Weed panicked and ran, as fast as his stubby legs and crippled limb could move, to his vehicle. He had left the key in the ignition and the motor started immediately.

As he swung into the track with spinning wheels, the bulldust almost engulfed the vehicle. Something slammed into the passenger door with a dull thud, followed immediately by a stinging pain in his right leg. Blood spurted out from it.

'Oh, fuck, I've been shot,' he cried, wiping at his leg and feeling something sharp. He pulled it out noting it was a sliver of steel, all the time fighting the steering wheel to keep the 4WD on the track. The pain was intense and the bleeding bad.

There was another thud, this time in the rear, followed by another a second later. The offside mirror suddenly shattered with a loud bang, and he saw the dust of a bullet kicking up in the grassless plain ahead of him a split second later.

'Fuck it, the bastards are shooting at me,' he screamed in panic. 'They will blow the fucking fuel up.'

In answer, the smell of petrol rose into the cabin, but somewhere in his foggy mind, he remembered that only an incendiary bullet could blow up a drum of fuel. He pushed the vehicle as it had never been driven before, bile of pure terror rising in his throat at the thought of a bullet slamming into his body.

He had left the gate open, and he almost rolled the tray back as he turned onto the bitumen and turned north. He noted a big mushroom shaped hole in the passenger door where the bullet had come through and broken up, showering the cabin with metal, a piece hitting him in his thigh. It was bleeding profusely, the warm blood running down onto the seat. He held a smelly oily rag against the wound with his left hand and fought to control the heavy vehicle with the other.

Tears were streaming from his eyes and by the time he saw the advertising signs he had lost control of his body function, the warm urine wetting his stubby shorts. Weed was no coward, but a soldier, used to taking orders. He had gone out on a limb, and he did not know what to do when things turned on him. He needed a fix more so than any other time in his life. The smell of petrol flooded the cabin.

He turned past the advertising signs and entered the slow corner, before the junction, at speed. Ahead of him were flashing lights on blue and white police vehicles that were blocking the road. He tried to stop but he could not his reactions were too slow. Weed slammed into the vehicle roadblock at full speed as Warren and Simpson "headed bush" as they later reported.

There was an almighty crash, followed by a huge explosion that was heard at the golf club where the regular patrons were settling down for the day for some serious drinking. Only when the town fire engine raced past, its sirens blaring, did someone look and report that there was a smoke pall at the junction.

'Fucking busy day, first the cops and now the fire engine,' he cried for everyone to hear.

'Probably a bushfire,' came the unconcerned reply from another patron. 'who's turn to shout? I'm empty.'

'Shit! What a fucking mess,' Simpson shouted to Warren who was lying in a shallow depression nearby where he had taken cover. 'You okay?'

In answer, Warren stood up and nodded as he brushed dust and dry grass from his uniform. In front of them was a smoking chaos of vehicles, the vehicles burning fiercely. As they later discovered, the spilled fuel from a drum on the back of the tray back ignited on impact, taking the other drum, vehicles, and the police vehicles with it, the diesel fuel added to the heat of the fire.

'Fuck all we can do, Sergeant,' Warren yelled above the noise of the roaring flames.

He was covered in dust, his blue uniform the colour of the landscape. Simpson thought he looked funny and laughed.

'You should fucking see yourself,' he said. 'I'm glad I don't have to fill in the paperwork for a new uniform.'

'Bloody simple job, really,' Warren replied. 'compared to you losing our vehicles and equipment. Shit, I forgot, I still have my mobile. I'll get the fire brigade to put the fire out. Give the boys something to do.'

They waited as a couple of cars, the drivers attracted by the smoke, arrived. They offered help, but Simpson turned them away. The volunteer fire brigade arrived soon after, but the officer in charge elected to let the cars burn out, as there was nothing to be saved. They sprayed some water on a couple of small grass fires near the road, even though there was not enough grass for a proper fire.

A grey Landcruiser wagon with two men also arrived from the Normanton side and pulled up behind the Normanton police vehicles. They stepped out, one man taking photos of the burning vehicles. A few minutes later two Normanton police units pulled up behind them.

Simpson recognized the man with the camera as Vic Hawkins, a journalist, and someone of interest who had been involved in a shootout up north. The other he did not know, nor did Warren. He vowed he would find out, as his police training told him that the men knew more about the day's incident than he did. Borrowing Warren's phone, he called Jackson at Normanton, who confirmed that no vehicles have been allowed to travel to Karumba.

'There is also a roadblock at Maggieville. You better check-up where they came from.'

Simpson nodded to Warren to follow him to where one of the two men was leaning against their 4WD. Hawkins was taking photos and joined them when Simpson waved him over.

'G'day. I'm Sergeant Simpson. I'd like you to tell me where you blokes have come from.'

'Simple, Sergeant,' Hawkins answered. 'We were pig shooting at the 21-Mile Hole. Left here at daylight and just got back. What happened here, anyone hurt?'

'Yes, the driver of the tray back ploughed into our roadblock and was probably killed on impact. Wouldn't know whose vehicle it is by any change?'

'No, I am a visitor myself. Vic Hawkins is my name. This is Bill Madsen. He is from Brisbane and has moved to Karumba for the fishing. He bought the Wilson's place.'

The policemen shook hands with the men. One thing Simpson had learned as a bush cop was to be polite too everyone as one got more cooperation from bush people that way. Hawkins directed a few questions at Simpson, but he was evasive having a natural wariness about journalists. The fire had burned out, and when Hawkins asked if he could drive around it, Simpson gave him permission to do so.

'By the way, any chance of getting copies of those pictures you took. I'll need some for my report to the boss. I suppose you are staying with Madsen?'

'No mate, I'm staying at Harry Douglas's place. When I get there, I'll download those pics for you on my laptop and will drop a scandisk into the station.'

'Don't want you to go to any trouble, mate. I will pick it up later this afternoon,' Simpson replied, surprised at the man's cooperation. Journalists never gave anything away.

'Fuck what a mess,' Bill exclaimed as they headed towards town. 'But it's a stroke of luck really. My cover is intact, and we were never involved with that chaos as far as anyone knows.'

'Not true, Bill, I saw a bullet hole in the tailgate of the tray back and another in one of those blown drums remains. The fuel must have leaked into the back and caused the explosion on impact. If they find a bullet, they will know where it came from. Ballistics has the rifling record of the Weatherby.'

'Fuck, never thought of that. Don't worry I'll inform the boss. He can put a lid on it before the can opens. Hell, what a fucking day and only one boar to show for it.'

'I don't know about you Bill, but all this shit has made me hungry. What say we have an early lunch at the Point before we do anything else? They serve the best fish and chips in town.'

After lunch, Hawkins pulled in at the Douglas residence. Jim King and Harry were watching a fishing action video and asked what all the siren noise was about, as unlike most other residents they had not bothered to move.

'Only because we're too fucking pissed,' Harry laughed. 'Hey, you pricks, like a cold beer?'

Hawkins told the men about the accident near the junction, and the sniper attack. He had complete trust in his mates to keep it to themselves, noted Bill. As both men now knew he was an undercover police officer, Bill told them why he was in the Gulf town.

'I wish you luck,' Harry said slowly. 'But be very, very careful. Remember what happened to that poor bastard Sheppard. If anyone finds out who you are and the barra mafia learns about it you will end up the same way, or as croc shit, and us too if they know we are helping you.'

Hawkins downloaded the camera images from the Nikon camera's scandisk onto his laptop. The boar and the crocodile attack were of great interest. He cut a scandisk for Simpson and another for Bill, before backing up onto another. He gave Bill the second disk, "with that other stuff on it."

They removed the tyre in Harry's workshop and found the bullet inside it. It was almost intact with the rifling standing out clearly.

'We have the bullet but will never be able to find out if Weed fired the shots because there is no way we can fire his rifle when it's recovered. Still, ballistics will know what type of rifle it was fired from,' Bill informed the men.

A car pulled up in the driveway. It was Simpson, still dressed in his gardening outfit, though the police belt and his hat were missing.

'Came for the photos,' he greeted. 'all hell has broken loose. The inspector is on his way from Mount Isa and wants the tray back wreck checked. We have recovered the remains of a body and a melted rifle. It looks like a slide action Remington centrefire. We also found a bullet hole in a drum, one in the tailgate of the 4WD, and another in a rear vision mirror. We also recovered a bullet that was lodged in the cab. You blokes wouldn't know about it, would you? By the way what sort of rifles were you using for shooting pigs?'

They told Simpson, who wrote the details down in his book. He informed them that the rifles could be required for ballistic testing later.

'Cunning bastard,' Bill mused. 'he is trying to bait us because he knows we know more than he does. He is a bloody good cop, the reason that they transferred him to Karumba after the Shepard killing.'

Following Simpson's departure, Grace arrived home and asked Bill if he wanted to join them for dinner in the evening at the Point's Tavern, where the close-knit group were going to celebrate Julie's birthday.

'But I hardly know her, besides I don't even have a card, let alone a present,' he protested, but she insisted that he was invited.

Hawkins drove Bill to his house, where a tail wagging Bluey made him very welcome.

'Looks as if the neighbours are down at the bar,' Hawkins noted. 'Bert is a fucking pisspot. Shame really, she works all day cleaning business premises and houses, and he drinks her wages. The prick is a parasite on that poor woman. See you at seven.'

Bill went over the day's events before emailing his report and recommendations to Farrell in far off Brisbane. He left the laptop running and checked it after having a shower. The answer was on it. Understood.

Chapter 10
GOOD TIMES

Bill was busy about the house setting the furniture, household items, and personal belongings that had been delivered the day before. He had forgotten how much gear he had, and in hindsight wondered why he trucked it all to Karumba, instead of storing most of it. Still, he had to make an impression of being part of the community. There was much to do, but the task became easier when Hawkins and King arrived for a coffee and helped him move the heavy stuff in place. Harry and Grace pulled up next.

'You must have made an impression on Harry,' King said. 'He hates cops.'

After the work was done, they relaxed on the rear patio, the cool breeze of the fans a respite from the oppressive humid heat boiled up by the overhead sun. Bill handed out cold beers for everyone out of his car fridge that had found a home in the kitchen for the time being. Across the river, a dozen or more fishing vessels were anchored. The river was calm with only a lazy current disturbing its surface.

'Bloody slack tide,' Harry swore. 'most people reckon it's the worst for barra fishing because there is little run in the river, but I reckon they are the best tides to target barra in the deep holes and about snags and with the weather being the way it is there should be good fishing now. There was a little lighting to the north in the Gulf last night. It may be a sign of an early "build up", but it needs to get hotter before we get any rainstorms.'

'Hotter!' Bill exclaimed. 'It's forty plus now I reckon.'

They all laughed as someone got another round of cold beers from the fridge.

'They will be pulling those boats out as soon as the tide is high enough,' Grace said. 'Old "Barra" Turnbull, who lives up the road from us, said that he is tying his boat down because we are going to get a cyclone this season. He should know as he was born and bred in Karumba. The only thing he knows is barra fishing, he's one of the best netters in the Gulf.'

That opened the door to compare other commercial fishers that made a living from netting barramundi, crabbing, or chasing mackerel and other pelagics in the waters of the Gulf. They reminisced about the birthday party at the Tavern on Saturday evening and the good times that everyone had. Bill had danced most of the night with Julie. She had looked radiant when she arrived. He found that they had much in common, but the evening had ended without him taking her home. He liked her. Jan's memories slipped into the past when he was with Julie. He found that odd, as he had loved Jan so much, but when he had held Julie's firm body and slim waist, he found himself aroused. He wanted her but did not know how to capitalize on his feelings.

With smoko over, and the cold beer running out, everyone left, leaving Bill alone to sort his stuff out. It was hot and humid, and he was sweating profusely. He had a little lunch before starting again on the household chores. He heard another vehicle pull up. It set Bluey into a barking frenzy. To his surprise, the visitors were a grim-faced Simpson and Warren. Bill felt dismay; no doubt, they wanted more information on the weekend events.

'G'day mate,' Simpson greeted in a curt manner. 'We'd like you to answer some questions.'

Bill directed the cops to the coolness of the rear patio where the river was showing signs of awakening as the tide turned. The police appeared ill at ease, noted Bill, as he poured three glasses of cold water as he had run out of cold beer.

'So how can I help you, sergeant?' Bill asked as he sat down facing them.

'What the fuck are you playing at, Madsen,' Simpson blurted angrily, his face red. 'We know who you are, so what the fuck is a senior sergeant of the CIB doing in Karumba without us knowing?'

'Who told you that?'

'Warren checked your name on the police records, so we want to know more about you. Are you keeping tabs on us or what?'

'No, I am not,' Bill replied firmly. 'look let me make a call to my boss and see if he allows me to inform you why I am here. It won't take long.'

He contacted Farrell on his mobile phone and explained that the local police had found out about him.

'Look Bill, we handpicked those two to clean Karumba up. Trust them. I did not want them to become involved this early, but there is no choice now. Tell them about the operation. God knows it is probably helpful if the local police shadow you. They are both good men, trustworthy and beyond approach.'

Bill sat down opposite the two men and told them of his undercover mission. He explained why they had been kept out of it. It angered Simpson.

'Fucking southern seat polishers,' he swore. 'don't they fucking trust us? For Christ's sake Madsen, what if you need help? Besides what the fuck happened yesterday and why is the District Inspector ignorant of this sting operation?'

'I'm not sure why the Inspector's is not involved,' Bill answered carefully. 'the Commissioner does not explain such things to me. He said that no one else must know that I am here. That includes you two, not a word to anyone about me. Is that clear? The boss is adamant that I go through him only. Now about the weekend events'

The two cops were silent as Bill told them about Weed's threat in the Animal Bar, and the events of the pig hunt. He got his laptop out and displayed the images that Hawkins had taken of the footprints, shells, and wheel tracks.

'I have the shells and the projectile,' he informed them. 'Now that you blokes are involved, I would appreciate if you sent them down with what remains of the rifle to ballistics.'

'With the remains of a bigger bullet we found in the 4WD?' Simpson asked.

'No, I would appreciate if you kept it in a safe place for the time being and say nothing. Hawkins is in enough strife already. Fuck that old prick can shoot. No wonder those arseholes up north didn't have a chance. However, I'm worried about his welfare as those crims hate him for what he did and are looking for payback. He asked me about getting a permit for a concealed carry firearm for his own protection. The boss has no problems with it. Can you arrange that, Jack?'

'I can, but Firearms won't like the idea of someone openly carrying a pistol on his belt,' Simpson remarked. 'It's only recently they took all handguns off graziers, even though they need them when handling wild cattle. However, I will investigate it, and can I refer the matter to the Commissioner if there are objections?'

'Yes, but get it moving because if someone does him in, the press and the public will ask us why we did not protect him. He is a hero. Giving him a permit to carry one of his handguns will put the onus on him for his own protection instead of on us.'

The two men bid farewell, Bill noted they called him by his first name, he had been accepted and they were happy to be part of the sting operation now that all the cards were on the table. He also felt good about knowing that these men would back him anytime he needed help, though he advised them to treat him like a local and only to contact him in an emergency.

The heat was tiring, and an afternoon nap was in order. Bill woke up hot and sweaty, even though he had turned the air conditioner on in the bedroom. He had a cold shower. It was Bluey's persistent barking that alerted him when he was drying off that he had another visitor. It was followed by the sound of a car door slamming and someone coming up the stairs and knocking on the door.

Still dripping wet, he wrapped the towel about his waist and opened the door and was surprised to see Julie there, looking beautiful and radiant. Bill cursing himself for being dressed in only a skimpy towel.

'Wow!' she explained coyly. 'now that is how a girl should be welcomed. Nice body and tan, you look as if you work out.'

'Come on in,' he invited, a little red-faced. 'excuse the mess. I am still unpacking. Go through to the back, while I put some clothes on. I just had a cold shower,' he explained sheepishly.

'Why cover that beautiful body up,' she smiled. 'it does not bother me one bit.'

Something in her eyes made Bill reach for her. She made no effort to fight him off as she slipped into his arms, her lips meeting his as if she was hungry. He slipped his tongue between her lips, and she met it with passion. He felt his penis grow hard as she reached down and grabbed it as he groped for her blouse and lifted it up over her head. He had problems with the clasp on her bra, but she obligingly slipped her hands behind the back and unclipped it. The bra fell between them as Bill pushed his face into the taut breasts and sucked on her nipples, her breathing heavy in response.

He picked her up, the towel falling away from his waist, his hard penis throbbed on her shapely bottom. As he laid her on the bed, she pushed her bottom up and he pulled her panties down, revealing a trimmed bush of black hair. Bill liked that as bare pussies left him cold. He kissed her belly before going down and nuzzling her furry vagina. She arched her back and lifted her legs, moving her hips and made moaning sounds of pleasure. He moved up and prepared to enter her. But she pushed her hands onto his chest.

118

'Hold it, get my purse. I don't want to get pregnant.'

He grabbed the purse she had left on the kitchen table and gave it to her. She took a packet from it and used her teeth to open it. Before putting the condom on, she slipped her mouth over penis, sucking it even harder. Bill could hardly control himself as she slipped the rubber over his throbbing member.

'Wow, you are a big boy,' she complimented. 'careful with that thing when you put it in. It's been a long time since I have had sex.'

She laughed and rolled on her back. Bill kissed her passionately and nuzzled her breasts.

'Put it in, now, please,' she moaned.

Bill dropped between her legs and pushed slowly into her, her body moving up to match his thrusting. They slammed together with almost frantic urgency, both desperate for climax. She came with a force that surprised them both with its intenseness that shook their joined bodies. Her sobbing contractions were as if all the emotions she had stored for long months were suddenly released. Bill came a few seconds later, her body meeting his with a passion that aroused him even more. Later he laid on her, kissing her face and lips until their heartbeats and breathing returned to normal before he rolled off her and lay on his back. She turned and pushed up against him, her head on his chest and her leg over his.

They slept and when they woke the sun had set and it was dark. Both were thirsty. Bill grabbed a couple of stubbie bottles of beer from the fridge that felt cool. She had followed him into the kitchen, naked as the day she was born, except for that attractive little bush below her belly, he noted. He took her in a gently embrace, her firm body feeling cool and fresh against his. She melted against him kissing his hairy chest.

'I'm hungry,' she said, looking into his eyes. 'for food,' she added. 'What do you have to eat?'

He had shopped at the supermarket and there was plenty of food. They made a salad and cold meat dish, not bothering to dress. It was hot and humid, even with the dining room air conditioner on. They showered together, letting the cool water run down their naked bodies. After drying they were back on the bed. This time their loving was more enduring as they explored each other's bodies. A long time later, both exhausted, she lay in his arms, their passions tamed for the time being.

'Wow, what a day,' she whispered. 'I thought I would never feel this way again, but Alex seems a distant memory now.'

'Yes,' he replied. 'I know the feeling. It's been many months now since I let Jan go, but the pain has been with me ever since. But I must admit it you got my blood boiling and my loins lusting when I first saw you.'

'Thank you, Bill, I felt the same way when we met.'

They fell asleep and when he woke up, she was gone. Her 4WD was missing. There was a note on the kitchen sink, telling him that she would be in touch later. He stared at it for a long time. The house felt empty. He felt very lonely and emotional.

Chapter 11
THE STORM

The Gulf country dies a little under the onslaught of sun and wind during the dry season. It becomes hotter and the humidity unbearable as the days move into the build-up period, a time of intense electrical storms that bring little rain. Bill and Julie loved sitting on the rear patio watching the disorganised storm clouds as they built up over the Gulf of Carpentaria almost every afternoon, the evening skies alive with electric lighting on the far horizon. Some storms were close enough near land to hear the moaning of thunder, but while the odd one had raged inland, Karumba had missed out on rain.

Like many residents, Bill was in the habit of rising early at daylight before the heat set in and going for a run and a brisk walk, followed by breakfast, before heading out for a day's fishing. When he was not on the water, he remained mostly indoors where fans and the air conditioner made life bearable. Julie was a regular visitor and she often stayed overnight, while Bill slept over at her house between her visits. They had become inseparable, and both had confessed a deep love for each other. She moved into Bill's house one weekend, ably assisted by Harry and Grace.

Hawkins and King had departed weeks before, fleeing the increasingly hot weather.

'My wife reckons I should come home,' Hawkins told Bill. 'Not a bad idea. Man needs a good woman occasionally, even at my age, and besides the Atherton Tablelands are five degrees cooler than the Gulf country during the summer.'

Bill missed the company of the two men, as between them they had managed to cull the local pig population down considerably.

His boat had seen plenty of water also as he had taken the men, and sometimes Harry, fishing in the river and along the coast as far as the Smithburne River to the north and the Leichhardt River to the west. They had camped on narrow sand dunes under whispering casuarinas, rifles and pistols on hand against possible crocodile attack from the water.

The reptiles were about in numbers in various sizes, and they had seen one that was at least six metres long near their camp on the Flinders River. Hawkins had said that during the build-up crocodiles were most active as it was their breeding season.

'All that mating makes them hungry and bad tempered and if you are destined to be taken by a croc this is the most likely time. Most people that have been killed or attacked by savage crocs has been during the build-up and in the Wet.'

Inland, on drying billabongs, they shot wildfowl for a change of diet from fish. Pigs were numerous about the drying swamps and billabongs, and they had great sport hunting taking some huge boars with trophy tusks. It was hot and dusty on the plains, the grasses had burned off under the onslaught of the hot sun and the only movements were the flocks of noisy brolgas, Sarus cranes and small mobs of cattle trudging tiredly to the watering places each morning, their hooves kicking up the dust.

The barramundi fishing season was closed, but it did not prevent them catching barra for sport and releasing the magnificent fish, some over a metre in length. Other fish – salmon, queenfish, and grunter – were plentiful and there was no shortage of fish barbeques.

The trips had a purpose for Bill because they were important journeys of discoveries as the two men knew the coast and the rivers like the back of their hand. They knew where invisible rocks, sand, and mud bars were, or the submerged trees where barramundi ambushed trolled lures, and more important to Bill, the seasonal fishing camps of the commercial barramundi fishers.

Bill had always insisted on being back for the weekend as it gave him a chance to be with Julie for at least two days. He was looking forward to the school holidays so that they could spend more time together.

During the weekends, Bill and Julie often fished on remote beaches, or sat in the boat under the shady canopy dangling baited hooks for javelin grunter and pikey bream on the shallow tidal flats, watching the sun rise. Sometimes they camped overnight at a lonely beach, enjoying each other's company by the dim light of a lazy campfire and staring out over the Gulf where the flickering of lightening on dark horizons heralded the start of the coming monsoon. Often the moaning of thunder would follow. It was hot and humid; the wet season was near. Before they had left, Hawkins and King came to his house and bid goodbye.

'Look Bill, if you ever get into trouble and need help, you give me a call,' Hawkins offered.

'Nothing much happening now because most people are on holidays, but once the Wet is over, this town rages, especially the Animal Bar.'

The day they departed the town was alive with rumours that a biker, who worked for Bull Antinus, had been found dead about twenty kilometres from town. It was said he had come off his Harley-Davidson bike and broken his neck. Bill rang the police station. Warren answered the phone but told him that he would call back later as he was busy. But it was Simpson who rang back.

'Interesting, the bloke who was killed had a record a mile long. His name is André Jolic. Our records show that he was mixed up with those mafia drug killings in Melbourne a few years back. He may have fled up here to hide from payback. An officer from the Victorian CIB reckons that Jolic was a hit man for the biker mob. He worked for the GBC for a couple of seasons. He never caused any trouble, and he was seldom in town, so we had no reason to notice him.'

They talked for a while before Simpson terminated the call. Bill switched his computer on and checked his email, before entering Jolic's name in the official police search engine.

'He is a hardened criminal,' Bill mumbled to himself. 'The bastard has spent almost half of his thirty-eight adult years in jail for theft, bank robbery, bribery, protection, assault, but no murder was ever proven. But why did an experienced rider like him come off his bike just after leaving town.'

On impulse, he drove to where the official police tapes were still on the ground. There were no skid marks on the hot bitumen to indicate Jolic had braked before running off the road and into a deep drain. Bill walked about when he noted something shiny on the edge of the road about one hundred metres away from where Jolic had crashed.

'Or was it untimely,' Bill mused aloud to himself as he picked up a shiny freshly fired .22 rimfire shell case. 'This might be nothing, but then again there might be more to this than meets the eye.'

His mobile phone rang. It was Simpson.

'Funny thing, Bill. Bull Antinus walked in a few minutes ago. He said that Jolic was holding a package with a large sum of money for him. He wants it back, but when we found Jolic he had only a bit of loose change and about thirty bucks in his wallet. He also had a loaded .22 Ruger pistol magazine in his bum pack and a box of ammo, but no gun.'

'Thanks for the information, Jack,' Bill replied. 'I'm at the site and I have found a fired .22 shell near where he left the road. There is nothing else. Waste of time and money to get the crime scene boys in, though will check with the commissioner first. I'll ring you back later.'

Farrell told him what he thought was best and agreed with him that it would indeed be a waste of resources.

'Do what you can and give the shell to Warren, Bill. He can send it onto forensics,' was Simpson's last remark as he hung up.

There was a party at the Animal Bar that Saturday night. Bill, Julie, the Douglas and Gregory couples met at the venue. Being early they managed to get their favourite table on the outskirts of the activity. Later, after enjoying a counter tea, someone turned the music up loud. The catchy rock and roll tunes had couples on the floor to dance the night away. It was a hot night and beer flowed freely. By eight pm the music drowned out the voices and cheers of all. Thunder rumbled overhead, and lightning flashes lit up the anchored boats in the river.

'The first rain for the season,' Julie whispered in Bill's ear. 'I just love making love when it rains. What say we go home and do it?'

He hugged her, but she suddenly froze.

'Oh my God, it's Bull and his mob,' she blurted out. 'They always cause trouble.'

Bill had only seen Antinus from a distance when he was heading out to his boat across the river. He was a huge hulking man, with a permanent stoop as if trying to appear shorter. He had wide drooping shoulders, and massive arms that hung along an overhanging well cultivated beer gut. But it was the huge bare shaved head with jowls like a bull mastiff, and matched by piglike eyes, that made Bull stand out from the crowd. A plain gold ring hung from his right ear, and he had another above his left eye. Bill mentioned to Julie that Bull was the ugliest man he had ever seen.

'He looks like a pirate, the only thing missing is the parrot and the hook,' Julie replied. 'but he makes up for that in bad temper.'

Antinus was not alone. Three other people accompanied him. Bill recognized one man as James "Animal" Hardens, a tall dour looking fellow with deep eyes set between a hawklike nose that matched a long, lean face. The other man was tall, slim and handsome with typical southern Italian features. Compared to the other men he was well dressed and looked articulate. Bill felt excited as he recognized him as Don Morossi, alias the Wog.

But what got his eye was the strikingly beautiful Eurasian woman who was holding tightly onto Morossi's hand. She was tall, with shoulder length jet-black hair and wore an open tank top that revealed a set of firm breasts, while a pair of white tight shorts cheekily exposed the lovely shape of her butt. Her legs were the type that men dreamed about. Long and slender they were, like her butt, exposed for maximum attention in a set of high stiletto shoes. Her almond eyes flitted across the room and rested on Bill's for a moment before passing on. It had not escaped Julie.

'That's Wog's woman, Suzie,' she said, holding his arm tightly. 'Beautiful, isn't she?'

'Yes, she is, but don't fret, I'm not going to hit on her,' he assured her with a laugh.

The group ordered drinks at the bar and found a table and seats not far away from theirs. Antinus looked about and spotted Harry Douglas. He shoved his chair back and lumbered over like a great ape.

'Where is that fucking mate of yours, arsehole?' he asked Harry in a throaty wheezing voice as if he was not getting enough air. 'Heard he left this morning. You tell him that Bull Antinus wants to see him and break his fucking neck as he's got something that belongs to me. I want it back.'

For the first time he appeared to see Julie. He laughed loudly, his body racking and his belly quivering. He leered at her.

'So, Julie my darling, you got over the loss of that worthless piece of shit you were married too, yet? Don't fret. I'm willing to give you a good fuck anytime you want it. Here give me a cuddle.'

He leaned over and reached out to her, but Bill pushed his hand down hard and slammed it painfully on the table.

He moved quickly kicking his chair away from under him, as he dodged a haymaker from the giant that would have taken his head off had it connected. He leapt into the clearing behind the table, where he had a little room to fight the man on his own ground. Antinus roared like a wounded bull and charged at him, fists and arms swinging wildly. Bill easily moved out of his way and kicked him in the fat cheeks of his butt as he passed by. It propelled the giant into a brick wall. He hit it with aloud thud, his bald head making first contact with a loud bang.

To everyone's surprised, he slowly stood up and wiped his head, blood seeping through his fingers. He licked it as if tasting it and Bill knew that he was going to be in the fight of his life. Everything that he had read in the police reports and heard about the man was true. He was a tough bastard who would break his neck given a chance. Bill backed away as Bull stalked him, slowly and timed this time. Behind him, Bill heard Harry cry to get out on the road for more room. As Bull charged, Bill turned and fled through the parked cars and onto the road, Bull hot on his heels and roaring loudly in anger.

'Fucking gutless cunt, stand and fight you bastard.'

Lighting slashed across the heavens and a light rain began to fall as the two combatants faced off in the dim illumination under the streetlights.

'Not gutless at all, he just needs room to move,' someone said as Bill dodged a swinging right fist and replied with a short right powerful jab that broke one of Bull's lower ribs.

Antinus cried out in pain and turned around as Bill swung about on the ball of his left foot and came up with a vicious high karate kick with his right foot that split the man's eye left eye open and tore out the gold ring. Bull stumbled, as Bill reversed the kick and hit him on the left temple with his left foot. The heavens opened as Antinus soundlessly dropped onto the wet bitumen like an oversized sack of wheat.

'Fuck,' someone in the crowd exclaimed in awe. 'The bastard is a kickboxing expert. Fuck taking him on!'

Animal rushed up but held up his hands as Bill moved forwards.

'Not me mate, I'm not into that shit. Only seeing if Bull is alive. Fuck! You killed him.'

He leaned over the man and felt for his pulse. He rolled him onto his side and yelled for someone to get an ambulance. Bill turned away and came face to face with the beautiful Eurasian, Suzie.

'Nice moves,' she murmured softly, tongue in cheek. 'interesting, we must do it sometime.'

Before Bill could reply a rough hand pushed him away and an authoritative voice said loudly. 'Back away sir or you will be arrested.'

He recognized Warren's voice and raised his arms in meek surrender. Simpson was also there, dressed in stubby shorts and a singlet and wearing a pair of tongs. But he was ready for business and wore the police gun belt and his hat.

'So, can anyone tell me what is going on here?'

It was Douglas who spoke.

'Look Sarge, Bull started this. He insulted Julie and Bill came to her rescue. Bull copped a flogging and that is about it.'

Antinus groaned as Animal helped him sit up. The ambulance arrived, the officer checked Bull who was moaning with pain and holding his blood-soaked head and rib cage. The rain was now heavy, and most people, having lost interest and run out of beer, returned to the bar to discuss the fight. Lightning slashed across the heavens and deafening thunder rolled overhead. Animal and another man helped the paramedics put Bull into the ambulance and it drove off to the Normanton hospital, its emergency lights flashing.

Bill was holding a trembling Julie. They were both soaking wet from being out in the rain. Her firm breasts under her light blouse were shiny and smooth and he wanted to hold her.

'Not now, you are in enough trouble as it is,' she replied, anger in her voice.

The cops were still busy asking questions and taking notes. Simpson walked over.

'Okay Madsen, follow me to the police station, or do I have to cuff you?' he snapped in an official and loud voice. 'You need to help us with our inquiries.'

Julie insisted on coming along even though Bill protested. She drove, and they walked into the station where Simpson was already waiting in the office.

'Care to tell me what really went off in there,' he asked Bill.

Before Bill could answer, Julie chipped in.

'It was not his fault, Bull tried to molest me, and Bill stopped him. It was self-defence.'

'For Christ's sake Bill, haven't you told her who you are and what you are doing here. If not, it is time you did. Stuff it. Julie, I'll tell you instead, this bloke is a high-ranking CIB officer and here on a deep cover sting operation to find out what the hell makes this place tick and who killed Sheppard. You might be compromised if the wrong people find out who he is. It is best you know.'

She looked at Bill as if seeing a stranger.

'How could you? Am I part of your plan? Don't you love and trust me? Fuck you, Bill, I don't know you at all. You almost killed the toughest man in the Gulf country without even working up a sweat and now I find out you are a cop. Who are you?'

Her eyes watered, and tears flowed freely. Bill reached out to her, but she pulled away with a look of dismay on her face. Without another word, she ran outside into the rain and drove away.

'Thanks very much Jack, that is just what she needed at the moment,' Bill shouted angrily at Simpson. 'Fuck mate, she has had enough happen to her life. I was going to tell her but in my own way.'

'Look Bill, I'm sorry about that but she needs to be told. If they find out who you are, they might try something on her, or worse still when she is at school and that could place the kids in danger. It is best that she knows and if anything happens, she can now at least recognize it. This is my town, and I am responsible for everyone's welfare, including yours.'

'Okay Jack, point taken, but hell she walked out, and it may be the end of our relationship. I'm not using her as you may be thinking. I truly love her and that is the truth.'

'Right, I'll talk to her later, but now I need you to listen to what I have to say. Rumours have it that Bull Antinus paid Jolic $50,000 for a hit on Hawkins and King. My informant told me that half the money was paid with the other half payable when the job was done. It's all about town.'

He paused and looked at Bill.

'A mate of Jolic has been talking. We are concerned about Hawkins' safety because Bull is looking for him; the reason we responded so quickly when we got word there was fight at the pub involving Bull. Warren and I got the shock of our lives to find you there, though.'

'So, what actually did happen out on that lonely stretch of road,' mused Bill. 'you reckon that Hawkins and King had something to do with?'

'Possible, and if they did, they will have a lot of unanswered money on them, or where Jolic's missing .22 Ruger pistol is. I'll bet the magazine we have is a spare for it. What do you reckon, should we issue a search warrant?'

'Not sure, but I'll ring the Commissioner in the morning and let him decide. Personally, I reckon that if they do have the money good luck to them, but they are in big trouble because Antinus will arrange another hit to get his money back.'

Simpson straightened up behind the counter and stretched his belly.

'Feel the same way, but if they have the money, I expect a carton of piss to keep them out of jail,' he said, a smile on his face. 'Those two good old boys are getting into so much shit around here that I prefer they stay home next season.'

'They won't,' Bill replied. 'They both love the Gulf and the lifestyle. Look, any chance of a lift home. Julie took the vehicle. I hope she is at home.'

They ran out into the pouring rain of the rumbling slashing storm that showed no sign of abating. Bill was happy to see Julie's SUV parked under the house behind his Landcruiser when he hopped out of the police vehicle. He was not looking forward to explaining to her about his job. He had found that his relationship with Julie had helped in being accepted into the small community. He loved her dearly and did not want to hurt her.

She met him at the door, her eyes red from crying.

'I'm sorry about my outburst,' she sobbed. 'but I feel so hurt. Why didn't you tell me?'

'Because I needed to protect you. I failed with Jan and don't want to lose anyone else. I love you and want to marry you when this is over. Will you?'

'Oh yes, darling, yes. I love you,' she sobbed, her tears tasting salty as he kissed her.

'Come on then, I'll tell you why I am here and who I truly am.'

Chapter 12
THE BIG WET

Julie had told Bill that she owned a barramundi fishing boat that her grandfather had started in the early 1960s. As a kid she had worked on the boat and later with her husband, Alex Grant, who took the business over when her dad had a heart attack and was forced to move to Townsville for constant medical care. When Alex and her son, Jason vanished, she had leased their new boat to "Dutch" Verhoeven, who contrary to his name had been born in Normanton. Dutch had worked for Alex for several seasons and was totally trustworthy.

Bill was fascinated when Julie spoke about her childhood days in Karumba, the fishing trips with her mum and dad, days of huge barra catches when only a few people fished the Gulf, and dozens of trawlers lining up in the river waiting to unload their catches at the Craig Mostyn wharf. She had attended the James Cook University at Cairns and years later she came home with a teacher's degree. They were sitting on the rear patio, watching the river sliding past like a muddy wave. The stormy weather had dropped much rain in the upper regions of the river, and it was flooding with red dirt washed in from the upstream cattle stations.

'I taught school at Cairns for three years. I met Alex there, the captain of a game fishing boat. We fell in love and married, and when dad died, we came to Karumba. Alex took a job on my barra boat as a deckie. He did it hard for a couple of seasons in getting to know how to fish in the

Gulf and may have failed had it not been for Dutch, who took him under his wing. Lucky, I got a job teaching at the school and made enough money to keep us going.'

'You really loved Alex, didn't you?' Bill asked softly.

'Oh, yes. He was a good husband and father to Jason. Oh God, what happened to them?' she cried in anguish looking at Bill helplessly with tears welling up in her eyes.

Bill hugged her tightly, her tears flowing on his chest. He had read the police reports how they vanished into the wilderness of the Gulf and learned more from Harry who had his own theory. In fact, Harry had a theory about everything, but they were surprisingly accurate as Bill had learned.

'Alex, Jason, and Dutch took the boat over to the Mitchell River' she explained. 'Dutch said they set the barra nets in the morning and remained in the vicinity. Alex and Jason took off downstream in the dinghy to go fishing for grunter with lines and hooks, while Dutch remained on the boat. He did so, because an Aboriginal family, who were camped on the bank near the anchored boat, told the police that Dutch never left the boat.'

She looked at Bill, her eyes wet with tears.

'When they did not return by mid-afternoon Dutch checked the nets and filleted the fish. He gave the catfish to the Aborigines and told them he was worried about Alex and Jason. One offered to go with him and look about as he knew the delta well. They travelled all the way to the mouth and along the coast, stopping often, calling, and firing shots with the rifle, but there was nothing. Dutch raised the alarm when they got back to the boat about midnight. When the tide was high enough, he and the Aboriginal took the fishing boat out to sea and along the coast, but they found no one.'

Bill knew of the long days of searching by police, the local Indigenous people, fishermen, and SES volunteers. Nothing. The dinghy and its occupants had vanished into thin air.

'Bull's boat, the Bonanza was first on the scene, and they had two dinghies out in the delta channels all day before the official police search commenced.'

'Bonanza, are you sure?' Bill asked as he had not seen a mention of the boat in the official reports. 'Yes Dutch, told me. The Gregory's boat Catfish, and Animal's Gulf Catch were also there. Why?'

'Oh nothing, but I just can't recall any mention of the Bonanza being involved in the search that early.'

'Well, I reckon that Bull and Weed had something to do with it. There were whispers that they were up to no good and that Alex and Jason saw it. But why kill a little boy?' she cried, her tears running freely. 'Surely men are not that evil.'

'I am not sure,' he whispered. 'but what about crocodiles, sharks, and gropers.'

'No way, they would have found the dinghy. It was five metres long, unsinkable and had a 60 hp Yamaha outboard motor on it. Even in the Gulf wilderness someone would find it eventually. It's been almost two years now. I was going mad until I met you.'

Thunder moaned in the distance and lighting slashed the skies where giant clouds were massing over the Gulf as the storm gods lined up for battle.

'Looks as if the weather is going to turn serious,' Bill said, attempting to take her mind of her sorrows.

'Yes, it is, a monsoon trough is hanging all the way from Broome to Weipa,' she replied in a changed tone. 'I love the Wet, but I always look forward to the dry season. The old timers reckon we are in for a cyclone this season.'

There was a great cloud war raging over the Gulf. Giant masses of clouds were banking high, only to retreat from others that stormed up from underneath them, creating upswelling that reminded Bill of the river tidal currents hitting submerged rocks. The masses piled higher until they reached into the very gates of heaven. Lighting flashed continuously across the deep black blue clouds and into the Gulf below under the failing light.

The land was breathless and still. Bill noticed that no birds were twittering and asked Julie as she knew about the birds and how they survived big storms. Even though there had been some rain days before, the ground had dried out again and the smell of salty dust, whipped by the wind from the tidal saltpans, lingered in the air.

'Most birds go to ground and shelter under grass and bushes,' she said. 'Those big storms are like mini cyclones. I am glad that Dutch insisted on pulling the boat out and tying it down.'

Bill had met Dutch and his wife Lara, who helped him on the boat. Like most bush and sea people in the Gulf, they were pleasant and forthright. Lara was plump and bubbly in an attractive way, while Dutch was a tall stringy beanpole redheaded man, with a ready smile that underlined a large nose on his ruddy face and unruly hair.

Most of the smaller barramundi fishing boats had been pulled out of the water days before and were now tied down in an industrial park and back yards where the skippers would busy themselves during the off season getting the ships ready for the next barramundi season. Most were about ten metres long, but they appeared much larger when moored on land. A few bigger vessels remained anchored in the river, awaiting their turn at the busy slipway yard in the harbour, where the hulls were cleaned, repaired, and had new antifouling applied.

The tide was coming in, speeded up by the wind, flooding the fringing mangroves, and forcing the muddy flood water upstream, the colliding forces of the two currents creating small stubborn waves trying to stop the tide, but they failed as the saltwater pushed up under the muddy water and headed inland. They talked about the 24hour tide and how the Gulf is one of the few places in the world where there is only one high and one low tide every twelve hours instead of the usual six hours tides that occur elsewhere.

The wind came up, whipping up dust on the saltpan that divides the town from the Point. The storm carried slashing lighting and deafening thunder. The rain came down like a solid wall making visibility impossible. Only when the rain whipped under the patio did they hurry indoors, as more thunderclaps shook the very foundations of the house. The rain thundered on the iron roof so loud that it stopped normal conversation.

The power went off, but they had prepared for such an event with an emergency generator under the house ensuring that the cold food supplies in the fridge and freezer did not go bad. They cooked a meal on the gas stove, the room lit by the light of a bright LED lantern. By the time they finished the meal, the thunder gods had galloped off inland leaving a vanguard to mop up behind them. But the rain never lessened.

It rained nonstop for four days with the occasional clap of thunder breaking the constant drumming of rain on the roof. They woke on the fifth morning to a grey dawn, the silence almost deafening. The patio was wet and the rushing river so swollen that it backed onto the rear of the house fence.

The river was in a hurry, the urgent current carrying flotsam, that nature had no need for, into the Gulf waters. The monsoon burst had passed for the time being, though the sky remained heavily overcast with banks of clouds pushing inland.

A ray of sunshine drove like a spear onto the floodwater, lighting it up with colourful reflections. The flooded mangroves stood out starkly against a dark and brooding black sky. Birds twittered nervously nearby, a restless sound in the otherwise silent morning.

'Beautiful, isn't it,' Julie whispered, as he stood behind her holding her firmly, his strong arms across her breasts. 'I just love it and there is nothing like it in the world. Look at those clouds, there is more rain coming.'

A little zebra finch landed on the rail like a colourful ray of sunshine, but it soon flew away. The sun was still clinging to the gap it had sliced through the cloud, but it vanished as suddenly as it had appeared. The mains power was back on. They cooked breakfast and ate on the patio talking on how high the river would rise. Logs and debris bobbed up and down on the crest of the red mud coloured stream that was moving rapidly out to sea on a dropping tide.

They went for a walk, the countryside already greening as new growth surfaced from the earth that a few days earlier resembled a dust bowl. The transformation was incredible. Birds sat on dead trees that had been killed by some unknown disease. Some said it was from climate change, others reckoned it was from a former mine zinc treatment plant that was now in mothballs, though management denied it saying that they had controls in place to prevent such happenings, but of course no one was convinced.

Julie told Bill all this as she pointed out the different birds and named each one. He was impressed. The other person that knew so much about birds was Vic Hawkins. It reminded him to call him and see how he was doing. He had a call from Hawkins a few days after leaving, but he had been noncommittal and did not mention anything about dead bikers. A police car drove up the road and stopped opposite them. It was Simpson.

'Great rain wasn't it,' he greeted. 'Was going to call you today, Bill, but now I can tell you. We found one of Jolic's ship mates near the airport beach. It appears as if he drowned but an autopsy might tell another story. Better watch it. From what I hear Bull is looking for blood, yours. Warren has warned him to keep away from both of you.'

When they returned home, Julie looked worried.

'Bill, stay away from the pub and particularly Bull,' she warned him. 'You might not be so lucky next time, especially if you are alone. His mates will gang up on you.'

'Yes love, I agree, but I reckon that I do need to be more professional about this. I will let Simpson or Warren know when I am at the pub so that they can respond if anything happens.'

'But you might be dead by the time they get there. Can't you carry your gun or something?'

'I could, but if I used it my cover would be blown, and months of undercover work would be wasted. I am not alone in this, there are others working along the coast, maybe even here in Karumba. If someone makes a wrong move, it will all be for nothing. I must go to the pub because that is where the information is.'

The rain returned that evening. Christmas and the New Year came and went and still the rain fell, with only a few days of sunshine experienced. The road to Normanton was cut, not that it mattered much as every road into the Gulf country was under water. Bill was summoned to headquarters and seeing that Julie was on school holidays, they both took a light aircraft flight to Normanton where they transferred to Mount Isa and caught a commercial flight to Brisbane the next day.

Bill had never liked the city and he loathed it even more so after they booked in at the comfortable hotel within easy distance of police headquarters. But they were happy to be away from the rain that continued to hammer the Gulf country without let up. He guided Julie about the city, and they went to movies and fancy restaurants when his police duties were not required.

There was much going on and Commissioner Farrell told him that there would be a workshop of interested parties the coming Wednesday.

'You better not miss it,' he growled. 'This is why you are here. All interested agencies are getting together to combine information and you are an important link in the chain.'

Chapter 13
THE WORKSHOP

Bill received a phone call from Farrell to attend the workshop at ten am and that the venue was at the Enoggera army camp. Farrell said he would pick him up at his hotel. The traffic was light, and they arrived on time. There was heavy security at the gate, and after checking their IDs and car, they were directed to the conference hall.

'Bloody over the top security,' Bill remarked.

'Yes, you will find out why later. I offered to have it at police headquarters, but the Federal Police believe it may be bugged, though we found nothing to support it.'

In a training room they were introduced to others who were present and to later arrivals. The meeting commenced at ten am sharp. Bill was surprised to see that high-ranking officers from the Australian navy, army, and air forces were present, as well as customs, border protection and antiterrorist units. Beside himself, and Farrell, two other State police undercover officers who were working in Weipa and Bamaga were part of the men and women present. The meeting was chaired by Tom Osborne, the Federal Police Commissioner.

'Ladies and gentlemen, thank you all for coming to this meeting. You may wonder why, but it's all about national security, organised crime and terrorists. For the last five months we have been gathering information on a smuggling operation that is without par. Combined National, State, and Territory Government regulations have made things very tough for materials like explosives, guns and drugs to be imported. On top of that we have an illegal immigrant operation that has gone undetected until recently.'

A drink of water appeared to be in order as the Commissioner rustled his papers.

Again, he paused and glared at someone who was whispering to the person sitting next to him. Osborne raised his voice to another level to ensure people were listening.

'Organised crime is very organised, especially in our larger cities. Police in all parts of the country have been undertaking many successful raids and removed drugs, guns, explosives, and uncovered prostitution dens manned with smuggled Asian women, even children, some barely ten years old, but these raids are akin to clipping your fingernails. The main source of supply and distribution remains open, and this is what this meeting is all about. We want to get rid of it and are working with overseas agencies and Interpol to find this source and shut it down once and for all.'

He took another sip from the glass before continuing.

'For the last five years or more, there has been an increase in hard drugs like heroin and ice while people smuggling, explosives and firearms are also of concern. A few days ago, a North Queensland police response team unearthed C4 explosives during a raid on an Atherton Tablelands farm and drug lab. Unfortunately, there was a shootout, and the occupants were killed.'

There was more ruffling of notes. No one spoke, the Commissioner now had everyone's attention noted Bill, as he shifted in his seat to a more comfortable position. Osborne stared about the room at the people he was addressing.

'As I mentioned the increase of other dangerous substances and materials appear to have been smuggled into the country, via the Gulf of

Carpentaria. Previously we had a minor network controlled by a small, but efficient smuggling group operating from New Guinea into Cape York. They used fishing boats, prawn trawlers, and small privately-owned banana boats. We have closed that door and jailed the offenders, only to find that another has opened. This one has proven to be more durable, and we have been unable to find the source, or how distribution takes place. So far, we have been working from rumours without any evidence, or a base. However, we have had undercover officers slowly, but surely, gathering information and now have moved from a small sapling to a whole family tree that involves organized crime, and we now fear, terrorism. Time for questions, people.'

The questions came thick and fast, and Osborne answered most, or let others answer them. Farrell gave a long talk on how his police were involved, though Bill noted that he was very guarded on how much information he passed on. Others in charge were probably also keeping something back in order to claim credit later.

'A failure of human nature,' Bill mused to himself.

The criminal tree was being drawn on a large whiteboard as each delegate added his or her findings to it. It took most of the morning, but an objective and plan had been achieved by lunchtime. Again, it was Osborne who took the stand after lunch.

'Right, now we have some idea what is going one. As you can see from the tree, we believe that goods and people are smuggled into this country, via the Gulf of Carpentaria, and from a port somewhere in Indonesia, possibly a remote island under the control of corrupt officials, or a war lord. We assume it is by a ship, or, possibly fishing boats, that deliver the goods ashore somewhere between Cape York and the Gove Peninsula. We also think that this "sea road" is used to smuggle huge sums of drug money to Asia for laundering and native wildlife. Several cattle stations between the Mitchell and the Norman Rivers were purchased several years back by a syndicate that also owns the Gulf Barramundi Company. We are aware that the company has criminal connections. The stations have been fenced and are closed off tighter than a drum to pig shooters, bird watchers, campers and recreational fishers. A few commercial fishing camps on the coast and the rivers were burned with only 24hours' notice being given to the occupants to get their gear out. Some had been squatting there for thirty years a more.'

He pointed the various place names and rivers out on a huge rear projection screen that displayed a map of the region.

'This was legal as the squatters had no right to be there. The only places that are still accessible are privately owned Remote Island on the Staaten River, and several recreational fishing camps on the Mitchell River and Topsy Creek owned and operated by the traditional owners based here at Kowanyama.'

He switched slides to show a satellite photo of a large cattle station.

'This is Blood Gulley Station, the head station where the other properties are controlled from. Yes, they run cattle and each season they muster them and send the stock to the markets. They use contract mustering teams and there is nothing sinister in this. However, two years ago this new complex was completed on Blood Creek. It has two huge hangers that can house planes or helicopters. This is the airstrip. It is sealed and uncommonly large for a station property because the owners fly small private jets in from the Middle East and Asia, via Darwin or Horn Island. They clear customs and it's all legal. There is even a well-maintained golf course and swimming pool. The homestead is huge, and so are a number of these outbuildings, possible workshops. The complex is surrounded by an electric fence to keep intruders out, while there is a security gate at the road entrance, about two kilometres away from the buildings.'

He changed the photo, this time it showed a security gatehouse and two uniformed armed guards.

'This photo was taken by two officers of the Queensland Police Stock Squad who visited last dry season. They were cordially received by the manager and were invited for lunch in the big house, but they were not taken anywhere else, as these photos show that were taken with a hidden body camera. We also know that the station is used as a holiday resort by invited guests only, and from the little we know most have criminal connections.'

He switched the unit off and directed someone to turn the lights back on.

'Thus, this is the picture,' said Osborne, as he pointed back to the family tree image. 'The source is Asia; arrival on the shore of the Gulf is by ship, the transfer of goods, as our deep cover police officer suspects, is to local fishing vessels for transportation to shore. But exactly how and where and when we do not know.'

He pointed to the main branches.

'This is Tony Broggetti, a well-known criminal with Mafia connections, and our sources say he is the Australian godfather. This here is "Axel" Shute, who heads the criminal biker groups we know are involved and may possibly be partners on the east coast. They are one of the main distributors of illegal substances. One of our undercover officers has supplied us with the Karumba connections on the transfer of goods from sea to shore. He suspects that there are six or more barramundi fishing boats involved. They belong to the Gulf Barramundi Company, or GBC, which is headed by Don "Wog" Marotsi. His lieutenant is Alexander Antinus, also known as "Bull" or "Bull ant." His cohorts are Michael "Animal" Hardens, and others of a minor nature who work for the GBC. Most have criminal records, have done time, and are well known to the police. These photos were taken by our officers.'

He flicked the images of the various people involved on the screen and paused.

'Hardens took over the "Raider" after the previous skipper was killed in a gun fight with a couple of pig hunters on the Staaten River. We are unsure of their motive, but believe white slavery was involved. Our sources indicate that goods are transferred to Blood Gulley Station from somewhere on the coast and distributed from there to the capital cities.

It's a smooth operation that so far has evaded us, but due to the latest development, we must urgently action this because we now suspect that a terrorist group may be using this door to smuggle men, drugs and guns into the country.'

Osborne introduced Major Jack Knag, who told the gathering that he had three SAS teams in the Gulf country at three locations.

'They are ready to respond immediately when requested by the police,' the major said. 'We initially wanted the police to handle this, but the police are not trained to camp and survive in the bush for long periods of time. We are. The teams were in the Gulf all last dry season, but we pulled them back to Townsville for the Wet. However, as soon as conditions become favourable, they will be back in the northern Gulf country.'

Other officers informed the workshop group the part they had in the operation. The Navy was patrolling offshore ready to respond with deadly intent, while Customs were in the air watching for ships. The air force was supplying satellite images direct to Osborne who was overall in charge of the operation.

Immigration said they had contacts overseas that were providing valuable information, while a secretive antiterrorist unit and Border Protection were on standby. In all mused Bill, things were moving well. The meeting ended with Osborne directing all and sundry that under no circumstances was anything discussed in the room to leave it.

'What was said in this room stays in it. Officers' lives are in danger,' he warned. 'Even a whisper may mean a person's life. Keeping quiet is protecting the lives of your men and the safety of our country. And most of all we need to cut the operational head off, not its legs or arms, thus no one makes a move until we can yard the lot.'

Chapter 14
EXPLANATIONS

Bill and Julie left Brisbane two days later for Cairns where they overnighted before catching the Gulf Air Normanton flight. The rain was still falling from brooding scudding clouds that brought heavy falls to the Gulf country and kept the rivers full to the brim. All roads into the Gulf country were still inundated. With the school holidays over, Julie went back to work, while Bill gave Dutch a hand to get the boat ready for the barramundi fishing season. There was much to do, but Dutch was not worried.

'Won't be anyone fishing for a couple more weeks,' he stated. 'There is still too much water and the floating flood debris will clog and sink the nets. We are having the best wet in years and the rivers will be full of fat barra when they subside. There is going to be a swag of money to be made when we pull the nets up. By the way, Bill, Lara is taking time off for a month or more to look after our granddaughter. Our daughter, Emily is having another child soon. Interested in helping me out? I'll teach you the ropes.'

'Yes mate, I would love too,' Bill replied. 'I'll talk to Julie about it tonight. Where are you fishing this season?'

'Up north mate, we will fish all the way to the Staaten River if we have too. We begin fishing from Duck Creek north. When the hold is full, we'll come back, offload, and get new supplies before heading out again. Be away for up to ten days, less if the catch is good or until we fill the hold. It's good money for you also.'

'What about the GBC boats that fish up north? I thought that you blokes kept away from them?'

'Well, so far, they have left me alone. I'm not sure why, though I avoid the waters north of the Staaten like the plaque. Wog's boats normally fish as far south as the Nassau River from their Mitchell Rive base, but they sometimes fish further south along the coast. They don't move about much, while people like me fish a system until we get bored and move to another for change of scenery. Call it freelancing if you like.'

Julie was not happy about Bill being away for a couple of weeks, but she knew that he would go regardless of what she said and pushed the issue no further. They finished the boat and Dutch said it was now a matter of waiting for the weather to clear up. Bill busied himself about the house yard mowing the lawn and generally tidying everything up. He worked out on the punching bag daily until his fists were calloused and rock hard. As always, the high kicks on the bag took their toll as he felt stiff and sore after a training session. He told Harry, who surprised him one day during a workout that he was getting too old for this sort of stuff.

'Bullshit, wait till you get my age. Came to see if you like a beer,' Harry greeted him. 'Wog and his boys are back in town, and I hear that they are all at the bar. Bit like a rattlesnake den I reckon.'

'Yes, I would, but I might get into another blue with Bull,' Bill replied. 'I don't want you to get hurt either as they will target you also if you are with me.'

'Don't worry about me. I have about thirty mates of mine in the bar who will sort Bull's mob out if they start anything. Most are sick and tired of sitting around waiting for the floods to subside and are heading out tomorrow. The Plummer boys are there also and if anything starts, they will sort out Bull's mob with the help of others. Besides the cops are keeping a watch on the bar, I reckon.'

The bar was alive with noise from jostling men and women that looked as if they were trying to drink it dry. The road had opened only six days earlier after having been closed for two months from flooding, resulting in some brands of alcohol running out. New supplies had arrived a day earlier.

'The boys are sampling them.' Harry told Bill.

George and Pearl Gregory were with an older couple at their favourite table. They waved the two men over to join them.

'Bill, meet Norm and Gloria Plummer. Norm, this is the bloke that broke Bull's ribs and put him in hospital,' George said.

'Bloody good on you,' Plummer replied with a genuine smile on his face. 'I would have loved to have been there. I never got on with that bastard since the day he pushed his ugly mug into this bar. I reckon they must have named the bar after him. By the way, he is over there with some of his cronies.'

Bull was mingling in with a small group of men, Bill noted as he sat down and joined in on the small talk of the fishing days ahead. Dutch and Lara came in and joined them.

'We called into your place to tell you that the boat is going into the water tomorrow arvo on the high tide,' Dutch said to Bill. 'If the river is too muddy, we can always set the nets off beaches and on tidal flats. I will need a hand. We'll fuel her up and load the rest of the supplies on and we'll be on our way on the incoming tide the next day. Okay with you?'

'Yes, no worries. I'll be there.'

Bill and George walked to the bar for another round of drinks. The bar girl took their order and as they waited for it another man had joined Bull's crowd.

Bill recognised him as "Wog" Marotsi. Up close he noted that Wog was unlike most southern Italian men he had met and was as tall as himself. He looked very fit and had a long lean muscular body. He was a very handsome man, with a touch of grey on the temples of his well-groomed hair, Bill noted. He met Bill's eyes with no sign of hostility, only curiosity, in them. To Bill's surprise he walked over.

'So, you are the man that almost killed my first mate, Bull,' he introduced himself, holding his hand out to Bill. 'I'm Don Marotsi, but everyone calls me Wog. I don't like it much, but I have got used to it. Fuck it mate, I am as Australian as anyone,' he complained somewhat bitterly.

Bill shook his hand.

'Bill Madsen,' he greeted. 'getting ready to go fishing?'

'Yes, tomorrow I'll be taking the fleet to our Mitchell River base and hopefully we'll catch enough barra to keep the shareholders happy.'

Gregory gave Bill a tap on the shoulder and nodded to where Bull was getting up from his table and striding towards them, his face twisted in hate.

'Better make a bit of room for yourself mate, he is coming for you,' he said urgently.

'Fucking hell, I told the bastard not to make any trouble,' Marotsi exclaimed angrily as he pushed himself from the bar and strode towards Bull. He met him halfway, holding him at arm's length and said something to him. Bill wished he could have heard what, as Bull sullenly turned about in anger and walked back to his table. Everyone present saw that it humiliated him.

'I am sorry about that, but he will not be fighting you while I am around. I need him on his boat, not in hospital. His job is to catch barra and make money for the GBC,' Marotsi said as he returned to the bar. The drinks arrived and after bidding farewell to Marotsi, the men headed to their own table.

'I loved it when Bull had to back down,' Plummer said with a grin on his face. 'Wog is the boss. Don't let those good looks fool you, he is a rough as guts grass fighter and gives no quarter. Few miners in the Isa ever could stand up to him in a blue. He hated being called Wog at school and fought kids twice his size when he was a little feller.'

'So, you know him from another life?' Bill asked.

'Yes, we were both brought up in the Isa, though I am a few years older than him. He looked me up when he first arrived at Karumba and we were the best of mates until his cousin showed up, Tony someone, who backed him with pockets full of money,' Plummer said bitterly. 'The boats and net licenses are in Wog's charge, but he doesn't do much net fishing these days, though he is very good at it. Check out Wog's boat. It's a pleasure cruise vessel, not a barra boat. He spends most of his time entertaining and taking sleazy looking criminal types that fly in from outside sport fishing. They generally have a few loose women with them also.'

'Sounds like he has a good life,' Bill said.

'Yes, he does,' Plummer answered with a laugh. 'but mate, you've' got a lot to learn about this place. Wog's mob gets more money from other sources than the whole of the commercial fishing industry combined in the Gulf.'

'That sounds like bullshit, how would they do that?'

'Drugs, Bill, drugs in, wildlife out. It's as simple as that. If you don't believe me, check out the old prawn farm past the Staaten River if you ever get up there and see why there are so many bird cages since I was forced out of the place by Bull. Or the old World War 2 bunker system on Kangaroo Island on the Mitchell River that Bull has claimed as his headquarters. Tell you mate, those arseholes have something big going. But don't get caught asking questions; you won't live to tell the tale.'

Bill was almost speechless. Plummer had told him with a few words what he had been searching months for.

'How come the cops don't know about this or customs and fisheries?' he asked.

'You got to be joking, mate. They are all in on it and the fucking magistrates and politicians as well. The cops chase my boys, because they grow a bit of grass, to look good. Fisheries have no guts, though they are not allowed to arm themselves so you can't really blame them. Instead, they book kids for undersize fish, and grey nomads for lack of safety gear in their boats instead of patrolling the Gulf. I reckon the big boys pay them to look the other way.'

'Yep, he is right,' Harry said, who was taking a keen interest in the talk. 'These things have been reported before, but little action is ever taken. When they did, they never came back to tell the tale, and a few bodies have turned up to back me up on that. Both the cops and fisheries have lost men. One inspector vanished some years back. They found him wrapped in a barra net. He had become food for crabs. More recently, look at what happened to that poor bastard Sheppard. No man deserves that.'

Plummer rested his hand on Bill's shoulder.

'Tell you something, mate. I like you, but whatever I said is between us. It's grog talking. Karumba minds its own business or people vanish. It's that bloody simple. We suspect its Marotsi's mob, but proving it is another thing.'

That night Bill called Farrell and reported what Plummer had said.

'It might just be piss talk, but in this town, rumours have foundations.'

'Right, what I want you to do is get a helicopter and check out the coast all the way to Kangaroo Island ASAP. Pay for it and I'll refund you when I get your invoice.'

Chapter 15
THE CROCODILE COAST

The local helicopter operator, Clive Burrows, was more than happy to take the charter but said he would have to fuel up at Kowanyama for the return trip. They arranged take-off as soon as the boat was in the water. Dutch had jumped at the invite of coming along when Bill asked him as it would give him an idea what the state of the still flooded rivers were. He had explained to Dutch that he wanted photos of the coastline and the rivers under flood conditions for his collection.

They had the Karumba Calcarifer in the water, fuelled, and supplies loaded by noon. After anchoring the boat in the deeper water across the river, they took the dinghy back to the ramp, showered, had an early lunch, and drove to the airport. Both men carried small backpacks. Bill had packed his 9 mm Glock, two loaded spare magazines, 10x20 field glasses, and his Nikon 500 digital camera fitted with an 18-300 mm Nikon zoom lens, and several bottles of water.

After ensuring that safety belts were secured, and headphones fitted, Burrows lifted the Robinson R44 helicopter into the air and turned north along the coast. Ahead the flood plains extended to far horizons where a scattering of blue-black storms and showers complimented the colours of the green plains and the yellow-brown and blue-green watercourses.

'That is a good colour change. It indicates where the flood water meets the incoming tide,' said Burrows over the headphones as he pointed to a collision of brown and clear water in a large creek. 'The floods are receding and the plains draining. That is Brannigan's Creek up ahead. Beyond it is Accident Inlet, while that big inlet in the distance is the Smithburne River.'

'This is fantastic,' Bill replied in awe. 'All that water, you wonder where it all comes from.'

'From the sky, mate,' Dutch answered seriously. 'This is the best flood water runoff I have seen in years.'

'Look at that, there,' Burrows pointed to where a couple of big crocodiles were basking on a small beach. 'We will be seeing plenty of those. The floodwaters are cold, and they are spending time basking in the sun. The big one is over five metres long, it's a male. That's his mate to the right.'

Duck and Snake Creek passed under them. Both were swollen by brown coloured flood waters and hardly recognizable as creeks, being more like rivers in appearance, thought Bill. The mangroves that fringed the Smithburne River were isolated and surrounded by water and looked like tiny islets.

'The tide is coming in, pushing back the flood waters onto the plains,' Dutch explained. 'this is all tidal flat country, and many watercourses unite during big floods. Over there, off that point, is where we will be hanging our nets in a couple of days.'

He pointed to where a low stand of mangroves marked a creek inlet. There was a small boat in the river. Burrows swooped low over it and a couple of people waved.

'Fucking amateur fishermen,' Dutch swore vehemently. 'they catch more fish than us.'

'But they can only take five barra home,' Bill argued. 'I am amateur, and I have fished with Hawkins, King and Harry, and we caught nowhere as many as you blokes catch in nets.'

'You're right, but still, they spook the barra, so they don't move about as much.'

'Yeah, right, you ever think that fish are evolving and now avoiding nets. Hawkins told me that they do that with different lures in heavily fished areas.'

'Might be, but those pricks have no right to be there,' Dutch protested in a surly tone.

Bill had heard it all before, the long war between the two camps that sometimes came to blows in the pubs. Still both camps had rights, so he pushed the subject no further. Ahead a big afternoon storm was moving out into the Gulf. It was blue-black in colour and had streaks of intermittent lighting flashing through it. The scudding, disorganized layer of clouds in the tail of the storm broke open, allowing a beam of sunshine to penetrate onto the floodplain below, turning it into gold with dark shadows that flitted across it.

'It's too dangerous to go on, we'll have to land and wait until it passes out into the Gulf,' Burrows advised soon after leaving the Gilbert River behind them.

He pushed the stick down and guided the Robinson to a narrow strip of golden sand that separated the Gulf and the grassy flood plains. The chopper landed, the struts sinking a little into the soft wet sand. Burrows shut the motor down and the men hopped out, the heat and humidity hitting them like a wave.

'Fuck, this is beautiful,' Bill exclaimed as he looked out across the calm water of the Gulf to where the storm clouds were piling high into the heavens, a living thing, alive with lighting.

Moaning thunderous reverberations rolled across the sea in a series of almost continuous sonic waves. Ahead the sky broke through the clouds, revealing a startling blue sky, but as quickly as it had appeared the gap was sealed by swift moving clouds.

Bill walked to the plain where only a few small scrubs broke the monotony of the grasslands. The rain had renewed the land and he felt as if he was the first man to walk on it. On impulse, he turned and composed a photo of his footprints on the beach that led back to the helicopter that stood starkly out against the backdrop of the blue-black tropical storm. The chopper resembled an alien thing in a surreal land of water. The storm had passed here, and tiny raindrops clung to scrubs and grass leaves, resembling minute slivers of quicksilver.

Somewhere in the distance came the sweat call of a grass bird and the royal trumpeting of brolgas and sarus cranes. A clean fresh smell lingered in the air, though there was a hint of decay from dying swamp grasses that faced death when the dry set in. The grass was damp when Bill walked into it for a little distance to compose another shot with the camera. To the east a pair of kite hawks circled against the stormy sky, while a pair of cheeky crows were harassing a sea eagle. Bill wanted to be nowhere else and wished that he had been able to bring Julie to witness this wonderful display of nature's own, but unfortunately it was a school day.

'Hey, come on we'd better move. A hole in the sky is open,' Burrows called.

Soon they were back in the air, the Robinson akin to a little dragon fly flitting aimlessly in an endless sky in this land of crocodiles, thought Bill as Dutch pointed out another one on a small beach ahead.

'They are getting bigger and more common,' Bill noted.

'Only babies, there are larger and more crocs further north,' Burrows replied. 'With luck we may see a real big one.'

The Staaten River was wide and in full flood, Burrows flew some distance upstream on a request from Dutch.

'There, that is Van Rook Creek.' Dutch pointed at a large creek that joined the river below. 'Good place for a net next week. Fucking hell, look at that monster.'

They looked at where he pointed and saw a huge saurian slipping into the yellow flood water.

'Fuck,' Dutch exclaimed. 'that thing is as big as Krys. Bit of a worry putting a net in.'

'Been about for years,' Burrows said. 'I saw him about eight years ago at the Wyaaba Creek junction up the river. I believe old Hawkins has photos of it, but he won't publish them because he reckons every idiot with a gun will be out to poach and kill it. Funny old prick, he shoots every pig he sees, but is very protective against something like this. That mate of his, King, thinks along the same lines.'

'I know,' Bill replied. 'they are the same with fish. They take photos of their catch and take only a few home or to eat in their camp, unlike most fishers who come to Kurumba and fill their iceboxes and freezers under the nose of the fishing inspectors.'

'Bloody hopeless mob those inspectors,' Dutch swore. 'They should be on the road booking those pricks when they leave with full freezers and iceboxes. The law ignores arseholes like Bull and his mob who often fish before the season opens and turn up with full freezers a day later. They openly unload at the Coop and fisheries do nothing about it. Its bullshit. Fuck! Its two days travel to the Mitchell, or back, from Karumba, let alone have time to set nets for barra.'

Burrows turned back towards the coast, flying low over the Remote Island Fishing Lodge where the caretaker waved to them.

'That's old Joe, the caretaker, should land and say g'day,' Burrows said. 'good bloke, but we don't have the time. Dropped a load of tucker and booze off last week to keep him going until the road opens. They don't open the lodge until the road in from the Savannah Way is open. It will be fucking weeks yet by the looks of it as most of it is covered by flood water.'

Further north, they passed over a cluster of station buildings sited on high land and surrounded by the flooded plain.

'Bushy Plains,' Burrows informed. 'doesn't look as if anyone is home. Probably in Cairns living it up. Funny mob, fucking foreigners, they don't like visitors, but us bush pilots always pass over isolated homesteads in the Wet just in case there is a problem or something.'

He flew low over the buildings. A truck and a couple of Toyota tray backs were parked in the shed, but what surprised Bill was a camouflaged coloured 4WD tour bus with the name, "Gulf Savannah Adventures," on its side.

He had once seen it in Normanton when it was refuelling. The passengers were all beautiful Asian women and very young. Seeing the 4WD bus parked in an isolated station shed could be an indication that it was used to smuggle people to places south. He took some photos of the station and the shed, ensuring that the bus and its license plate were in focus.

'I would like to see the old prawn farm if possible. Can you take us there? I'm interested in old history and love a photo of it,' Bill asked Burrows.

'No worries, mate, it's your money. I think a GBC barra boat uses it as a base these days. It's easy to find, just a matter of following that half-drowned track ahead of us. It used to be the service road before the place was destroyed by Cyclone Max a few years back. They were also farming and there is lots of irrigation gear rusting away in the grass. The locals reckoned that they were growing funny grass, if you know what I mean.'

Ahead the coast came in sight. Long sinewy snakelike tidal channels, fringed by thick mangroves that ended at flooded tidal flats, reached inland from it. Little remained of the prawn farm. There was a dozen or more ponds, and some outbuildings that were partly overgrown by vines and tall grasses.

'I'll take her down so that you get a close look,' said Burrows as he picked a clearing of sand near one of the ponds. 'Don't get too close, there is a fucking big croc in it.'

They caught a glimpse of a four-metre reptile as it slipped off the pond bank and dived into clear water not deep enough to hide it. Burrows held the helicopter over it, and it nervously swam into deeper water where it refused to budge no matter how close the Robinson neared the surface. Tired of the game, Burrows landed the chopper on a cleared area nearby. Beyond the buildings a narrow strip of monsoon rainforest stretched in braided finger like links as far as the Nassau River. Bill was wary as he walked to the buildings, as both men had cautioned him about snakes.

'Especially fucking taipans,' Burrows warned as they picked their way through the tall grass. 'Cranky bastards that will go for you if you are too close. One bite and you will probably be dead before I can get you to the Normanton hospital. Be careful.'

One building had several army style stretchers, with the mattresses hanging from the rafters to keep rats out of them. The kitchen cupboards were stocked with tinned food, while oiled iron cooking pots and camp ovens hung from hooks attached to the ceiling above a gas stove. Movement near a ceiling beam caught Bill's eye. He stepped back in horror as a four-metre snake glided along it.

'Only a carpet python,' Burrows laughed. 'It is harmless as far as poison is concerned but they have big sharp teeth that can inflict a nasty wound. Shit, there is enough food here to feed an army. Whose camp is this, Dutch, any idea?'

'Not sure, though I have seen a GBC boat anchored in Salt Arm Creek. They use a dinghy in the channel at high tide to reach the buildings. They fish the creek, the coastline, and those little tidal creeks that penetrate inland all along this part of the coast. Most of all, they don't like visitors.'

There were several large aviaries behind one building and more inside it, but none held birds. Another shed had smaller cages.

'For holding reptiles, I reckon,' Dutch said.

'Looks as if old man Plummer was right,' Bill mused aloud. 'He reckoned that Bull's mob grow marijuana here and that they smuggle wildlife to Indonesia.'

'Could be right,' Dutch mused. 'Though I reckon that old prick probably built the cages before Wog's mob chased him out. Plummer is no fucking saint.'

Back in the air, they headed north, passing the Nassau and its sandy casuarina fringed inlet. It was a pretty river. Burrows swung the helicopter upstream pass an old barra boat abandoned in the mud.

He pointed to where a concrete pad was, all that remained of a fishing camp that had been burned out. The river was alive with crocodiles, seemingly hogging every bit of exposed land along it.

'Now that is a crocodile,' Bill exclaimed. 'Fuck look at the width of that thing. It's big enough to swallow a bloody draught horse.'

The big six and a half metre reptile showed no inclination to move until the copter was close. Only then did it slide across the mud and into the river with a great splash and vanished under the cloudy coloured water.

'Fuck,' Bill swore. 'You wouldn't want engine failure. I heard these Robinson's don't have a very good safety record.'

'Hey, we don't talk about things like that when in the air,' Burrows rebuked him. 'But they are safe enough or I would not be flying one. That is the Mitchell estuary coming up ahead of us.'

All the river estuaries that they had passed appeared to be concentrated into one system, thought Bill, as myriad tidal channels and wide estuaries of the delta came into view. The river appeared to have three mouths: each one several hundred metres wide. Burrows confirmed his observation.

'Yes Bill, you're right, the South Arm, Main Mitchell and the North Arm. Plus there is the Coleman River estuary that connects with the North Arm by a two-kilometre channel. In truth it is one large system, the largest in Australia. There are recreational fishing camps over there on Topsy Creek below us, and on Surprise Creek, which runs into the Main Mitchell. There are more camps on the Coleman from where they boat into the Mitchell River. You can just see the Kowanyama Community to our right. However, since the GBC took over, recreational anglers have been harassed and not too many come here anymore, unlike they used to some years back. That is a loss of income

158

to the community.'

Several large and small islands made up the river delta, the two larger ones abutting the Gulf.

'The farthest is Kangaroo Island,' Dutch said, pointing it out to Bill. 'There are old World War 2 bunkers on it and a barge landing. See there is Bull's barge near the old landing. It's his base and he moved down here from somewhere north of Weipa some years back. I think he uses the bunkers also. George Gregory is the only bloke who still fishes here, though only in the Coleman. Bull's mob intimidated others by cutting nets, burning their land-based camps and shooting up their boats. Nothing was ever proven though. Cops and fisheries blame amateur anglers, pig shooters, and the local blackfellers making war on white fellers. They don't have the guts to go after Bull.'

'So why not the Gregory's?' Bill asked. 'How come they allow them to fish here?'

'Not real sure,' Dutch said slowly. 'But pub lore has it that Bull woke up one night to find George standing over him with a knife blade across his throat. No one knows what was said, but Bull avoids him. George is part black feller, part white feller and part mongrel when he wants to be, a real tough bastard who fears no one. He is related to the Pormpuraaw mob. His wife is from Kowanyama. The Indigenous people stick together and have a system they call payback, which they enforce if anything happens to one of their clans. I reckon that George told Bull that is anything happens to him; his tribal brothers will be looking for revenge and it frighted the shit out of Bull.'

'That is an old car ferry barge from the Daintree River,' Burrows informed the men as he flew the Robinson close over the complex. 'It has demountable donga accommodation, generator, and fish freezer facilities on it. They say Bull's mother and a sister live in the old concrete bunkers.'

The barge looked comfortable. A couple of big tinnies were tied up alongside it. There were nets and fuel drums on shore and a well-used track extended from the concrete landing ramp into a low forested hill. Someone came out of the barge building and waved. The copter dipped from side to side in greeting. A flash on land near the tree clad hill attracted Bill's attention and he turned the field glasses to it. There were two people under the trees, one holding a scoped rifle.

'Better get the fuck out of here before they start shooting at us,' he warned Burrows, but the pilot was already turning the copter away and diving below the tree line.

'I saw it, happens every time when I get too close. Probably to discourage me from landing.'

'So where is the bunker,' Bill asked.

'Under that little scrub covered hill, I think. It only takes a couple of wet seasons to cover things up with growth in this country and the years can hide many things. Well, time to fuel up and head home.'

Burrows turned the Robinson upstream and followed Magnificent Creek up to the Indigenous community and the airstrip. After refuelling they found themselves heading south into a darkening sky. Bushy Plains Station came into view and fell behind them. Burrows pointed ahead and there was concern in his voice.

'That's a big storm front ahead of us. The radar shows it's a huge system and there is no way we can get through or around it. I'll try and reach Remote Island. Old Joe owes me. We should be able to scrounge a feed and a bed for the night. Sorry guys, but safety comes first.'

Burrows concerns were justified as in the south a blue-black curtain rose like a towering wall over the flooded savannah plains. Sulphurous flickers of lightening slashed amongst the boiling cauldron of sunlit clouds and through the black base that extended to far horizons. The helicopter was like a tiny gnat against the blackness of the storm as it raced it to the cluster of the island's buildings.

Severe wind gusts shuddered and shook the small craft as it dipped below the trees and touched down hard on the bottom of the airstrip, close to the first building. Someone raced towards them on a side-by-side buggy.

'Brought some rope and pegs,' he yelled at Burrows. 'you better tie her down. This storm might have a tornado travelling with it. There is plenty of shear wind already. Here, use the hammer.'

Burrows grabbed the sledgehammer and hammered a steel picket that Bill held for him into the sodden ground. The ground was soft and only a couple of hits were required to angle the pickets down into it. They roped the undercarriage of the Robinson to the pickets as tight as possible. The copter rocked back and forth and was in danger of being blown away by strong wind gusts. But the ropes held.

A sudden slash of lighting lit up the dim twilight of the failing day in a brilliant flash and noise as a nearby tree was shattered into match wood. As pieces of timber and branches were flung to earth, there came a thunderous clap of thunder as the tempestuous savannah storm broke over them.

'Fuck this,' Burrows shouted. 'get away from those iron pickets, we have done enough. Let's get under cover now.'

They ran for the buildings, close behind Joe on his buggy. Thunder and lightning were as one and then the rain came in so hard that it almost hid the pallid flickering of the lightening and damped the deafening thunderclaps. The storm burst with intensity beyond belief. Twilight turned into stygian darkness, penetrated and lit up only by streaks of lightening.

No one slept well that night as the rain drummed ceaselessly on the corrugated iron roofs, accompanied by the cannonade of thunder and lightning that continued well into the early hours of the morning before the thunder gods slowly galloped away across the savannah to the north. Daylight revealed a mindless brown flood sweeping past in the billabong that fringed the lodge, but the land was fresh and the skies blue. Broken and smashed trees and branches were scattered all about the complex, but the Robinson had escaped damage, though it was plastered with leaves.

'That is the end of the Wet, its last hurrah,' Joe informed the men. 'there'd be no more rain until the build-up.'

They knew he was right.

Chapter 16
BARRAMUNDI RIVER

They declined Joe's offer of breakfast, boarded the helicopter and landed at Kurumba later in the morning. Bill had called Julie on the lodge phone shortly after landing at Remote Island to assure her that they were safe and well. After bidding farewell to Burrows, Dutch and Bill planned to sail out on the next morning's high tide. Only a couple of boats remained at anchor in the river, most having departed earlier in the morning.

'That overnight stay cost us a day's fishing,' Dutch grumbled. 'Oh well, that gives us an extra day with our loving ladies.'

On the return flight they had spotted the Italia far out to sea, the big cruiser easily recognizable. Closer to the coast was Bull in Bonanza, while Animal's Raider was a couple of sea miles behind it. Four other GBC vessels were leaving the Norman River when they landed. The Gregory's Catfish was moored off the coast north of the Van Diemen Inlet, the couple setting nets from a narrow beach into the sea. Dutch reckoned that they were doing the right thing as it would be a waste of time in the river and inlets, because the big fresh from the night's storm would have washed a lot of debris into the nets.

'But by the time we get there it should be over with the worst flushed out to sea,' Dutch said. 'We will fish the tides off Point Austin for a day or so and then head north to the Staaten River.'

Bill called Commissioner Farrell and informed him what he had seen before emailing selected JPEG images of the trip. By the time he finished Julie arrived home. Seeing it was their last night for some time, they went out for tea at the Sunset Tavern and watched the sun set over the river in a great ball of fire in a sky that for the first time in many weeks was largely devoid of clouds.

Back home, they made love for much of the night. Bill was tired and weary when the alarm woke him from a deep sleep. Julie moaned and was still asleep when he closed the door. He left her a note saying he loved her and would call that night. Dutch and Lara were waiting outside the front gate to pick him up. Bill tossed his kit into the Toyota, and they headed to the wharf where Dutch kissed Lara farewell.

Calcarifer headed out of the channel, past the flickering pilot lights and into the Gulf proper, as the eastern sky turned to a rosy, red glow before the auto pilot changed course and turned the boat north into a calm sea. The two men sat back in the cabin, letting the auto pilot guide the vessel on the plotted Sat Navigation course. Dutch boiled the kettle on the little gas stove in the galley and made some buttered toast. Now they relaxed, sipping hot sweet black tea from enamel mugs.

'Fucking marvellous, the auto pilot,' Dutch said quietly. 'You set it on a selected course, and it will take you there, and back, using Global Positioning or GPS from overhead satellites. The old days of the compass made it much harder to navigate. Anyone with half a brain can do it these days.'

He took another sip of the strong liquid from the mug, his ruddy features cracking in a smile.

'The old man used neither compass, nor GPS. He shot crocs from the Roper River to the Jardine River and there was not one river or inlet that he missed. I reckon you could blindfold him, and he would sail into any of them without grounding.'

'You shot crocs with him on a professional basis?' Bill asked.

'No, not commercially, crocs were protected by the time I was old enough to shoot. Besides the old man had retired by then. He was a tough old bastard. He migrated from Holland after the war, but seldom spoke about it, though he once said he was in the Dutch underground. I did shoot a couple of crocs with Dad once. He is gone now.'

'So, you have fished for barramundi all your working life.'

'Yeah, I know nothing else. Hope to buy my own operation one day, even though there is no money in it. I suppose the lifestyle has got to me. Julie won't sell. I put it to her some time back, but she reckons that our current arrangement works fine. It does and it is better for me than wages and I am my own boss.'

Later in the morning they neared Point Austin and found another barra boat moored off it.

'Looks as if someone else beat us to my spot,' Dutch grumbled bitterly. 'We'll have a look and see if anyone is fishing in the inlet. No hurry, the tide won't be turning for a few hours yet.'

After rounding the Point, a gap in the low coastline indicated the inlet entrance. The tide was barely high enough to take the boat over the shallow mudflats and into the inlet.

'That is the northern channel of the Smithburne River, Bill. There is no one else in the inlet. The water flow is not too strong. We'll give it a try tonight when the tide is right.'

Dutch located a deep hole on the depth sounder and instructed Bill to release the safety shackle on the anchor chain. The anchor rattled into the depths and the boat hung in the current a little before swinging round and facing into the incoming tide.

'It's time for a bit of lunch before we have a look about in the dinghy,' Dutch announced as he switched the engine off. 'You'll get used to the noise of the generator, but we need it to keep the freezer and the ice slurry cold.'

After lunch, they boarded the five-metre net dinghy. Dutch kicked the 60 hp Yamaha motor into life and turned the dinghy upstream. The river was running high from the tide that forced the freshwater back upon itself, the overflow spilling across the floodplain. A few flooded mangroves and small inlets indicated the true banks of the river.

'This has been a good spot for me in the past,' Dutch informed Bill. 'We'll set one net downstream from this creek and another above it this afternoon. When the tide turns, the fish swim out and into our nets. We'll check them at daylight. We'll take a run and have a look about as it will give us a chance to find out if anyone else is in the river.'

They headed downstream and out to sea from the main channel. A barra boat was anchored near the mouth of the river. They waved to the two men on board but did not stop.

'Bloody pair of arseholes,' Dutch grunted. 'Fucking GBC boat, they are not to be trusted.'

Bill did not reply, but in the days ahead he found that when Dutch was fishing there was little rapport between them and other netters they encountered. The sea was slightly choppy, but the home run was close inshore and they escaped most of the chop in the open boat. The men were back in the dinghy, by evening, setting the nets.

'Four will do for the time being,' Dutch said when the last net was in the water. 'If we get any fish, we'll set two more on the next tide. No good busting our guts for no fish, we must find them first.'

The tide was on the turn by the time they were back to the boat, had dinner, and settled down for the night watching a movie on cable TV. Bill had noticed that most, if not all the boats had cable TV antennas and remarked about it to Dutch.

'Yes, Bill, things are not what they used to be. Most of us now enjoy TV anytime we want it. We also have excellent radio communication and satellite phones. Some of the boys have email also, but I can't stand fucking computers. Of course, some of the boats have more porn movies than most adult shops to keep the crew occupied.'

Later they sat on the rear deck, the night clear under a sky struck with twinkling stars that were strengthening as a waning moon sunk into the Gulf. Dutch switched the generator off.

'The freezer is cold enough. I'll switch it back on before we bed down. I love the silence of the river. Like another beer, Bill?'

The silence was almost deafening after the noisy generator until Bill's ears adjusted to it. Now he heard the current, lapping the sides of the boat, and out wide there were fish moving with the running tide, the splashes loud under the silent stars. There were sudden "boofs" that he recognized as barramundi feeding on panic-stricken mullet that were rushing about near the shore in noisy schools. From somewhere upstream came a dull cough.

'Bull crocodile,' Dutch muttered matter of fact. 'They carry on mating after the Wet. He is trying to attract a female. Late nests have a better chance of survival as many early nests are washed away by floods. However, the downside is that the babies have less food, so it all evens out in the end with probably only about two percent or less surviving.'

The men spread their swags on the rear deck, as it was much cooler than inside the cramped cabin. Dutch, an old hand, had a couple of mosquito nets to keep the biting annoyances at bay. He warned Bill not to sleep too close near the rails, as crocodiles were known to pull swags containing people into the water. Despite the warning, Bill slept blissfully. When he woke, Dutch was in the galley boiling the billy. Breakfast was over by the time daylight painted the eastern sky blood red. They headed upstream in the dinghy and found that the floats on the first net were partly under water.

'She's chockfull mate, plenty of barra or bloody catfish,' Dutch cried in delight. 'You grab the net when I line it up with the dinghy.'

He guided the boat toward the net and Bill grabbed the end float as Dutch switched the motor off. The net was heavy when they pulled it up and both men grunted under the strain. There was silver colour in the water and Dutch grinned in delight.

'Barra, Bill,' he grunted, a big smile cracking his ruddy face. 'This is where you begin to earn your keep, mate.'

There were a dozen barra in the first few metres of the net, along with threadfin salmon. Dutch showed Bill how to get the fish out of the monofilament gill net strands that securely had trapped and choked the fish.

'Watch the gill rakers and the spines on the barra. They are razor sharp. I don't want a trip back to Karumba to have your hand stitched up from a bad cut. They are sharp enough to cut through your gloves. Infection is also a problem with fish slime, so be careful. Here, have a go yourself. Quickest way to learn.'

They worked together removing the fish from the net and dropping them onto the dinghy floor, while most were dead, some were still alive and struggled violently, big fish, a couple over one metre in length that weighed fifteen kilos or more. They neared the middle of the long net and were pulling hard on the section that was mostly under water, when suddenly the net was pulled from their hands. Bill almost fell overboard as the net moved under him. Dutch grabbed and steadied him.

'Careful mate, this is no place for swimming. If the crocs don't get you sharks, and gropers will. There is something fucking big in the net. It's probably a big sawfish. Pull hard and don't let go.'

The men pulled harder on the net, the nose of the dinghy almost dipping under the water. Something big and black rose to the surface; the net partly rolled about it.

'Fuck!' Dutch swore loudly. 'Fucking big croc, about four and half metres long. Just our bloody luck and on the first drop for the season. We'll have to try and roll it out of the net so that it can free itself.'

The reptile's head was partly out of the water, its jaws entangled in the net. The men rolled the net away from the body.

It was a dangerous and difficult task as only the net line separated it from the dinghy. The croc lay still, as if knowing that the men were trying to help. Dutch leaned over, holding the net and used a gaff to pull the net mesh over the nose of the croc. It happened in a moment. One second, he was standing in the boat and in the next he was pulled over the croc's head and into the water behind it as the monster bit down hard on the gaff and propelled itself at the dinghy hitting it hard on the side and almost tipping it over. It took some water before balancing itself as the croc pushed against it and launched itself at Bill.

Bill pulled back from the slashing jaw, but the crocodile was just as quickly snapped back by the catapult effect of the heavy nylon net. The dinghy steadied, settled, slipped over the net and the croc and drifted away with the current. Bill kicked the motor into life looking about for Dutch. He was about forty metres downstream heading for the mangrove lined bank.

But Dutch was in dire danger as Bill to his horror saw another big croc swimming towards the fisherman at speed. Bill opened the throttle on the outboard motor, the dinghy's nose rising high before it settled and glided forward on the plane. The crocodile was close to Dutch, who, having seen it, turned back into midstream to avoid the reptile. But it quickly closed the gap, and it was only a few metres away before Dutch turned, his belt sheath knife in his hand.

Suddenly there was a mighty roar, as the dinghy hit the croc with a fleshy sounding thud and became airborne in front of Dutch, the propeller spinning freely and spraying him with blood and bits of skin and flesh.

The dinghy landed with a mighty splash about three metres away as the croc rose out of the water in a crescent shape, as if trying to bite its tail. Blood spurted from its back in a stream, colouring the water about it. Ahead, Bill turned the dinghy sharply and headed back at Dutch at high speed before slowing and spacing it between the wounded crocodile and its intended victim. Bill reached over and pulled Dutch on board. He flopped in the dinghy on his back on top of the dead fish, his body shaking.

'Fuck, mate,' Dutch muttered. 'Who wants to be a fucking fisherman?'

'Are you okay, Dutch, anything broken. Fuck, you scared the crap out of me when you went in.'

'The body feels okay Bill, but my pride is hurting. Hell mate, you saved my worthless fucking life. I would have been a goner if I had been alone as I had originally planned.'

Dutch sat up, fish slime draining off him. They had drifted about three hundred metres downstream from the net.

'Mate, head back to the boat for my revolver. There is only one way to get a fucker like that out of the net and that is to shoot it.'

At the boat they tossed the barra in the brine bin noting, for the first time, that the sun was well up. Dutch used the deck hose to wash the slime of his clothing. Bill noticed that his hands were shaking when Dutch handed him a holstered .357 Magnum Ruger revolver before climbing into the boat.

The big croc was still trapped in the net, its head above the water line. There was no sign of the other reptile. Bill held the dinghy steady about three metres away from the saurian as Dutch aimed and squeezed the trigger. As the shot erupted the torpor of the morning a thousand birds rose from the fringing flood plains in alarm.

The croc went crazy, trashing the water to a boil. Again, the gun bellowed, a spurt of flame erupting from the barrel. Once more, Dutch pulled the trigger and the crocodile's skull exploded into flesh and bone. He holstered the gun and handed it to Bill who placed it in the dinghy's storage box.

'Hate to shoot a big crocodile like this one,' Dutch said in a sorry tone. 'But there is no other choice. We must make a living. Let's empty this net.'

The men pulled on the net until the shattered head of the croc was alongside the dinghy. Dutch swore at the damage the old croc had done to the net as he tugged to remove the monofilament strands from around its mouth.

'Grab the tail and hold it Bill, there is a little job I have to do before we let him go.'

Bill held the massive tail as Dutch hooked the net on the dinghy's tie off hook. Bill noticed that the saurian was longer than the dinghy and almost as wide. Dutch drew his knife and with a couple of deft slashes disembowelled the beast, its bowels spilling out into the current.

'Okay mate, you can let go now,' he advised Bill, as he slipped the net from the reptile's nose. 'Crocs are protected Bill, and we must release them unharmed when they are caught in a net. We tried our best, but we could just as easy have been killed. It will sink to the bottom, and no one will ever know.'

The reptile's body swirled away with the current and vanished under it. It seemed a waste to Bill, but he understood what Dutch said. Ignorant urban seat polishers made crocodile protection policy in airconditioned offices in far-off Brisbane without having a clue, but for those working and living in the wilds of the Gulf country, crocodiles were a daily gamble with death. The men pulled the net in, removing dozens of big barra and salmon. Dutch reckoned that it was good for another drop, and they left it set for the afternoon tide.

The other nets had fewer fish and thankfully no crocodiles, thought Bill, as they removed the barra from it, and several large unwanted dead catfish, their carcasses drifting away with the tide.

'I don't want catfish, not worth the trouble, though when the barra are not running I do take them for mixed fillets,' Dutch informed Bill when asked about the fish. 'Nothing wrong with catties, they taste okay, it's just that barra fillets are worth much more money and easier to handle.'

'We used to fillet all our fish once, but most boats now have brine bins installed,' Dutch informed Bill. 'We just toss whole fish in the bin, unload them at the Coop and they are transported to the southern markets as they are.'

With the job done and the deck hosed and washed spotless, they sat back and relaxed on the shady deck enjoying a light lunch of fried barbequed salmon fillets washed down with a couple of cold beers. A sea breeze sweeping in from the Gulf heralded the turn of the tide and the ship slowly swung around until it faced downstream. The day was hot and humid with disorganised clouds drifting over the green wild land that fringed the crocodile coast.

Chapter 17
TERROR IN THE NIGHT

Two days later, after the barramundi run ended in the Gilbert River, Dutch decided to move north and fish the Staaten River and its large tributary, Van Rook Creek. They cruised out into the Gulf on a rising tide, the night stygian black with only a starlit sky showing any lights, their route guided by the GPS unit.

'We can't get in or out at low tide in the Staaten,' Dutch explained. 'During the dry season the high tide is at night and the shallow river entrances are only navigable on a high tide. With a bit of luck, we should enter the Staaten just before daylight. We can't use the GPS to guide us, because every wet season flood changes the main channel and depths. We must see our way and hope we don't end up on a sandbar.'

The Gulf waters were choppy, but the big boat rode comfortable in the swell as she sailed north, the engine throbbing in her wake. Bill made coffee and handed a mug to Dutch.

'Go ahead and have a camp, mate,' Dutch offered. 'There is nothing to do until daylight anyway. The auto pilot and the GPS are doing the driving. All I have to do is to keep an eye on the radar to make sure we don't run into a ship or a floating obstruction, providing it is big enough to show up on the radar.'

'No, I am okay Dutch. This is all new to me and I don't want to miss anything. I am looking forward to seeing new country, especially the

Staaten River. Hawkins and King told me a great deal about it.'

'Yes, they know it well and most other rivers hereabouts also. I have often seen them fishing the river in the past, though I don't think they will be there for a while yet. The road will be closed a few more weeks seeing we had that late downpour the other night, though the Remote Island Fishing Lodge is probably operational now as they fly most of their clients in.'

There were no lights to indicate that other ships were in the vicinity. There was a promise of daylight when the ship turned towards the mouth of the river. The tide was slack and on the verge of turning when she slowly entered the wide river mouth and headed upstream. They passed another boat anchored up the river, though only the mast light was on.

'Matt and Emily Jackson's boat,' Dutch answered when Bill asked him about it. 'Good people, they have been fishing the river for years. They won't like it too much with us coming in here, but no one owns the fishing rights to these rivers, though the GBC thinks otherwise. But Matt is a rough customer and a good knuckle man, while Emily is a deft hand with a gun. They don't take shit from anyone, the probable reason that the GBC has left them alone.'

The sun rose above the tree line when the ship dropped anchor in a deep hole just inside Van Rook Creek. The men had the nets in the water an hour later before returning to the ship for a late breakfast and a well needed nap. They checked the nets by midday, and while the catch was not what Dutch had hoped for, he reckoned it showed promise. The Jacksons dropped by in the afternoon and said they were doing just fine and that they would be returning to port too offload their catch in a day or two.

Bill took an instant liking to the couple, a hardworking pair born and bred in the Gulf country. Both their parents had been pioneering net fishermen. They warned them that Bull's Bonanza had been in the river twice and that the crew were far from friendly.

'Keep the guns handy and the powder dry,' Matt warned as the couple headed downstream after enjoying a few drinks and snacks. Bill noted that a rifle case was in the dinghy, backed by a holstered revolver on Matt's waist belt. It was a bad sign that people were carrying guns for protection, and he felt sad that the police could do little to protect those making a living in this harsh land.

The tides were kind and bringing fish in. So much in fact that they pulled one net out as they were flat out keeping up to it. Two days later Dutch announced that another drop would fill the brine bin.

'We will move out to the mouth on the next tide and drop the nets in at the point. We don't need many fish to fill up and it will give us an early start for home on tomorrow night's tide.'

They were anchored off the right bank of the Staaten River by late evening, the sea breeze welcome after the hot humid days and nights in the creek. They set the nets and enjoyed a late tea, followed by a few cold beers. As was his usual habit, Dutch checked the instruments before retiring.

'Come and have a look at this, Bill,' he called out to Bill who was laying his swag out on the rear deck. 'We got a large ship on the radar and should be able to see her lights, but she is not showing any. No one runs around these seas without lights. If they are caught the skipper could lose his license. I reckon it is that GBC boat Matt spoke about. I better keep the Ruger handy. I don't trust them, though I don't think they will bother us as they have enough country to the north to keep them busy. Still, you never know, we better be on guard instead of being sorry later, or dead,' he added as an afterthought.

Bill got his 9 mm Glock out of his pack and checked the magazines before fitting the Surefire Executive Elite tactical light under the barrel. When he pressed the switch, the light lit up instantly, the beam of the laser sight directly in its centre. Dutch, who was loading his licensed Ruger Single Action .357 Magnum looked up in amazement.

'Fuck Bill', he exclaimed. 'That is some weapon you got there. You don't want the cops to find it on you. They would send you away for life. I didn't even know you owned a pistol or had it on board.'

'Well, I don't exactly want people to know about it, Dutch. But you haven't seen it. It is all in your imagination. Right?'

'No worries, mate. I get it but if you ever want to sell it, I want first offer.'

Both men slept fitfully, knowing that in the darkness of the Gulf waters was a boat that by its intentions was not friendly, but the droning generator engine, coupled with the lapping of lazy waves against the hull and the splashes of hunted fish about the boat, was a restful lullaby. Above the sleeping men the dim glow of the mooring light on the radio mast did little to break the almost total darkness or that of the distant pinpoints of the stars in galaxies far away.

Bill woke up, his eyes trying to focus on the gloom near the deck railing. Something had alerted him, something like the squeak of the deck gate hinges. Suddenly he was wide awake as again the tiny squeak broke the silence. His right hand found the Glock under his pillow; he gripped the butt firmly and place his finger on the trigger. His heart was thumping rapidly in his chest and even though he had trained for this he found that his hands were shaking.

The night was moving, something black was silhouetted against the railing that moments before had been slightly outlined by the dim glow of the mooring light. The smell of rotten fish was in the air. He knew that Dutch was also awake, as his breathing had changed.

Suddenly Bill quickly rolled away from his swag against the rail as he felt something coming at him. It struck the air mattress with a dull thud as he switched the pistol light on, its beam highlighting a tall man with an axe his hand, its head buried in the air mattress where moments before Bill had been sleeping.

At the same time Dutch fired, the boom of the big revolver deafening, the muzzle flash blinding. Someone gave out a hoarse gurgling cry of pain followed by a splash by a body falling in the water.

Seconds passed before Bill's eyes overcame the muzzle flash, but the man with the axe had vanished as silently and invisibly as he had come. Below the deck came the noise of someone starting an outboard motor near the bow and a roar as a dinghy sped away into the night with two men in it.

Bill fired and emptied the magazine at the boat, the target difficult and weaving under the limited beam of the Surefire. The weapon light was designed only for closeup combat. Dutch switched the deck lights on, the welcome glow flooding it with brightness. There was nothing to indicate they had an unwelcome visitor only moments before. Nothing, but the hissing air mattress split by the sharp axe and a smear of blood on the rail.

'Fuck Bill, that was close. That bastard almost got you, just as well you woke up. I think I got him. He let the rail go and fell into the water. If he didn't make it into his boat the crocs and sharks will eat him for sure, especially if he is bleeding. And I reckon he is. Even I don't miss at this range. Did you hit anyone?'

'Not sure Dutch, but that bastard with the axe almost got me. I was ready to shoot him, but the muzzle blast of your revolver saved his life I reckon. It frightened the fuck out of me, also. Fuck, my ears are still ringing. Not too sure if I hit anyone in the boat though. This pistol light is designed for closeup combat, not for long range shooting. Thanks for the intervention.'

'Don't thank me mate, I owe you for the croc, remember?'

The men checked the deck, but apart from the blood and the deflated mattress, there was nothing else to indicate that they had been attacked. Dutch switched the radar on.

'He is heading straight for that big boat, Bill. I reckon it will take off as soon as the dinghy reaches it. By the way did you smell that rotten fish. I reckon that is what woke me up. The only bloke who stinks like that is Bull's brother, Slime. It would explain why he vanished so quickly. He once turned up in a fishing camp on the Smithburne where I was having a few beers with some mates. They had two watch dogs that would tear an intruder to bits, but Slime walked pass them and they took no notice at all. Evil fucking stuff! I was sitting on a log near the campfire, and he was standing behind me before I smelled him. He scared the fuck out of me and the other people in the camp. Turned out his outboard had broken down and he wanted a tow to Bull's boat. He is a real low piece of shit, believe me. Bill, when daylight comes, we pull the nets out and catch the outgoing tide. We are going home as soon as we can get out of here. How about a coffee?'

Bull had never seen Wog so angry. It frightened him to see his boss in such a state, his eyes fierce, the veins almost bursting from his forehead and muscular neck. He was glad that Wog did not have a gun in his hand as there was no doubt in his mind that he would use it.

'Fuck, fuck you Bull, you and you're useless fucking vendetta against Madsen. For fuck's sake, get over it. You have put at risk the whole organization and lost a good man because you want fucking payback. Well, let me tell you, I order you now to forget about Madsen in company time. If I hear as much as a whisper that you have used company resources on Madsen, I will personally feed you to that fucking pet croc of yours. Get out of my fucking sight, now.'

Bull climbed into his boat and headed back to the Bonanza riding gently at anchor in the mouth of the Nassau River a short distance away. They had barely made the runoff of the tide and the boat had scraped the bottom in the shallow channel a few times.

His half-brother, Slime was waiting for him on the deck railing, his yellow eyes strangely tame looking thought Bull as he tossed a rope to him. Tame looking was right; it reminded him of a dog waiting to be punished and wanting to make up to its master after doing wrong. Slime was an animal mused Bull as he looked at him. He was mad, Bull knew that, but he was mostly controllable; mostly, and Bull cursed as he remembered that sometime during the night Slime and the deckie, had taken a dinghy and taken it upon themselves to attack the Calcarifer in the hope of killing or capturing Madsen and bringing him back to Bull. Only Slime had returned, his eyes red from crying and blubbering that someone had shot the deck hand.

Bull had bashed Slime all over the deck and would have killed him had reason not set in. Now he was in the bad books with Wog, his mate who could do no wrong in his eyes. Bull's rage was almost uncontrollable as he stepped onto the boat and again smashed Slime to the deck, before grasping him by the throat and heaving him up on his feet.

'You senseless fucking stupid idiot,' he cried. 'Why the fucking hell did you go after Madsen. He is my business and mine only. You keep away from him unless I tell you, do you fucking hear?'

Slime struggled to speak, Bull's grip on his throat choking him. Bull felt him go limp and dropped him to the deck, kicked him in the ribs and turned away. He did not see the hate filled eyes of the man gasping on the deck for air. If so, he might have killed him. Slime was close to going over the edge.

'Hide the fucking dinghy in the mangroves, no better still, sink it. If the cops come and see the bullet holes in it, we're fucked,' were Bull's last words as he stepped into the cabin and slammed the door behind him. He thumped the table with his fist, the rage within him abating.

'Pity one of those bullets did not fucking kill him.'

Chapter 18
THE BIG BLUE

The sun was setting over the river and it and the Gulf were linked as one, the tide creating great ripples of orange and gold across the surface. Overhead a sea eagle floated on wide silent wings across the water, its last chance for a meal before nightfall. It gave up and settled on a channel marker, some distance away from the boat. It perched there; a feathered statue almost ebony under the colour of the setting sun as it looked down on the intruders in the fishing boat.

'Beautiful darling isn't it,' Julie smiled. 'but I wish the fish would bite. I haven't even had a touch.'

'Whoa, you're not complaining, are you?' Bill asked as he reeled his line in. 'All this nature about, but you are right of course. I reckon we ought to pull the boat out and get fish and chips at the Tavern on our way home.'

'Let's do it, darling, fish and chips are fine as I had my heart set on a fresh fish fillet tonight.'

Bill started the motor and moved the boat forward to slacken the anchor chain for Julie to pull it up. The sun was a red orb that hung suspended over the Gulf for a few seconds before vanishing in it. By the time they winched the boat on the trailer it was almost dark. There were others at the ramp waiting to get their boats out of the water, grey nomads that had been arriving days before on their annual pilgrimage from the Deep South to enjoy the balmy winter season of the Gulf country. Several caravans, towed by flashy expensive 4WDs, were lined up at the caravan park, waiting their turn to book in. Bill parked the Landcruiser past the tavern, ensuring that the trailer and boat did not stick out onto the road.

'Hello, looks as if we have got another visit from a biker's club,' Julie observed. 'There are over a dozen Harley Davidson bikes parked in front of the tavern.'

'Do you get many biker visits?' Bill asked.

'Yes, we do. But they mostly stay at the GBC compound out of town. A few live there, even during the Wet. They work on the barra boats and often have visitors, probably fellow club members judging by the colours.'

'They probably do, most have close links, especially those from the same chapter. Not too sure about this mob though,' Bill said as he noted the name Gulf Rebels on a couple of bike tanks.

The Tavern sounded like a beehive with noise from locals, grey nomads, and the bikers that included several women. The bikers had taken over the bottom end of the bar. They were noisy and boisterous. Bill and Julie ordered their meals, and a couple of beers. Someone called out to them. It was Harry Douglas and his wife Grace, who were sitting at a table overlooking the river.

'Saw you come in from the sand bar,' Harry greeted. 'Did you catch any fish.'

'Not a one, dead as a door nail out there, wrong tide I guess, at least Julie says so.'

'Well, she should know as she spent more time on a fishing boat with her old man than at school. Not that it harmed her any, did it my dear?'

'Aww shut up Harry,' Julie rebuked him. 'You know that the tide is wrong, otherwise you both would have been out there yourself.'

They enjoyed another round of drinks before their meals arrived. As they ate, the harsh roar of more Harley Davidson motor bikes coming from the Town raised the ire of The Point residents. A dozen or more bikes pulled up in a noisy display of showing off and sky larking when the new arrivals were greeted by those already present.

'Fucking wankers,' Harry swore. 'They should ban those fucking noisy Harley Davison bikes. We get booked for noisy mufflers and these arseholes get away with it. They are fucking leather, ear, nose, and eyebrow rings, and gold chains people. What a fucking bunch of losers. Even the women look like dogs and probably have rings in their pus'

'That's enough Harry,' Grace interrupted sharply. 'How would you know anyway?'

'Well, I do,' Harry scowled as Bill and Julie burst out laughing.

'Tell you something Bill,' Harry said, suddenly very serious. 'there is something going on. I'll bet that Wog and Bull will be in town soon. They always turn up when this mob arrives. Big secret meeting at the compound to look at more ways to smuggle drugs and guns in I reckon. That is what these biker gangs do. You know that.'

'You're probably right Harry, but unless they invite me to the meeting I won't know.'

'I reckon. I need a piss, be back soon.'

Bill noted that Harry had trouble getting through the bikers as he headed to the toilet. He saw that three big men walked in behind him a few seconds later.

'Fuck!' he swore. 'Julie, call the police and tell them to be quick. There is going to be trouble.'

He got up and walked quickly past the bar. He had to force his way between the bikers, excusing himself as he pushed past them. He was surprised that no one made a move to stop him. They did not know him or cared what his urgency was.

He pushed the door open and saw that two men were in the process of pushing Harry into the urinal, while the other had his penis out and obviously was going to piss on him. There was blood running from the man's nose, while Harry had a cut eyebrow that was bleeding profusely.

He obviously had made a stand.

'Fuck off, mate,' the biker with the penis in his hand snarled. 'This is a private party, so fucking walk away now, arsehole.'

'Busting for a piss,' Bill said as he raised himself on the ball of his feet and swung a mighty drop kick with his right foot that caught the man on his temple. Still clutching his cock, he slumped unconscious to the floor as the other two released Harry and rushed at Bill. Only one made it to Bill who met him with a twohanded closed fist hit in the chest. His face turned ash grey, and he gasped for breath as Bill hit him with open palms across his temples. He went down as if he had been hit with a sledgehammer. Harry had a chokehold on the other man, who was turning a bright red. Bill kicked him in the stomach and chopped him hard across the throat as Harry pushed him forward. He slumped to the floor clutching at his throat and gasped for breath.

'Fuck Bill am I glad that you turned up. Hang on mate, but I still need that piss I came in for.'

Harry pulled his penis out and promptly pissed all over the biker who was going to do it to him.

'Karma, mate, Karma will always get you. Wish I had more piss for those two bastards. How about you Bill, are you joining me?'

Bill laughed. 'No thanks Harry, the ethics committee would have my guts for garters if they found out. Let's get out of here, before their mates come looking for them.'

Bill opened the door to find surprised faces staring at them.

'Shit!' a big bald biker who had rings in his ears and a gold chain hanging on his bare chest swore loudly. 'The fuckers have done the boys over.'

He charged at Bill with swinging arms, his face red with rage. Bill smashed him hard under the nose with an open palm that sat him on the floor on his backside, were he moaned in pain, blood from his smashed nose running freely through his fingers.

Another biker charged at Bill, a murderous look in his eyes. His

183

swinging arm was suddenly stopped as Bill's hands locked about his wrist. Bill ducked under the arm and pushed down hard, and the biker's body was suddenly air borne as he did a complete somersault. He landed hard on his back on the tiled floor and promptly lost interested in the scenario missing, what locals later said, was the best bar room fight ever seen in Karumba.

One man was wrestling with Harry, but he dropped to the floor as Bill punched him in the side of his head. He grunted in agony and slumped on his knees where Harry's kick lifted him as he fell. Harry stepped over the man and sparred up to another who had taken his place. Bill avoided the full contact of a huge fist that painfully grazed him along the cheekbone. He recognized that the bikers were becoming organized and attempting to surround the two men. Harry dropped onto one knee as a blow caught him on the chin. He managed to raise himself on his feet and at the same moment brought his right fist up from the floor to make hard contact with his assailant's testicles. A scream of pure pain erupted from the man's lips before a crashing left on his chin shut him up.

The two men faced their attackers, backs against the wall. Bill lunged forward on the balls of his feet, his body airborne and his right foot coming to a sudden violent stop on the ugly bloodshot face of a crewcut biker who had stepped forward. As he dropped soundlessly to the floor, another rushed in swinging a heavy chain that grazed Bill's shoulder and tore away his shirt and flesh. Before the biker could be ready for another swing his face made sudden contact with a rock-hard fist that broke his right cheek bone.

Bill lunged forward, ripping the heavy chain from the biker's hand. It was almost a metre long.

Holding it in his right hand he flicked it like a recoiling snake's tongue at a man's face who was moving forward in a classical boxer's stand.

The chain hit him fully in his mouth, blood, teeth and pieces of skin coming away with it. Before the cursing bikers could rally Bill was amongst them swinging the chain in controlled movement. They paused and moved away quickly, except for one who came at him with a bar stool. Bill rolled under it, doubled and swung the chain, hitting the man across his lower legs. He screamed in agony. The bikers fell back to regroup, their women screaming and encouraging them on.

'Get the cunt,' a woman shrieked in a bansheelike wail. 'Cut his fucking nuts out.'

Bill dodged a blow, but the man managed to grab his shirt, tearing it away from his body as he fell to the floor. For the first time, they halted their attack, fearing the corded muscular man who for all appearances was enjoying the fight as a workout. Even though he was bleeding from his shoulder and face, it made him look even more dangerous.

'Police, stand back, all of you,' suddenly commanded someone in a loud voice. 'Police, stand back.'

Bill recognised Simpson's voice. He was more than happy to hear it. Warren was on the left side of him moving into the biker group. Bill noted that both men were holding taser guns. He dropped back to the wall where Harry had slipped down to the floor, his old legs no longer able to bear him. He was breathing heavily, his hands shaking.

'You okay mate?' Bill asked resting his hand on the older man's shoulder.

'Fuck yeah, mate, just fucking legless. Not used to this shit anymore. Fuck a man is getting old, but it's the best fun I have had in years, apart from giving the old woman a good loving that is.'

Simpson and Warren had moved themselves between the warring factions.

'Okay you people move back, it's over. Move!'

Bill helped Harry onto his feet, and they beat a slow retreat from the threatening faces and curses of the menacing biker mob as the two cops separated the combatants.

When he was outside Julie and Sarah rushed over and helped Harry to his 4WD.

The police officers stood firm, holding back several bikers wanting to carry on the fight in the street, mostly women who were screaming and cursing for blood.

'Okay,' Simpson shouted. 'Any more trouble and you'll spend the night in the slammer. There is an ambulance on the way to treat injuries, and if any of you give us any problems, we will end it and belief me it won't be pleasant. Back off, now!'

They fell back, recognizing that the officers would not stand any nonsense. But mostly they feared Bill who had returned and was standing behind the police, still holding the chain, his body tense and alert, a brutal look in his eyes. Simpson noted it. He turned about.

'Sir, you, and your friends leave now. I will see you later in case anyone presses charges. Now go.'

He winked at Bill as he nodded his head, secretly pleased at the carnage this one-man force had done to the bikers. In line with most police officers, bikers rated on the low order of things as far as he was concerned. Julie drove the 4WD, closely following Grace and Harry, who was in no condition to drive. As they drove away, Bill let his breath out and suddenly felt like Harry must have done when the adrenalin rush had abandoned him.

'Are you hurt, darling,' Julie asked, concern in her voice. 'I have never been so scared in my life. I thought they were going to kill you.'

'Don't worry about that, they would have kicked our guts in if they had managed to get us down,' Bill replied gruffly. 'Bikers are like dingoes and attack in a mob.'

They pulled up at Harry's place and helped Grace to get him into the shower to wash the blood and grime off him. Bill marvelled at the old man's courage and skill. He must have been a great fighter when he was younger and fitter.

The women scolded and told them that they were not to go anywhere near the local waterholes until the bikers left town. Bill and Julie said good night and drove home. Grace had a loaded double barrel shotgun in her hands "just in case they come here." Bill knew that she would use it.

Bill moaned in agony as he stood under the shower, the water painful as it flowed over his torn shoulder skin, cheekbone, and knuckles. He also discovered a few bruises that he didn't know he had. After Julie applied antiseptic liquid to the wounds, and ice packs to the bruises, he felt almost human again. However, before they went to bed, he opened the gun safe, pushed a loaded magazine in the Glock and chambered a round home. Julia looked at him oddly, as he placed the pistol on the bed drawer beside him but said nothing. Bill lay down on the bed, his muscular body aching and smarting. He felt very tired and sore.

Chapter 19
KIDNAPPED

In the morning Bill felt as if a road train had run over him. Looking in the mirror, he saw that more than a few hits had connected on his body and face. His left eye was partly closed, but in all he got out of it better than expected, he thought, though had it not been for the timely arrival of the police, things might have turned out different. Julie had prepared breakfast and as usual they ate it on the rear patio overlooking the river. The tide was running in high and close to reaching its peak. Several barramundi fishing boats were coming down the channel. Julie was looking through the powerful telescope. It was part of the patio furniture and used to spy on everything and anything on the river.

'That is Wog's boat and Bull is not far behind them,' she informed Bill. 'Harry was right when he said they would be in for a meeting with the bikers. Have a look darling.'

'Yes, something is happening. I reckon we'll go for a drive later and just sit back to see who meets who.'

By the time they had finished breakfast the boats were anchored on the other side of the river. Bill grabbed his camera bag and field glasses and tossed the holstered Glock pistol in the camera bag, while Julie insisted on taking along her Remington slide action .223 Remington Magnum rifle. She placed the cased rifle behind the seat of the Landcruiser and they drove to the Town boat ramp. Several visiting anglers were waiting their turn to launch their boats in the river.

'Oh look, Catfish is back,' Julie enthused, pointing to a boat that was cruising up the river. 'George and Sandra must have a full load as they were not due back until the middle of the week.'

'I hope so,' Bill replied. 'Look, Bull and that slime ball deckie of his are pulling away from the Bonanza. Wog's tender is also being launched.'

'You're right about the slime ball bit,' Julie giggled. 'They actually call him Slime. He is Bull's brother. They reckon that Bull is also his father if you can work that one out. He is a very repulsive man and rarely seen in town.'

Slime pushed the bow of his dinghy onto the ramp, totally ignoring a recreational angler who was backing down his dinghy for launching. His mate, who was directing him asked Slime to move, but Bull told him to "fuck off." Bill and Julie could hear the argument from where they were sitting on the bank overlooking the busy ramp.

The man told Bull and Slime they were a pair of "ignorant arseholes." His mate got out of the vehicle and asked Slime to move the dinghy over but was also told to "fuck off." A woman, the wife of a local recreational fisherman, walked over and said something to the two anglers. They took note of her and turned away, resigned to the fact that they had to wait for Slime to move the dinghy in his own time. One of the men took a mobile phone from the car and made a call.

'He is calling the cops,' Bill observed. 'I reckon that they will be here very soon.'

Wog's sport fishing boat came in on full plane and slipped alongside the ramp. Bill noted that the beautiful Eurasian was on the console steering wheel. Wog ordered Slime to get his boat off the ramp. The man reluctantly did as he was told. Both boats were then tied up upstream from the ramp.

'Cunning bastard that Wog,' Bill mused. 'He wants no trouble, the reason he told Slime to move his boat. The last thing he wants is a confrontation with amateurs who call the police at the slightest bit of trouble. Yep, I was right, Constable Warren just pulled up.'

Warren walked down the ramp to where one of the men, who had now backed the boat trailer into the water, pointed to Slime and Bull who pretended that they were not there. Warren walked over and spoke to them; they shook their heads and nodded. He also said hello to Wog, who as usual was very pleasant, while the Eurasian smiled and distracted the police officer's attention.

Bull and Slime walked pass Bill and Julie. Bull gave them a hateful look but said nothing. Bill mused that Slime was well named. He was an average height man, with long scruffy reddish hair and a full beard, both needing attention. A hooked nose matched his thin lips, but it was his yellow eyes that made him stand out from the crowd. They were the eyes of a madman, and a very dangerous one at that, thought Bill. His clothes looked as if they had been worn forever, and even from where they were sitting Slime smelled like rotting fish. The smell brought back memories of the Staaten River attack when the night had come alive with evil. Now he was looking at Slime directly, but the man looked away and gazed at Julie instead. She shuddered as her eyes met Slime's and turned away as if given a sudden fright. After the two were out of earshot, she held Bill's hand tightly.

'That dirty man gives me the creeps. Bull is a gentleman compared to Slime. Bull never lets him out of sight when they are in town.'

Warren came over and said hello.

'Looks as if they got a few in on you last night. But after you left, they were as tame as pussy cats. Three were taken to Normanton for hospital treatment, nothing serious as they were not admitted, though they are sporting a few stitches. You're in the clear Bill, no one is pressing charges. They reckon it was a misunderstanding but watch your back. The same goes for Harry.'

Wog walked pass, the Eurasian alongside him.

'Hello Julie, you are looking lovely as always,' he greeted them. 'Bill, I heard that you have been fighting again. Perhaps you should work for me to keep my men in line. I have a bit trouble with some.'

They laughed; the Eurasian sounding like a tingling bell thought Bill. Seeing her in daylight enforced his earlier observations that she was the most beautiful woman he had ever seen. Again, she was dressed to kill, a tank top and her trademark pair of cheeky shorts complimenting her figure. She was almost as tall as Wog noted Bill as they walked away after a bit of small talk.

'You know, Wog walks proud, like a dog with two pricks, when he is with her,' he said to Julie and Warren, almost sounding envious.

'Bill, you're rude,' she laughed. 'But yes, she is beautiful, isn't she? She could be a movie star or model. Makes you wonder why she lives with someone like Wog and his shithouse crew.'

Warren bid farewell, again warning Bill to watch his back. Catfish had anchored, and the Gregory's were heading towards the ramp in the dinghy. Julie ran down and grabbed the tie-up rope when Sandra tossed it to her and secured the dinghy.

'G'day Bill,' George greeted him. 'you don't look too bad. From what I heard you and Harry are lucky to be alive.'

'Shit! How come everyone knows,' Bill lamented.

'Because it came over the UHF air waves last night, mate. I reckon we had a word-by-word commentary of it. Everyone is talking about it this morning. Hell, I wish I had been there.'

'So, what the hell are you doing back so early?'

'Full hold mate, will be unloading in the morning, refuelling and loading stores before heading back up north. The barra are really running this year.'

'Let me know, and I will come and give you a hand to unload, nothing much else on now. I need the exercise.'

'No worries, Bill. Meet you at the Coop at ten tomorrow. I'll put you to work.'

Later, Bill and Julie drove to the Point, avoiding the pods of 4WDs towing caravans and camper vans. Karumba's caravan parks were filling rapidly.

'They are early this year,' Julie informed Bill. 'The weather must be cold already in the deep south. There are plenty of amateur anglers in town also, the word is out the barra are biting. It's all good for local business. I can't wait for the school holidays to start so we can get away for some good fishing ourselves.'

They had morning smoko at the Point TakeAway before driving along the airport and onto a bush track that ended at the ruins of an abandoned mango plantation. Gnarled old mango trees remained as a mute testimony of yet another failed pioneering venture in the Gulf. Bill found a couple of rusty old cans. He placed them on a log some twenty-five metres away and they had an impromptu target session on the tins with the Glock. Julie was a good shot as she had grown up with firearms. She could beat Bill almost every time with both rifle and handgun. They turned for home when the shooting session ended and passed a dozen or more Harley Davidson motor bikes at the road junction, the riders leaning back against the wind, their women holding tightly onto them. The roar of the powerful engines was harsh on their ears.

'Heading for the Tavern,' Julie stated. 'They are probably camped at the compound.'

'I would like to the check the compound out. Just drive past slowly and I'll have a look with the field glasses,' Bill said. 'Don't worry they won't know who we are, besides it's about one hundred metres off the bypass track. It's used by fishermen every day, so we won't even be noticed.'

Bill had found out that the Compound, as the locals called it, had been a former outstation, part of a cattle station. It was about three kilometres out of town and situated along a good connecting dirt track. While it was still part of the station property, Bill had discovered it was rented out to Wog for staff accommodation though he never lived there, preferring the luxury of his boat.

There were several bikes parked near the open shed, and a couple of

4WD tray backs, while a handful of people were seated about a long table under the shed shade drinking beer. Even though Bill and Julie passed well away from the complex, it stirred the dogs up who raced along the fence until they were out of sight.

Bill recognized Wog and Bull as they passed and lost sight of the complex where the track entered a patch of low bushy scrubs before turning back to the town. Julie drove down it for some distance before Bill asked her to pull up. A helicopter was hovering over the complex and slowly settling down to land in a cloud of dust. Bill directed Julie to pull up in the scrub. Grabbing his camera, he jumped out and asked her to wait. He quickly made his way to the edge of the scrub, which ended close, near the fence. It gave him an unobstructed view of the open shed.

A dozen men were walking about shaking hands with what appeared to be new arrivals from the R44 helicopter. Bill took a few photos with the telephoto lens when he paused and cursed as one of the newcomers cropped up in the viewfinder. Dropping the camera, he swapped if for the field glasses and swore loudly.

'Fucking hell, it's Broggetti. Wonder who those other bastards are?'

The memories of his dealings with Broggetti came flooding back, the arrest, vanishing witnesses, and his wife's death, followed by him giving the gangster the beating of his life. He was almost lost in grief at the memory when he saw that one of the dogs had seen him and was alerting the others. He pulled back into the scrub and walked swiftly to where Julie was waiting, the motor still running.

'Go, I have seen enough,' he ordered brusquely, the tone upsetting her. She put the vehicle in gear and headed to where the ugly grey roof of the mine zinc treatment plant blemished the beauty of the land.

'What's wrong?' she asked. 'Did someone see you?'

'Only the dogs. But I saw Tony Broggetti, the Australian Mafia Godfather. I know he ordered the murder of my wife, but I was never able to prove it. Her friend was a star witness, who saw a shooting that Broggetti was involved with. Both she and Jan were killed in a car bombing. Fuck, this time I'm going to get that bastard and fry him.'

At home, Bill talked for a long time to Commissioner Farrell, informing him what was happening in town.

'According to the locals, every time the Gulf Rebel bikers come to town, Wog and Bull turn up within a day for clandestine meetings, but when I saw Broggetti at the meeting this whole thing fell into place. This group is the core of every big shipment of drugs, guns, and Asian prostitution smuggled into this country. I now know how it is done, but we must catch them in the act, and I reckon that the time is close, very close.'

'You're right Bill. The Feds have reports of a ship that, Customs suspect is running the goods, left Sulawesi some days ago. They expect it to arrive in our waters soon. Both the navy and customs say that they are short on ships as the waters around the Wessell Islands and in the Torres Strait are suddenly under siege by Indonesian poachers and the politicians are screaming for action. I was going to call you later tonight on the matter, but this whole puzzle is coming together from what you tell me. The army has been keeping the Mitchell River base under observation. They report that little actual fishing is taking place.'

'I need to get to the Mitchell River, Boss. One of the local netters is leaving within a day. I reckon that he might tow my boat up and from there I can move about the area. I know a bloke that might guide me about the delta, Vic Hawkins. If I want backup he will give it to me, besides I also want to work with the army, providing they are not tied down with red tape when it comes to their version of "Rules of Engagement" with civilians.'

'Not too sure about having Hawkins along, Bill. After all he is a civilian and if he gets into another shootout, we might have some explaining to do.'

'He is also a Justice of the Peace, Steve, and as such does have certain legal rights and protection when assisting police in their duties when called upon. He is the only guide I can trust.'

194

'You're right, Bill. But is he available?'

'Not sure but I will contact him when I get off the phone. I'll get back to you later. I also need to see if the Gregorys will tow my boat up north first.'

'Righto, call me later, Bill.'

Bill called the Gregorys, and they said that they were more than happy to tow the boat up and back and to carry his fuel and supplies. They planned to leave as soon as they unloaded, refuelled, and stocked up with new supplies the next day.

'Mate, the barra are running and the sooner we get out there, the better our change of another big catch,' George enthusiastically said. 'We will cruise all night and should arrive on Tuesday noon with luck.'

'No worries, George, by the way do you know what old Hawkins is doing these days. I would like to catch up and fish with him if possible. They reckon that he sees you at least once a year somewhere on the Coleman River.'

'As far as I know he might even be there. The track opened last week. Old prick never tells me anything, him and Jim just appear on the river as if they like to surprise us.'

'Thanks mate, I'll see you at the Coop tomorrow morning to unload. I must get the boat and gear ready and in the water. Bye.'

Bill rang Hawkins next. He sounded delighted to hear from him again.

'Lucky to catch me, mate,' informed Hawkins. 'Jim and I are loading up and leaving for the Coleman at first light tomorrow. Whoever wakes up first for the morning's piss lets the other know. It's usually me, weak bladder I reckon. Regular as clockwork at four am. What are you up to?'

'Well mate, I'm also leaving for the Coleman. The Gregorys have offered to tow my boat up and back, so I'll meet you there. Mind if I camp with you guys, there is not a great deal of privacy on the Catfish.'

'No worries, mate. You're most welcome. Can you toss in a couple of cartons of beer and a couple of bottles of Bundy rum in the boat?

We'll bring the coke and ice. We can't bring alcohol onto Aboriginal land and the cops often check us. Its legal to have it on the water, though and they never come down to the camp at night.'

'Fuck Vic, you're asking me to break the law,' Bill groaned. 'but I'll see what I can do.'

Julie backed the Landcruiser down the ramp and the trailer into the river. Bill pushed the boat off the trailer and tied it up alongside some dinghies. He kissed Julie goodbye and told her that he would be in touch in the evening and for her not to worry. He knew that she was not convinced. She was concerned, and he understood she had reason to be.

As she drove away, Wog, the Eurasian and two young girls arrived in a Toyota trayback loaded with supplies. They waved to Bill, and he gave them a hand to unload the supplies in their tender. It was bigger than Bill's fishing boat. Wog introduced him to the girls. They were German back packers. Both were blonde and nice looking. One thing about the Wog he loved all the good things in life, including women, thought Bill. But he hardly noticed the German girls as the presence of the Eurasian ruled them out. Her expensive perfume scent hung into the air, and he was most conscious of her presence. She smelled good, mused Bill, like a bitch on heat.

'Ah, the Coleman, it is a great sport fishing river,' Wog remarked. 'You will be close to where I fish in the Mitchell. Why don't you join us for dinner on my boat one night and enjoy some fine wine? Do you have a sat phone? Call me first, please, but not for a week or so as I will be very busy until then.'

He handed Bill a business card with his sat phone number on it. Bill thanked him and backed his boat into the river. The big outboard purred like a kitten, but it was like a racehorse erupting from a barrier gate as it leapt onto the plane when he pushed the throttle lever down. He ran up the river past the old boat wreck at full throttle before turning about and heading to Catfish, happy with the boat's performance.

Catfish sailed out of the river at three pm on an incoming tide. After clearing the channel, she turned north into a light southeast wind, keeping well offshore to avoid the shallow shoals. They cruised into the Coleman on a changing tide late the next day. The Catfish dropped anchor some distance up the river in a deep pool wide enough to allow the boat to swing with the tide and the wind. George drew him a mud map to guide him up the river to the designated camping area used by visiting recreational anglers.

'This is Hawkins' favourite spot,' he pointed on the map. 'I don't expect they will be there yet. It's a slow trip to Pormpuraaw after the Wet because of washouts and bad roads. They will be looking forward to a cold beer by the time they get here. But don't get caught by the cops. There is a grog ban in place at the community and they are trying to stop the smuggling of booze on our land. As for me, I saw nothing.'

Bill bid farewell and headed up the river. He found the camping area easily where George said Hawkins and King normally camped. It took him a while to carry his gear up the muddy bank and to set his camp up. He gathered a pile of driftwood for a fire and stacked it near a bare spot that indicated a well-used fireplace, but the wet season floods had cleared it. Darkness fell and with it came the mosquitoes and sand flies, biting nuisances that could drive a man mad. But a liberal dose of Bushman insect repellent kept them at bay.

He cooked a big steak and fried potatoes on the open fire and had a couple of beers, enjoying being alone in the silent bush that surrounded him. Once he thought he heard an outboard motor, its sound carried on the wind.

'Must be George, setting his nets,' he mused. 'I should have stayed on the boat for the night and helped out.'

The night was cool, and he moved closer to the fire, pushing a couple of extra sticks into the coals for extra heat. He smelled something like a dead fish and sensed the presence of some one behind him. He quickly turned around. Something struck him on his head, and he slumped sideways, unconscious.

'Hope you didn't kill him with that rifle butt, Slime' Animal said as he stepped out of the shadows. 'Wog said that he was to be delivered in one piece.'

'Fuck him. I should take him to Bull, so that he can feed him to his crocodile in little pieces. He hurt Bull badly, the bastard and he killed Baldy.'

'Well, that might just happen when Wog is finished with him, so don't fret, mate.'

Animal always marvelled at the way that Slime moved in the bush. They had come up the river and walked along the bank for over a kilometre, guided by the glow of the campfire and the light. Bill was sitting silhouetted against the glow of the fire on a log, his back towards them. Slime cautioned Animal to stay and slowly stalked the figure at the fire. Animal saw it all in full silhouette, the stalk, and the slamming down of Slime's rifle butt on Madsen's head.

Slime would probably have killed him had it not been for Animal's intervention. Animal knew that Slime was mad, and apart from his mother and Bull, he was the only other person that could do anything with him, though Animal knew that no matter what, Slime was like a trapped taipan and just as unpredictable.

'Okay, you go back and get the dinghy, while I tie the bastard up,' Animal ordered. Slime vanished into the darkness as silently as he had come out of it. It made Animal shiver. He secured Bill's wrists and feet with rope before checking the head wound. Bill's face was covered in blood that oozed out of a deep cut on the side of his head. But he was breathing, and his heart was beating normally noted Animal as he checked the pulse. He could not understand why Wog wanted him unharmed or even wanted him at all, but orders were orders and he hoped that Slime had not gone too far. Wog was a dangerous and volatile man when his orders were ignored.

The sound of the dinghy traveling at high speed disturbed his thoughts. He tossed more sticks on the fire. The flames flared high into the sky and in the glow, he saw the dinghy with Slime at the tiller pushing the bow onto the muddy bank. Slime jumped out and dragged Bill by his legs down the bank and dumped him in the dinghy.

'Okay, wipe out our tracks and let's get out of here,' Animal urged. 'Don't touch or steal anything. Remember, Wog said it has got to look as if a croc got him.'

They busied themselves with branches and erased their tracks. Suddenly Slime paused and held up his hand.

'Listen, that is a Toyota V8 coming this way, no mistaking that sound,' he almost whispered. As if in answer, a set of powerful spotlights lit up the tidal flats to the north.

'Fuck, he was waiting for someone. Let's get the hell out of here. We have done enough,' Animal snapped urgently.

They slid down the riverbank, hurriedly wiping it clean before boarding the big dinghy. Slime pushed the starter button and the 60 hp Yamaha stuttered into life. He backed the dinghy into the river, its bow leaving a deep unnoticed furrow in the mud. Slime opened the throttle and the nose of the dinghy rose high before it began to plane. In seconds, it vanished into the darkness of the night.

Chapter 20
TRACKS

'Fuck, I'm glad that we made it, Vic,' King groaned. 'Shit of a drive on that washed-out road, especially the last few miles. Looks as if Bill is waiting and has a fire going. Cup of tea and a hot meal will be nice.'

'How about a cold beer instead?' Hawkins asked. 'I asked him to bring a couple of cartons of 4X Gold and two bottles of Bundy rum.'

'Mate, you're fucking unreal, asking a cop to bring booze into a DOGIT grog free zone. You reckon he will?'

'I think so. I could tell he wanted something that is why I put the hard word on him. It will save us bumming George for a drink.'

The powerful driving lights lit up the camp and swept over the fireplace and the small tent beyond it.

'Funny I wonder where he is,' King muttered. 'Maybe he is hiding in the bushes to scare the shit out of us.'

He stopped the Landcruiser, switched off the engine and pulled the hand brake on. The men alighted from the cabin and called loudly, but the night was silent. Hawkins grabbed a LED torch from the vehicle; its powerful beam searched the shadows for life. There was none. He walked to the riverbank where Bill's anchored boat floated silently. Hawkins came back, looking worried.

'I don't know mate, but there is something funny about this. He hasn't been away too long otherwise the fire would have died down.

There are no tracks, even about the fire. More importantly, there is a furrow from a boat bow in the mud below the camp, but again no tracks. Funny that, it looks as if someone went to great lengths to rid the area of footprints. Hell, I am going to call George on the sat phone and see if he is with him.'

George told him that Bill had departed that afternoon to set up camp on the river in anticipation of their arrival.

'No croc sign about?'

'No mate, excepting marks in the mud that indicate that another boat was here not so long ago. Looks like a flat nosed punt, or a net dinghy.'

'Yeah, that could be right. I heard one pass by during the night over the noise of the generator. I thought it might have been someone checking nets. We will come over for a run and help you look about. Give me a chance to check my nets on the way back. See you soon.'

Some fifteen minutes later the lights of the dinghy and a powerful spotlight sweeping the riverbanks heralded the Gregory's arrival. In the meantime, King had found tracks in the timber that indicated that at least two men had been there. George confirmed it after tracking the footsteps along the river to where a dinghy had been moored. When he came back, he said that two men had walked to Bill's camp, but only one had walked back.

'Probably to bring the dinghy up to here, 'ey,' he said. 'Funny thing, if I didn't know any better, I reckon someone kidnapped Bill. Fucked if I know why though?'

Hawkins told the Gregory's who Bill was and what he was doing. He also urged them to keep it to themselves as people's lives depended on it.

'That makes sense, 'ey' George mused. 'I reckon Wog has him on his boat, providing he is still alive. He left before us while we were loading. He knew that Bill was coming with us. Bill told us that they were talking at the ramp, 'ey. But why not kill him here?'

'Probably after information to find out how much he knows,' King replied. 'Bill is a tough bastard, and he won't talk. They will have to torture him, but he might still be alive.'

It was almost nine pm when Hawkins rang Commissioner Farrell's emergency number on Bill's sat phone. The gruff voice on the other end indicated that he was not happy about the late call.

'This is Farrell and it better be good.'

'Mister Farrell, this is Vic Hawkins. Sorry about this late call, but Bill Madsen has vanished. We arranged a meeting on the Coleman River earlier tonight, but when Jim King and I arrived, he was not here. His camp was set up and a campfire was burning brightly. I called George Gregory, he and his wife own the Catfish, a local barra boat. We have found tracks that indicated that two men were here, but they went to a lot of effort to hide their tracks and Bill's.'

'Oh shit, I hear what you say. I know that Bill told you some of the things that are going on and he was there to investigate and report on any illegal activities. He wanted you as a guide for the delta. Anything you can do? I can get assistance to you if you need it.'

'Not sure, I'd say that somehow his cover has been blown, but they want to know what he knows, otherwise they would have killed him on the spot, I reckon. What sort of assistance are you offering, those army boys that are hiding out hereabouts?'

'How did you know about that?' Farrell asked sounding surprised. 'Only a few select people know that they are there.'

'Oh, the locals have known about it since they first arrived last year, Mister Farrell. Even the army leaves tracks and believe me there is nothing you can hide in black feller country if you leave footprints. They have been under observation by the traditional owners since the day they arrived.'

'Look, I'll talk to someone about the army helping. Do you know your exact position?'

'I do, we are on the public camping area on the Coleman River. Hang on a second and I'll get Jim to give you an exact GPS position.'

King gave the position to Hawkins. Farrell asked them to be on standby, before ending the call. As they waited for the call, they set up their camp, cooked a meal, and ate it in silence. The Gregorys left after having a cup of tea and said they would be in touch in the morning to help with the search. The sat phone buzzed. It was Farrell.

'Vic, an army patrol should be with you soon. It appears they are camped nearby. Please give them any help they want. I am not sure what their intentions are or how they can assist. However, they know the danger of the mission and perhaps you will be kind enough to fill them in. Call me back if you have problems. Police are on their way from Pormpuraaw, and a Special Response team will be in the air at daylight from Cairns. Good night and good luck.'

They came out of the darkness, a group of seven well-armed men, dressed in camouflage, but unlike Slime's stealthy approach King had the beam of the LED torch on them when they were still eighty metres away.

'Good evening, men,' Hawkins greeted the men. 'I am Vic Hawkins, and this is Major Jim King, retired.'

'Hello, I am Lieutenant Tom Creole. These are my men. I believe you know who we are.'

'Yes, we do,' Hawkins replied. 'We need your help to rescue an undercover police officer who we believe was abducted from here and taken away to a boat somewhere in the delta or to Bull Antinus' bunker. I know where it is, and I believe you people do also.'

'Yes, we do, but the bunker is army property, not Mister Antinus'. We wanted to kick him out but were told not to.'

'Well, that is water under the bridge, but our priority is to rescue Madsen. I will launch my boat and take it, and I need a good man who can think for himself instead of acting on orders if you have one. My boat is fitted with an electric motor and that will give us stealth. If anyone hears an outboard coming down the river, they will kill Madsen for sure, cut his guts out and drop him in the river.'

Hawkins strapped his heavy .357 Magnum Ruger revolver on, the belt full of cartridges, and loaded his .270 WM Weatherby rifle, before pushing it into a soft case along with spare rounds. King was also putting his rifle in Bill's boat.

'I'm sorry, Vic, but I can't allow you to be armed. We will do the shooting if we have to,' Creole protested.

'Mate, if you want me to drive this boat and take you where Madsen is, you take us as we are, or we do it alone. My plan is to sneak up alongside Wog's boat, or wherever they have Bill, without being seen. We rescue Bill if he is there and get out. If there is any shooting to be done, believe me our guns will blow bigger holes in a man than those puny little calibres you blokes use.'

'Okay, it's your call, though I am not happy about it. But what about the rest of us?'

'Right, you follow in the big boat but give us about twenty minutes start. Jim will drive it and wait at the junction. Don't go any further. If you get a signal from your man, you come in fast because it means we need help, big time. Who is coming with me?'

'Stuart, you go. In case there is any shooting, silence your 9 mm UMP submachine gun and don't miss. If needed take orders from Vic here, but don't forget, civilians are involved, and we must abide by the "Rules of Engagement". Now go.'

The dinghy powered by a 50 hp outboard vanished into the dark of the night. Minutes later Bill's big Evinrude stuttered into life and loaded with the soldiers, headed downstream before turning into the Mitchell River side arm. Stars twinkled overhead as the men caught a little sleep as best as they could in the cramped confines of the moving boat. It was a long night and when the sat phone suddenly buzzed, all were instantly alert. It was 2.30 am.

'Get over here fast, we need help.'

Stuart was impressed how the older man handled the dinghy as it glided over the dark river, guided only by the lights from twinkling stars. The outboard engine purred like a kitten, its sound constant. They passed the Catfish riding at anchor but did not stop.

'We'll use the electric motor when we get to the junction,' Hawkins said. 'it and the tide will carry us silently to Bull's barge, or Wog's boat if it is there. With luck they will all be sleeping. I have full GPS bearings of the river delta, so hopefully we will not run aground, but you never know after a big flood.'

He suddenly turned the boat sharply to the left and the soldier saw the reflections of a wide stream that turned directly south. Dark brooding banks loomed alongside it. Sometime later they turned west into another channel and ran for a few kilometres before Hawkins slowed down and turned the motor off. He tilted it out of the water and dropped the electric motor down that was mounted on the front of the boat.

'Swap you seats, Stuart. I need to be up the front to control this thing. Lucky, we have a good current to help us. We should be in sight of the barge in a few minutes. Talk all you like. But don't raise your voice.'

The soldier was excited, the adrenalin had kicked in. Stuart thought back to silent night patrols in enemy territory in Iraq and Afghanistan, but for some reason this one felt more dangerous than the others.

'You know Vic, there is something about this place that gives me the creeps. I have fought wars with Islamic terrorists and the Taliban on their home grounds, served in Timor and New Caledonia, but nothing seemed as dangerous as being on this fucking silent croc infested river in the middle of the blackest night I have seen in donkey's years.'

'You are so right mate, but you get used to it. These rivers are dangerous at night believe me. I for one do not want to be here and rarely fish at night in a small boat like this. You need a big tinny like the one back at the camp. The rivers are full of sharks, gropers, and the world's largest crocodiles. Hello, there is a glow ahead. We must be nearing the barge. Is that gun of yours ready? Don't fire it behind me. My ears don't like gunshots.'

'Don't worry about the concussion Vic, I'm putting the suppressor on, call it a silencer if you like. Only small popping sounds come out when it is fired. You won't hear a thing.'

'Well, you'll hear the Weatherby if I have to touch one off, believe me. My revolver has a big blast also, but I have no intention of using my guns unless I have too.'

'Yes, hell of a thing shooting a man, but when your life is at stake, it does not feel that bad. Have you even shot anyone Vic?'

'Unfortunately, I have, Stuart, though not in a war. I had to defend myself against some of Bull's mates a couple of years back in the Staaten River. Some people were killed in the gun fight. Lucky for me the coroner said it was self-defence, so you can understand why I like you to do the dirty work if we have to.'

'Shit, I remember that shooting. Lot of talk about it in the army because one of our sea patrols was involved looking for the vessel. So, you're the man. You know Vic that sets me at ease because now I know if I need back up, I will have it. I thought you were an undercover cop when I got orders to work with you.'

The light was annoying Bill. It was bright, but it appeared distant. His head was splitting with pain, and he felt dizzy. He tried to lift his hand to rub the pain away but could not as it was restrained by something. Apart from the blurred light, he was unable to see anything. He tried to shake the annoying light away, but it only increased the pain in his head.

'Stop it, don't move,' came a voice he dimly recognized as Wog's mistress, the beautiful Suzie. 'Hold still and I'll clean you up. There is blood all over you, especially your head.'

She washed the matted hair that covered the wound, wiping away the dried blood with a soft damp cloth. He could hear her rinsing it out between wiping him. She slowly worked away, cleaning the wound. It hurt like hell, and he let her know it. However, she persisted, gently but firmly cleaning the wound before washing the blood from his eyes. At last, the dimness faded, and he could see that he was on the deck of a boat, Wog's boat. The discovery rocked him, and he suddenly remembered the fishy smell that Slime carried with him before the blow on his head had dumped him into nothingness.

He attempted to stand up, but she pushed him down. He found that he was sitting on a deck chair and that his wrists and his feet were secured with cable ties on the chair. The Eurasian stood in front of him, holding the wet cloth.

'Don't move about, I'll cut your shirt away. It's covered with blood.'

'What the fuck am I doing here,' Bill demanded, his voice hoarse.

'You are a guest on Wog's boat. Though I am not sure why he brought you here in this manner or why we must keep you like this until he gets back.'

Loud laughter came from inside the boat. It startled Bill.

'Don't worry about them, it's Animal and Slime. They brought you in like this. Now sit still while I cut your shirt away.'

She used a fishing knife to cut away his blood-soaked shirt and bathed him down with cool water. It brought him back to reality. It felt good and he asked her for a drink of water. She walked into the well-lit boat and returned with a bottle of cold water. She held it to his lips. He drank most of it before she pulled the bottle away.

'Okay that is enough, otherwise you'll end up being sick,' she admonished him. 'Now let me dress your wound properly. Do you remember what happened?'

'No, all I noticed was a rotten fish smell and a second later the sky fell in.'

'No doubt Slime's rifle butt. He always has it with him. Wog will be angry with them because they were told not to harm you.'

'Why the hell am I here?'

'Because Mr Broggetti wishes to meet you. He asked Wog to bring you here as he has a surprise for you. It all came about when Mr Broggetti asked one of the bikers you bashed who had done it. Wog told me that

Mr Broggetti got very excited when he found that the description of you could be his long-lost friend.'

'Friend my arse, more like he wants to feed me piece by piece to the local groper population.'

Bill noted that she was working with a well-stocked first aid chest, and in an expert fashion that indicated it was not the first time she had treated wounds. She applied some ointment to the wound before wrapping a gauze bandage about his head. He felt much better and asked for another drink. He drank greedily, the water clearing his head. He also noted that his smell had returned and that her powerful perfume was almost overbearing. She stood before him; her lithe body wrapped in a colourful sarong with dragons embossed on it. She wiped the water that had dripped of his chin and his chest away with the damp cloth, taking longer than she should, thought Bill.

'Oh, you have a beautiful hard body,' she whispered. 'I love men with muscles and lean bodies.'

She rubbed his chest with her hands, spending time on his stomach muscles before she dipped her hand inside his shorts and felt for his penis. Sore as he was, Bill could not help himself and he was already hard when she touched it. Bill knew that he was being raped by an expert, but somehow, he did not care, he wanted her as he had never wanted a woman before. He felt guilty when for a moment Julie's vision came to him, but it was just as quickly swept aside by an unbridled lust.

'My, you are huge. You could be a porn star with a cock like that,' Suzie complimented him as she opened his fly and pulled his rock-hard penis from it.

She slipped down on her knees, her tongue licking it expertly before she took it in her mouth. Bill groaned with desire at her expert touch. Suddenly she stood up and slipped the sarong from her body. She stood in front of him, her body like a swaying ivory statue, naked and hairless, like the day she was born. Bill feasted his eyes on her in the dim lights and groaned in frustration as he struggled against his bonds. She walked away before coming back to him with something from the first aid kit. She tore at it with her mouth before coming over to him and slipping a condom over his penis.

'I don't want to get pregnant,' she explained.

Her body was hard and muscled like a dancer, and she felt cool against his almost feverish arousal when she straddled him and moved over his rock-hard penis before guiding it into the dampness between her legs, moaning with pleasure. Slowly she worked herself on it before she pushed herself up and down with her legs, matching Bill's thrusting in almost hydraulic movements. She slipped under his arms and wrapped hers about his neck; her fingernails digging deep into his flesh. Her mouth met his. Their tongues entwined, and both were lost in a world of their own as their orgasms erupted in a primitive release of lust and passion. She rested her head on his chest, her body felt cool, his penis still inside her as she was in no hurry to move.

'My God, that was the best fuck I have ever had,' she moaned. 'I should keep you for myself instead of giving you up.'

'Cut me free and we will get away,' Bill urged.

'No, I can't do that. Wog will kill me.'

Animal and Slime were happy. Slime loved being on Wog's boat. Especially the comfortable leather chairs in the stateroom, which held a gun cabinet and a small library. He had never learned to read but he loved looking at the pictures of faraway places in the coffee table books. Wog never let him in the room when he was home, and he was only allowed on the deck. Slime did not know why and hated Wog because of it. But Animal was his drinking mate and an all-round good bloke as far as Slime was concerned.

They were drinking rum and coke and smoking a joint. Slime loved that. The bottle was empty when Animal decided that he had enough and slumped down on the sofa, snoring loudly. Slime tried to wake him, but Animal did not response. He opened another bottle and greedily drank the raw liquid, the rum spilling down his mouth.

Slime got up, the bottle in his hand. He took another long sip and walked unsteadily to the door, noting that the deck lights were off. He slowly opened the door and saw the Eurasian astride on Bill's lap in the dim light from the cabin door. Slime paused, his mind trying to work out what was happening. He had women before because Bull would sometime let him fuck one of the back packers they brought back from Karumba, but they were always tied up, screamed and fought him. This was different, Suzie was fucking Madsen as if she was possessed. Seeing a woman make love to a man was new to him and he wanted the same experience.

Slime stood there watching, his lust growing. He rubbed himself and knew that he was ready. He switched the light on and stepped out of the doorway onto the flood lit deck.

'Okay, now it is my turn,' he blurted in a slurred drunken voice.

'Fuck you Slime, get the fuck out of here,' the Eurasian screamed as she slipped off Bill's lap and faced the madman who stood there holding his hard penis in his hand.

'No, I want you to do what you did to him,' Slime yelled, suddenly very angry with her.

He approached her, but she struck out at him, hitting him hard along his face, the impact sitting him down on the deck.

'Cut me loose Suzie, he will kill you if you don't,' Bill cried.

She grabbed the knife she used to cut his shirt away and cut away at the ankle ties. They fell away and Bill stood up.

'My hands, Suzie cut the cables from my hands.'

But before she could, Slime hit her on the side of her head with the rum bottle, the impact scattering glass all over the deck.

'You damn bitch, I will kill you,' he screamed, his yellow tinted eyes blazing with madness.

He dropped between her legs, forcing them wide and fell on top of her, but suddenly discovered that his erection had gone down. He pulled on it and tried to raise it, but it would not, the moment had gone. It did not occur to him that she was unconscious from the cruel blow he had dealt her.

'Fuck you, fuck you,' he shouted, frothing at the mouth and shaking her roughly. 'You bloody bitch.'

He grabbed a length of rope from the rail and tied it around the ankles of the unconscious woman. Next, he tied the other end of the rope onto the hook of the crane jib used to lift heavy loads onto the rear deck and dinghy onto the upper deck. Bill saw what he was doing and cried out to him to stop.

'Fuck you, you're fucking next. Charley be here soon. He'll know what do.'

He got a fish frame from the deck freezer and began to slap it on the side of the boat.

'Charley, here Charley,' he crooned like a farmer offering his pet hens a handful of grain. Slime tried to work the crane before realizing that the motor needed to be running. He hurried to the top deck and turned the key on the port side engine. It roared into life, washing the deck with black choking fumes.

'Now I'll fucking teach you, you bitch,' Slime muttered when he appeared back on the deck and pulled on the crane controls, jerked the woman up from the floor. Bill screamed at him to stop, but he took no notice as he lifted the now conscious naked woman over the rail with the crane jib and hung her low over the dark water. Suzie screamed in fear and pain as her head went under water for a few seconds before she was heaved up high again.

'Here Charley, here boy, tucker time boy, come and get it,' Slime crooned. 'Come boy, come for tucker boy.'

Bill became aware of something big in the murky water alongside him. He looked hard and screamed in fear and terror at Slime to get the girl back on the deck as he saw the shape of the living nightmare of the tropics, a huge crocodile at least six metres in length. He suddenly knew why Broggetti wanted him in one piece. Slime worked the crane control letting the now conscious Suzie drop down to the water before jerking her up when the croc neared her.

'Fuck me like you fucked him,' he cried his eyes wet with tears. 'Fuck me like you did him and I will let you go.'

She screamed and tried to pull herself up as Bill struggled with his bonds.

In the cabin Animal stirred from his brief slumber, the vibration and noise of the motor making him sit up.

'What the fuck,' he said to himself as the screams from the deck rose over the engine noise. 'Oh shit, Slime's gone fucking mad again.'

He got up and stumbled unsteadily to the door. He stood there for a moment, his mind trying to comprehend the scene of the woman hanging high above the water from the crane jib and Slime and Bill screaming. In fact, everyone was screaming and yelling he thought. For a moment, he enjoyed it before his mind suddenly snapped to reality.

'Stop it Slime that is Wog's women. He'll fucking kill us both, stop it,' he cried in alarm as he rushed to the crying madman. Slime saw him coming and backhanded him onto the deck.

'Fuck you Animal, she got to fuck me first, or Charley gets her.'

'Come one Slime get away from those controls, now. Please mate, lift her back on deck, please.'

He slowly walked over to Slime when he suddenly noticed a darting red dot flitting about. A split second later came a thud and Slime groaned, let the controls go and clutched his chest, blood flowing out between his fingers. Animal leapt towards him as the red dot targeted him, and again the thud sounded. He gave a horrible cry and clutched at the deck wall before sliding down it, leaving a streak of blood on it.

Suzie was still screaming in terror when Hawkins grabbed her and held her up while Stuart cut the rope. She fell on top of Hawkins as Stuart grabbed the rails and pulled the boat against the cruiser, keeping a wary eye on the watching crocodile that surfaced only metres away. It had grudgingly given way to the boat, feeling the vibrations of the electric motor as it closed in. Stuart leaped over the railing and secured the dinghy to the rails. Hawkins passed the naked woman to him. He climbed over the rail and looked at Bill accusingly.

'Looks like you were having a lot of fun, Bill,' he said as he cut away the ropes with his hunting knife. 'Why is your cock hanging out of your pants, need a piss, mate?'

'Fuck mate, my hands were tied, but trust you to bring the bloody Australian Army,' Bill replied rubbing his bloodied and numbed wrists before zipping up his fly. 'Close mate, fucking close. You're the best sight I have ever seen. How is the girl?'

'In shock, mate,' Stuart answered. 'But she is young and will get over it. Is there anyone else on board?'

'No, that is about it as far as I know,' Bill responded. 'We better get her inside and have a look at her head. Slime broke a bottle on it.'

He held the door open, as Stuart entered the stateroom carrying the moaning Suzie. He laid the woman on the sofa while Bill covered her with the sarong she had tossed onto the deck table.

'Shame to do that,' Stuart remarked. 'best body I have seen for a long time. By the way I'm Stuart. You must be Bill Madsen.'

They shook hands as Hawkins came in with the first aid kit.

'Cleared the deck,' he announced. 'That croc won't go hungry tonight.'

'Vic, we need those bodies for evidence,' Bill blurted in surprise.

'Evidence, bodies, what the fuck are you talking about?' Hawkins exclaimed. 'No bodies here, they jumped over the side. After all we don't want young Stuart getting into trouble over that "Rules of Engagement" crap, do we?'

'I suppose so, besides Charley needs a feed. He sure looked hungry.'

'So that was the infamous Charley. Bull keeps him around. Charley is a legend in these parts, all the twenty odd feet of him. When they are cleaning fish on Bull's boat, they feed it the barra frames. It lies on the back of the transom board, and they toss fish frames into his jaws until he has had his fill. But why where those arseholes feeding Wog's lady to Charley?'

'Long story Vic, but there is lot's happening and I need to call the Commissioner now. Do you have a sat phone?'

'Yes, it's in the boat. But use the ship's phone. Wog won't mind paying for the call. By the way Stuart did you call your mob?'

'I did. They are on the way.'

'Well tell them to come in as silent as possible. There might be people on the barge and in the bunker.'

'Oh, there is no one on the barge, or they would have been over. There was a lot of yelling and screaming when Suzie was hanging over the water.'

'Yes, we know. We could hear it as we came in. I thought that you were being tortured like they did to that poor bastard Sheppard.'

'I was, but in a nice way, blokes,' Bill replied.

Chapter 21
AMBUSH

Hawkins gently bathed Suzie's head and wiped the blood away from her face. She stirred and moaned before attempting to sit up, but he pushed her tenderly back on the sofa. 'You are lucky, my girl, that he caught you with a glancing blow only. Hell of a bump, but it is only a small cut. Bloody waste of good rum though, I reckon.'

Bill came in and looked at her, thinking back about the passionate moments they had shared before Slime's interruption.

'Suzie, can you tell me where Wog and Bull are? It is important for me to know,' he said.

'I can't Bill, they will kill me,' she uttered, a look of fear on her face.

'Suzie, I am a senior investigating officer in the Queensland Police Service, and we have been investigating their activities for a long time. I can offer you witness protection, and have you protected 24/7 providing you tell me what you know and later give evidence on behalf of the Crown.'

'I did not know that you are a police officer, Bill. So that is why Don wanted you. But what will happen to me when it is over? Will they send me back to Malaysia? You see Bill I am a slave and was sold to Wog. It is what happens to girls like me, but when we get older, and when our use by date ends, we are sold off. If I go back my former boss will find me and sell me again to the highest bidder.'

'Hell, I thought that the slave days were dead,' Bill replied. 'Tell you what, I will get a good lawyer for you who will fight on your behalf to convince the Australian Government to allow you to stay as sending you back will be harmful to your welfare. Helping us will really help you also. But I do need you to tell me what Wog is up to and what his plans are.'

'Bill, the sex slave trade is very much alive. Wog has been kidnapping girls from all over the place. They are mostly backpackers and they never come back when he goes for a trip. Tonight, there were four girls, the German girls you met at the wharf, and another two that were kept in Bull's bunker for a long time.'

'Yes, we expected as much, Suzie, but where are they now?'

'Gone to meet an Asian boat that is carrying heroin, drugs, guns, and more sex slaves from Southeast Asia. There are also supposed to be some men coming from the Middle East also I think, but I don't know who they are, except that Wog is getting a lot of money from them. It is all on Wog's computer over there. He is very good with it and has all the details of his work on it. It has everything, what is received and paid for, where it goes, and who gets it.'

'Suzie, you are a doll. It is just what we need. Look after her Vic. I'll have a look at the computer and make a call to the boss. Do you have the security code for it?'

'Yes, it's WOG with capitals.'

'Shit, that's original. I would never have thought of it.'

The computer had more details of transactions that Bill could ever hope for. He noticed that Wog also had an external drive for backup for the files. The system was also connected to the satellite network, and it was a simple matter of emailing the files to Farrell. He left it running and walked out on deck. Stuart was hanging up the deck hose after having washed the deck clear of glass, rum, and blood. Bill called Farrell from the bridge on the ship sat phone.

'Thank Christ you're okay, Bill,' he blurted. 'What happened?'

'I will tell you later Steve, but things are happening fast. Wog and Bull's boats, and two others sailed out last night to meet a ship somewhere in the Gulf; no doubt it is close to shore as these barra boats are not seagoing vessels.'

'Yes, we know about the boat. The Navy is preparing to board it as soon as it turns back into the Gulf proper. We have a team flying in from Cairns at daylight to apprehend Wog if possible and that is where you come in.'

'Fuck, call the Navy off Steve. There are four kidnapped girls on board the vessel. Wog kidnaps them for the Asian sex trade, as there is a big demand for blonde, white women in Asia. If the navy closes in, they will be killed and tossed overboard.'

'Shit, I didn't know that. I will inform the Feds right away and let them decide. They are overall in charge of the operation. We might have to let the girls go and get the Indonesian authorities to rescue them at the other end.'

'Can we trust them to do that?'

'Yes, they have been extremely helpful and are working with both Interpol and the Feds on this case. They feel that this smuggling operation is a smack in their face. Probably because they are not getting a cut. Besides, they will shoot the bastards involved, while our weak gutted judiciary will give them a slap across the knuckles and have them back on the street within five years. Fucking frustrating believe me. But where are you now?'

'I'm on Wog's boat. Apparently, he does not use it for his smuggling operation. His sex slave, Suzie told me that all records of his dealings are on his computer. It's being downloaded now onto yours as an extra precaution. I will look after it and make sure we use it against him and Broggetti. Like most crooks, Wog is arrogant enough to believe that the police won't raid him. We expect him to return sometime early in the morning on the high tide. Suzie says that two planes generally land on the bush strip near the bunker and pick up what the boats bring in. They often do several trips to Blood Creek Station and back.'

'Bill, how many men do you have?'

'Currently there is only Hawkins, a soldier and me. There are six more soldiers on the way and Jim King. They should arrive any moment.'

'Okay, as far as I know two police officers from Pormpuraaw, and an Aboriginal police aid will leave by boat on the high tide. I can get two more to come down from Kowanyama, while the Cairns response team should be at Kowanyama at daylight. A Jet Ranger helicopter is waiting for them when they get there.'

'Okay, but tell them to hold back until I give the okay for them to come in. I am worried that too much activity might cause Wog to toss the loads overboard. Remember there are planes coming from Blood Creek Station also. It would be a good idea to raid it also, if you have the men on hand for it.'

'Yes, I am aware of that and will instruct the men. Good idea about raiding the station and will arrange the warrants ASAP. I will fly in with the Rapid Response team. Any idea what you intend to do?'

'Yes, I was brought here because Broggetti wants me. Suzie says he will be arriving on one of the planes. I plan to put the army boys ashore and a couple on the barge also. We will hide until the fishing boats tie up alongside it. I will stay with Hawkins and King on Wog's boat and let him bring Broggetti on board. Once that happens, we spring the trap.'

'Sounds good, how many men are you facing?'

'According to Suzie at least a dozen, not counting the plane crews and any passengers they may bring to help shift the gear. She also said that some Middle Eastern men may be on the boat, but she is unsure of their intentions.'

'They could be the people smugglers, or even terrorists. Be careful, they will be armed and highly trained in combat. Let the army boys sort them out. So, what makes you think that Wog will bring his boss onto the boat?'

'Suzie said that they never help with the unloading, and they always come back to his boat for breakfast and coffee while the work is being done.'

'Okay Bill, it is your call, but don't let civilians in the firing line if you can help it. Protect that computer and Suzie at all costs. Evidence like that comes along only once in lifetime.'

'Right boss I must go. King has arrived with the army. I will keep you in touch as this thing progresses.'

Bill had heard the boat as it docked. The men climbed out onto the deck, silent and grim as Stuart held it steady.

'Lieutenant, this is Bill Madsen. Bill, this is my team leader, Tom Creole.'

Bill shook hands with Creole, liking the strong grip of his handshake. He distrusted men with limb handgrips. Creole introduced him to the others. Like Creole, the handshakes were firm and strong. Bill saw that they were tough fighting men, battle hardened warriors who would give no quarter.

'Okay, let's get inside and plan this. It will be daylight soon and we must have a plan in place. Vic has the kettle on and is cooking breakfast for us all. G'day Jim, thanks for coming.'

King had tied the boat up and struggled over the gunnels and onto the transom. Bill held out his hand a steadied him.

'We will have to hide the boats,' Bill said. 'But we have a little time before daylight.'

The night had cooled a little, but it was warm in the, now overcrowded, cabin. He noted that Suzie was missing.

'I put her to bed,' Hawkins informed him as if reading his mind. 'She has a mild dose of concussion. It's a wonder that you don't have one. Apart from some abrasions she has no cuts, unlike you.'

'No brain, no pain,' Bill replied, touching the bandage around his head. 'but it is bloody sore.'

'You're still bleeding Bill. Here, come and sit down and I'll have a look at it. One thing about Wog he is totally organized, including having a Flying Doctor's first aid kit. I reckon that it might find its way on my boat later.'

'Fuck is there anything you can't do, Vic. First aid? Where did you learn that?'

'I used to work in mines years ago and first aid was everyone's job, Bill.'

Bill sat down at the dining table. Hawkins unwrapped the bandage and checked the wound.

'It's nice and clean and not too deep. It should heal okay, though it will leave you with a scar unless you want me to stitch it. Can do, but it will hurt like crap.'

'Do it Vic if it must be done. I can bear it.'

'I'll do it,' one of the soldiers offered. 'I'm the official paramedic on the team. Won't hurt at all this kit has plenty of stuff in it, including something for the pain. Vic, can you find me a razor? Shit, why would you want condoms in a first aid kit?'

The men laughed as he held a couple of packets up. Bill knew why but kept silent. He flinched as Cody inserted the needle. He shaved away the hair around the wound with a razor. Bill felt some slight tugging, before Cody dressed the wound and wrapped a bandage about his head.

'Done mate. All you need is to lie down and rest for a day or so and you'll be fine.'

Bill explained to the men what his plan was. Creole agreed that the plan appeared sound apart from a little fine turning. One of the men poured cups of coffee and they chatted as they enjoyed bacon, eggs, and buttered toast all cooked in the ship's well stocked galley.

'Okay, we need to get your team on the barge and under cover in the accommodation donga and on shore. Not sure, what is in the donga, because as far as I know Bull lives in the bunker with his mum and sister. They are probably used for staff quarters and storage. Jim will take you over in his boat with the electric motor. Be careful on the walkway that connects the barge to the shore as they have dogs at the bunker. I heard them barking earlier. Reckon you can handle that, Jim?'

'On the way, mate. The tide is slack and there is little current. Let's go men.'

Creole handed Bill a handheld radio for communication as the soldiers boarded the boat. It silently vanished into the darkness. King was back ten minutes later.

'There is no one on the barge, it's as silent as a morgue,' he reported. 'Though you can't hear it from here, there is a generator running at the bunker, probably why they didn't hear all that yelling. We better hide the boats into the mangroves because if Wog sees them, he will smell a rat. I'll use his dinghy to tow our boats into a little side arm downstream.'

Bill and Hawkins gave him a hand to rope the boats together and watched as King vanished into the darkness, the motor on Wog's dinghy at trolling speed. It was hardly audible. He sat on the dark deck with Hawkins, talking about the night's event. There was a glow in the east when King returned.

'Top spot,' he announced. 'there is a bend some distance inside the creek that hides the boats from the river. Unless someone flies over it or goes there, they won't be seen. You know boys I almost stayed there. The old mind is worried about self-preservation, especially number one – me.'

'Yeah, me and Bill were talking about doing the same,' Hawkins mused 'It's this fucking waiting game that gives me the shits. By the way, I checked up on Suzie, she is still sleeping. Will be for a while yet, I reckon, as I gave her a couple of knockout pills to make sure she rests. Might get some sleep myself, as I don't think much is going to happen. Who has first watch?'

'I'll do it,' King offered. 'Had a bit of a catnap doze in the boat when we were waiting upriver. You too Bill. I'll wake you quick smart if anything happens.'

Bill laid back on the lounge while Hawkins elected to use a bunk in one of the cabins. He called to Bill to have a look at one.

'Like a fucking cell,' he said. 'bars on the window and chains on the beds. What the fuck would Wog use this for?'

'For the backpacking girls that have been vanishing from Karumba and Cairns,' Bill replied. 'There are four on a ship heading for Indonesia right now, destination: the white slavery market, toys for rich Asian men.'

'You're fucking kidding me, is that right? That would explain the Staaten River fracas.'

'Yes, these are the type of people we are dealing with. They have no respect for human lives so don't spare the bullets if you have to shoot anyone.'

It was daylight when King woke Bill. He looked through the porthole where the barge was anchored silently along the open riverbank. Some three hundred metres inland he could see the outline of trees and the low hill where the bunker was. There was no sign of life, except wheeling flocks of corellas and brolgas dancing on the tidal flats. The tide was turning, and the boat was swinging about in the river with the current. The mangroves on the south bank were lightening up as the hues of pink and red of the rising sun filtered over the river and land. Hawkins came silently up behind him.

'Yes, this is a beautiful spot, the Mitchell River. It's too bad about the vermin though, they need exterminating. Suzie is up. I checked on her and she is looking much better. She is taking a shower. Hell, I'd give a King's ransom to spend the night with a body like hers. Christmas every night.'

'You silly old prick. You would be like a dog with a whale bone and wouldn't know where to start chewing,' King laughed loudly. 'Come and have a cup of tea instead. At least it won't kill you like a good fuck would.'

Suddenly the radio crackled and a few seconds later Wog's voice came over it.

'Suzie, are you there?'

'Quick, get Suzie,' Bill said urgently.

King knocked on the shower recess door. Suzie opened it, dripping wet. She gave him a good look at her body. His face went blood red and for a moment, he could not speak.

'Quick, it's the radio, Wog wants you,' he managed to croak.

She stepped out of the recess, and partly held a towel about her, before walking out in front of King, the firm cheeks of her shapely butt fully exposed and dripping with water droplets. Wog called again, but in a more urgent tone.

'Ask him what he wants, and above all sound normal,' Bill instructed her.

'Hello darling, welcome back,' she slurred in a soft voice that had King rubbing his crotch. Now he knew what Hawkins meant about a night with her being like Christmas.

'Good morning, Suzie, where are the boys?'

'Oh, they are asleep. I tried to wake them, but they had too much rum last night. We also have a guest on board.'

'Well done, Suzie, we should be there in another hour or so. Please have breakfast ready for my guest and me.'

'For Mr Madsen and you?'

'Fuck Madsen, no it is for Mr Broggetti and me. He should be flying in about the time of our arrival. Over and out.'

'Bye darling, see you soon.'

She hung the receiver up and turned facing Bill.

'How did you like that?' she asked cheekily, holding the towel up to her breasts. It only partly covered her. Hawkins was sitting back on the sofa, her back towards him, looking bemused while King leaned on the door as if struck dumb.

'You did well Suzie, now put some clothes on before you give us all a hardon.'

'Oh, I'm sorry, I had not noticed,' she giggled as she walked up the aisle and into the bow cabin.

'Maybe you'd like to contribute to a King's ransom now, Jim,' Hawkins said. The men burst out laughing. Bill called Creole on the UHF radio and told him what was happening.

'No worries, Bill, the boys are asleep on the bunks in the donga. Pretty comfortable workers quarters Wog has, though they could do with some cleaning.'

Next Bill called Farrell and informed him about the events.

'Good my troops are on the ground and ready to go as soon as you give the word. Let me know when those planes land and I'll order the rapid response team in the air. They are waiting in Kowanyama. I will also advise the ground teams to come in. The Pormpuraaw cops are in the Coleman and the Kowanyama cops somewhere in the north Mitchell, so they can respond in less than thirty minutes if they have too. The army has a Blackhawk heading your way with an SAS team from Weipa. They are expected to arrive in about 40 minutes. They also have a medical evacuation team on the way from Cairns. It should arrive midmorning.'

The waiting game appeared to go on forever but at last, King said that he could see a boat heading upriver. Hawkins used the binoculars to confirm it that it was Bull's boat with two more a few hundred metres behind it. He handed Bill the field glasses.

'Love to be on the bridge, but we got to keep out of sight,' Bill lamented. 'The portholes need cleaning. Hello, there is movement on shore also. There are people and dogs walking about near the trees.'

The boats appeared to take ages before they moored at the barge, but soon people were walking about it. Suddenly a twin-engine plane roared over the river and landed on the strip, leaving a cloud of dust in its wake. It swung around and parked on the river end of the strip, only metres from the barge. A few minutes later a similar plane landed and parked alongside it.

'Right on schedule,' Bill said. 'It is time to call the troops in.'

He rang Farrell and told him to get the backup moving.

'I'm onto it,' Farrell replied in an excited voice. 'What is happening now?'

'Well Wog is walking towards the planes and Broggetti is coming towards him. I reckon they will be here soon for breakfast while their pirate crew does all the work.'

'Righto Bill. Speak to you later. Stay safe.'

Wog shook hands with Broggetti.

'Welcome Tony. I have the package for you. It is on my boat. Suzie has breakfast waiting so we'll go and join her. I have had enough of that stinking fishing boat for a while. The wind was up, and it was a little rough out there last night.'

They boarded a dinghy that was tied onto the barge. The motor started with a bit of choke, the exhaust smoke blowing away on the breeze. Bill called Creole and instructed him that as soon as the two men were on the deck to take the initiative.

'I will arrest them when they are inside, but if they smell a rat they will bolt, and we will have to take drastic action. There are armed police parties and an SAS team on the way and the first should be here in about fifteen minutes or so. Until then it is up to us to stop the planes from taking off.'

'Roger Bill, I have two men on shore for that job, the others are well hidden, but so far no one had made a move to enter the donga. There are about fifteen men on the boats and more people on land, including two women. We will need the backup because if we get into a fire fight, we are vastly outnumbered. Hell, wait on. There are a dozen Asian girls coming from one of the boats. Must be the slave girls you mentioned. We must let them get out of harm's way first.'

'Okay, it's your call, I have to go, Wog just pulled up at alongside the boat. We have visitors.'

Wog swore as he brought the dinghy alongside the transom and climbed out of it, holding it for Broggetti to step onto the deck of the Italia. Normally Suzie would be there to tie the tender up. She was getting too big for her boots, and he would have to teach her a lesson he promised himself. Perhaps it was time to bush her and get another concubine. They were cheaper by the dozen, he mused to himself, laughing at his own joke. He tied the dinghy up and followed Broggetti who had gone ahead and into the cabin. He swore as someone grabbed him by the shoulder and propelled him forward. He stumbled over Broggetti who lay slumped on the floor.

'Welcome Wog, we have been waiting for you,' greeted Bill, pulling him back on his feet and expertly frisking him.

'Fucking knife. I should have known. You wog boys love sticking people, don't you?'

Bill pushed him roughly back on the floor and pulled Broggetti in a sitting position. He was having breathing difficulties, a victim of a hard karate chop across his throat when he entered the cabin, one that for Bill had a lot of pleasure and feeling in it.

'Come one Tony, wake up you arsehole.' Bill slapped the man hard across his face and patted him down looking for weapons. He pulled a shiny stainless steel 9 mm Smith & Wesson pistol out from a concealed belt holster behind Broggetti's back and handed it to King who was holding a rifle. Hawkins pushed the curtain back that covered the aisle door, his .357 Magnum revolver in his hand as he stepped out.

'Come to visit us, Wog, have you?' he greeted, the bore of the revolver menacing Wog.

'Well mate, the game is over. You're under arrest in case Bill hasn't told you, anything you say will be used in evidence against you. Now lie on the floor and don't move a muscle. You're going to find out the hard way about the cable ties you arseholes use on people.'

Wog did as he was told, noticing that his boss was being trussed up like a dog. He cringed as the cable ties tightened around his wrists and ankles. They were very painful.

'Don't worry Wog, they won't cut off your circulation. We want you alive to serve the rest of your fucking life in jail. If it was up to me, I'd feed you to Bull's pet croc, one limb at the time, you mongrel,' swore Hawkins vehemently as he pulled hard on a tie.

Bill reefed Broggetti onto his feet and pushed the still dazed man into the aisle and into the jail cabin and secured him to the wall with the chains.

'This will give you a taste of your own medicine. I'm on Hawkins side and I would hang you from the crane jib and slowly let Charlie rip you to pieces. Might fucking do it yet.'

'Fuck you Madsen, you got fucking nothing on me. Let me go. I'm on a fishing trip with Wog and what he does in his spare time is none of my business. You know that.'

'Maybe so, arsehole, but the courts will decide that. Your name is on Wog's computer and believe me that stuff alone will get you twenty years.'

He backed out the door and padlocked it behind him before pocketing the key. Wog was still on the floor. King and Hawkins looked down on him with amusement.

'What's so funny?' Bill asked.

'Nothing much Bill, the big fucking criminal pissed himself. What do you want to do with him, put him in the jail cabin with his boss?'

'No, from now on they won't be seeing each other. I'll tie him up in another cabin for now. Come on Wog, on your feet. There is enough slack for you to shuffle.'

He pushed the hapless man ahead of him and secured him in a cabin with a length of rope before cutting the cable ties.

'Fuck you Madsen. I can't move. I have rights,' Wog swore.

'Yes, the same rights as you give to those poor girls you have been kidnapping for Asian criminals. If you don't shut up, I'll have Hawkins do it. He'll slit your throat if I give him the word, though I reckon he would love to feed you to Charlie first.'

As he locked the door, a burst of gunfire erupted across the serene river, driving the brolgas and the corellas into the air where they wheeled over the tidal flat like snowflakes with cries of alarm. Hawkins cried out.

'Get up here Bill, the war has started.'

Chapter 22
BATTLE OF THE MITCHELL

Creole had hidden his men well, with himself and four others in the donga, while the others were concealed in the scrubby foreshore beyond the thin mangrove fringe. They watched as the girls were walked past them to a plane. The guard dogs had come up from the bunker when the boats moored and one of the mongrels discovered a soldier hidden in the mangroves and commenced barking. It attracted others and they circled about him before attacking. He had no choice but to open fire on the dogs, the burst of 5.56 mm ammo from his rifle cutting several down. The yelping survivors fled in terror.

'That's its men, let's go,' Creole cried as he kicked the donga door open and rushed onto the barge deck, his men at his heels.

The gunfire had alerted Bull and the others, who were running back onto the boats. Someone pointed a pistol at the SAS men, but a burst from a rifle cut him down before he could pull the trigger. Rapid pistol fire from one of the boats splattered the iron deck of the barge with bullets. One soldier was hit in the leg. Another grabbed him and pulled him behind the donga for cover, before re-joining the others. Concentrated gunfire now came from the boats and forced Creole to order his men to take cover behind the donga, cursing himself and knowing that they had lost the element of surprise.

'Fuck it,' he cursed. 'Okay men, try and stop them from taking off.

They need to come onto the barge to unhook the ropes. Shoot anyone that moves and watch your back. We are in for a fight.'

He called out loudly when there was a lull in the gunfire.

'This is the Australian Army. You are under arrest. Lay down your arms and step onto the deck.' In reply, bursts of automatic gunfire shredded the galvanized iron and timber from the donga's frame.

'Come and get us, you fucking arseholes,' someone cried from a boat. Creole recognised that they were in a bad position because they were unable to get on the boats without suffering casualties, though fire from his men on shore, who had the advantage of higher ground, kept the men in the boats under cover.

Suddenly a red streak shot out of a boat, ricocheted across the deck in a brilliance of sparks and slammed into a dozen fuel drums at the end of the barge. The explosion rocked the barge and a sheet of flame erupted into the air like that of a flamethrower. Drums of petrol exploded as others containing diesel ruptured and spilled across the deck and into the river. The SAS team felt the heat searing their skin.

'Give us covering fire,' Creole ordered his shore-based men over the radio. 'Right men, we got to get out of here and onto high ground. You there, help the wounded and the rest of you spray the boats with bullets. Now go.'

Two men grabbed the wounded soldier as the others turned their automatic weapons on the boats laying down a withering hail of fire that had everyone ducking for cover amongst the boxes of cargo stashed on the decks. The bullets punched through the timber deck planks, spraying lethal wood splinters and lead across the decks. Two men died in the deadly hail as the soldiers fled up the gangway and onto high ground where they dived for cover into any little hollows they could find. More drums exploded, while part of the barge deck was burning fiercely, the fire threatening the donga and the securely moored boats. Someone jumped from the rear boat and raced towards the mooring ring, but he was shot down by a soldier.

Creole took stock of the situation. He had two wounded men and was in no position to take the advantage, even though he held the high ground. The gunfire from the boats was spasmodic but accurate enough to prevent the SAS team from responding effectively. Suddenly another red streak erupted from the front boat.

'Get down men, another rocket,' Creole roared loudly as he pushed his body deeper into the low depression that barely hid him. The rocket whizzed over their heads and exploded somewhere on the saltpan behind them.

When the first burst of gunfire struck, Bull, who was on the rear deck of his boat, rushed back inside the cabin. He quickly unlocked a panel to a hidden gun locker and loaded a charged magazine into a Mini light machine gun. Grabbing a spare magazine, he turned back to the deck in time to see the fuel drums exploding in a ball of flame. The explosion was near enough to feel the hot caress of flames and heat on his face. There was thick smoke on the barge and lots of gunfire. He did not know where it was coming from. Suddenly bullets stitched the sides of the boat splashing pieces of timber and lead all about him.

Bull fell back in the cabin, a piece of timber sticking in his leg. He howled with pain and rage as he pulled at the splinter. It came out with a rush of blood. Someone helped him to stand up and he became aware that others were in the cabin also, some of his men and three of the Middle East men they had picked up and were armed with pistols. One of his men held a lever action Marlin hunting rifle; the others were empty handed.

'Get the weapons from the locker,' Bull cried. 'Use the AK-47's. They are much better than hunting rifles. Let's give the fuckers hell.'

The fuel fire had eased off, though the barge deck was still burning fiercely. Bull noted that if the donga caught fire the boats could be engulfed by it. He ordered one of the men to untie the mooring ropes, but as soon as he leapt on the barge deck, he was shot. Bull saw the man's head explode as if in slow motion, before he collapsed on the deck, his blood turning the deck red.

The fire was clearing a little as most of the fuel had spilled into the river and was drifting away with the incoming tide, lessening the danger of the donga catching fire. Bull could see someone's head on the shore about sixty metres away. The boat was just below the line of sight of land. There was a streak of smoke as a rocket sped away from one of the boats and exploded on shore a second later.

'Fucking stupid bastard,' Bull roared. 'Stop firing that fucking thing, you'll blow us all up, or hit my mum.'

A curse came in reply. Bull knew it was one of the Middle Eastern men they had picked up from the smuggler's boat. It had been against his grain to bring them into the country, but Broggetti was the boss, and their money was as good as anyone else's. They had lots of luggage and some heavy cases.

Bull did not know what was is in them, but now he knew. Bull yelled at the rocket man to stop shooting, as there were planes and his mum on land behind the soldiers. The man was surly but dropped the tube down.

Bull looked about, being careful not to stick his head out to where he could be seen from shore. But he saw no one; everyone was hiding either below the deck walls or in the cabin. He noted that Wog's boat was pulling up anchor.

'Probably making a run for it, the gutless bastard,' he swore aloud, ducking down as several bullets slammed into the boat near him.

However, there were more pressing things on his mind, and he lost interest in the Italia.

'Fuck you, arseholes,' Bull cursed, suddenly stepping onto the deck, the machine gun held in his big arms. The 5.56 mm bullets swept across the barge and punched into the riverbank raising little dust clouds. A soldier lying prone behind a mound of dirt was shot in the head, the dull thud of the bullet hitting its target loud and clear to the others nearby.

'Fuck, they have a machine gun,' Creole swore loudly. 'We must pull

232

back. We can't fight against machine guns and rockets. Oh fuck, where the hell did that come from?'

Behind him came more gunfire and bullets thudded into the dirt about the soldiers, followed by spasmodic bursts of what he recognized as 5.56 mm gunfire sounding in return.

'It's okay, Lieutenant, we have it under control,' reported the soldier who had been attacked by the dogs. 'The pilots decided to join the battle, but they have permanently lost interest, though there are still some shots coming from the bunker, but it's too far away to be effective. How are things over there?'

'Not good Cody, we have lost men and are in an exposed position and under fire from a machine gun and rockets. We must pull back. Is there anywhere we can defend ourselves and hold out?'

'Nothing where we are, excepting the bunker, but it has at least four people in it who are shooting at us. Besides it is a long run, and we would be shot down like dogs as there is no cover at all.'

The UHF radio crackled into life.

'Creole, are you there? Bill here. Can you hold on a little longer? We are putting the boat into a position from where we can better direct and hit targets on Bull's boat. It will take us a few more minutes.'

'Bill, I had forgotten about you guys. If you can that would be great and may give us a chance for a counterattack. Be careful someone has a machine gun and an RPG launcher.'

'We know, that's the reason we are getting out of range. Hawkins and King reckon they can hit man-sized targets out to three hundred metres or more with their hunting rifles. I have seen them shoot and believe me they can.'

Bull fired another burst of fire over the bank and changed the magazine, telling one of the men to recharge the empty one.

'Okay, one of you blokes get those ropes off the mooring now. We are getting out of here,' he ordered. 'I'll cover you.'

Someone leapt over the side onto to the deck and grabbed the stern rope, but he was unable to pull it off the mooring as the boat's weight was heavy against the current. Bull ordered another man to help as he fired a burst over the bank. Both men pulled hard and managed to slip the rope over. It dropped into the water and the boat's stern began to swing about, the bow rope still holding firm.

The two men heaved on the rope when one suddenly dropped down on the deck as a bullet slammed into his body. A split second later the second man slumped alongside him as the twin reports of heavy calibre rifles sounded across the river.

'Fuck,' Bull cursed. 'They have snipers, but where the fuck are they?'

The boat swung around into the current and was now facing the barge, still held firmly by the nose rope. One of the men pushed past Bull onto the rear deck, thinking he was no longer in sight from the shore. The thud of a bullet hitting flesh was like a hammer blow to Bull. It splattered him with blood and bone as the man's chest literally exploded in front of him. Bull felt a dull blow on his right shoulder a split second later before could duck back into the cabin for safety.

He fell back against the wall, the gun slipping from his arms, his right arm hanging down from a smashed shoulder. Bone protruded from his shirt. He tried vainly to stand up and cried for someone to help, but no one did. Darkness fell over him and he slipped into unconsciousness.

The Italia was holding anchor and had swung around, the rear facing towards the smoking barge and the three boats. King suggested they move the boat upstream and away from the machine gun and the possibility of more rocket fire.

'About three hundred metres is fine,' he advised. 'We can shoot right down onto the rear decks if we pick the right angle. We can use our deck table as a benchrest for our rifles and take out anyone out who comes out on the boat decks.'

Hawkins started the engines and pulled the anchor up with the electric anchor motor. In the meantime, Bull fired a burst with the machine gun and killed a soldier. Hawkins turned the Italia upstream before slowing down a safe distance away. The anchor went down and held firmly in the river mud, the boat swinging about and holding steady in the current. He switched the engines off and joined the others on the rear deck. Bill had taken a .308 Winchester rifle from Wog's gun cabinet. King said it would be fine for long range sniping.

'However, we need someone to call the shots and keep an eye on things with the binoculars as we only have a narrow point of view with our rifle scopes. I prefer you to do that.'

As they readied to fire, a man leapt over the Bonanza's side and laboured to pull the stern rope off the mooring. Another joined him. They succeeded in freeing the rope before the men could fire. Only when they began to pull on the nose mooring did Hawkins's fire, followed a split second later by King's shot. Both men dropped to the barge deck. The boat swung around in the current and it gave them a view directly on the exposed rear deck of the boat and the cabin entrance. King shot a man who'd stepped in front of Bull. Hawkins got a shot away before Bull managed to get to cover. King fired another shot into the cabin, hitting a man in the stomach. The rest sought cover or hugged the floor.

'The Evelyn,' Bill shouted. 'someone has a rocket launcher.'

The rocket seared towards them, but it went over the top of the Italia and struck the mangroves on the other side of the river with a loud explosion. At the same moment, the rocket man was slammed against the cabin wall by a bullet that drove into his chest, the blood and bone exploding from his shattered back splattering the men inside the cabin.

'Fuck that was close,' King swore as he fired another round into the open cabin door. 'That should keep their heads down. Lucky for us it's a Chinese made 69 RPG. They are not very accurate.'

'How the fuck would you know that?' Bill asked.

'He is a war vet and is an expert on military history and arms,' Hawkins answered. 'Nothing much he doesn't know about military arms.'

'Now why does that not surprise me,' Bill lamented as he glassed the boats, but there was no sign of anyone moving about. Hawkins fired another shot through the open cabin door at a fleeting movement inside the cabin, but there was nothing. They waited a few minutes as Bill called Creole up.

'Tom, we have shot both the machine gun and rocket operators, and a couple of others, and no one is moving about anymore. What do you think?'

'We are still under fire from the bunker,' was the reply. 'though they have their heads down and are more of a nuisance value rather than deadly. It is probably the women shooting at us with .22 rimfire rifles. The boys took the pilots out. Our backup should be here soon. Hang on there is a boat moving up now. Looks like the Kowanyama police. I suggest they hang back a little.'

'How is your group, any wounded?'

'Bad Bill, we have two badly wounded men and two dead. Can you ensure that the medivac is on its way?'

'Will do Tom, I'll call the boss and inform him what is going on. I better let the new arrivals know that we are friendly before they start shooting at us.'

The police boat cautiously came alongside, the two police officers holding ready to use Ruger Mini-14 rifles as the Aboriginal police aide grabbed the Italia deck rails.

'I am Sergeant Bill Madsen,' Bill said. 'come on board but keep away from the back as we are shooting at hostile targets.'

Bill filled the new arrivals in on the morning events and the sudden stalemate that had occurred. They were interrupted as Hawkins and King shot someone who appeared in the doorway of the Evelyn for a split second and paid for his stupidity with his life.

'Fuck,' cried one of the cops rubbing his ears. 'What the fuck are you boys shooting with and at what.'

'Sorry mate,' King apologized. 'but that bloke went for the rocket launcher that is on the deck. They almost hit us last time and we might run out of luck. Better him than us.'

'Rocket launcher,' the cop exclaimed. 'you're fucking joking, aren't you?'

'No, he is not,' Bill said sharply. 'They also have a machine gun and God knows what else on board those boats. The SAS have two wounded men and two dead, so believe me this is not a good place to be. If you blokes have families and want to leave, do so now. No one will blame for it. Better still, get in your boat, and stay out of range until you are called or needed. It will be much safer for all concerned. It's currently a stalemate with no one going anywhere and we can afford to wait for the arrival of an SAS team.'

The men obeyed under protest, but Bill insisted. He handed over a note with a phone number on it.

'Use your sat phone and call this number. It's Commissioner Farrell's number. Tell him what is happening here and that I don't have time to call. Inform him we need help and especially medical help urgently. Also call the Pormpuraaw police and tell them to stay out of range until they are called in. Now go.'

The boat pulled away and Bill breathed a sigh of relief as Hawkins gave him an odd look.

'You've got your priorities wrong, Bill. The civilians should have been evacuated first, remember.'

'I know, but I feel safer with you blokes than those three. They were shitting themselves. Besides you blokes wouldn't leave anyway, right?'

'Right. By the way that sounds like a helicopter in the distance.'

'You're right, that must be the police task force or the SAS.'

'Police,' King stated. 'That is a Jet Ranger.'

The helicopter circled wide, and the phone rang. It was a police officer in the helicopter asking for instructions. Bill called Creole and asked if there was a suitable safe place for them to land.

'Yes, to the west of us. Still some fire coming from the bunker, but they have only .22 rimfire rifles. It is too far away to do much harm. Besides, my men don't believe in shooting women. The cops can sort that out.'

'Righto, I will inform the copter. Any sign of life on the boats?'

'Nothing, the way those boys of yours shoot there probably won't be anyone alive. Any chance of signing them up for the army?'

'None, Tom, the police force wants them first. Catch you later.'

The helicopter vanished behind the trees and landed almost a kilometre away, a dust cloud rising high into the sky. King fired a shot as someone moved on the rear boat towards the rocket launcher.

'Did you hit him,' Bill asked, becoming used to the sporadic shooting of the two men.

'I think so, but we got to get that thing before someone else does and uses it on us.'

'I'll have a go at it and see if I can put a bullet up its spout,' said Hawkins. 'Need you to watch it Bill and see if it moves when I fire. Jim, you keep an eye on that door because if they wake up to what I am doing, they will try and get it.'

Bill watched the launcher through the powerful field glasses as Hawkins steadied himself down behind the rifle stock. Even though he knew the old man could shoot, it was a very difficult shot. The rifle roared. Bill saw a little splatter on the deck where the bullet hit.

'You're about ten centimetres too low,' he advised.

'Thought so, I'll try again.'

King's rifle suddenly bellowed as someone dived for the launcher. He died in mid-air, partly falling across the tube.

'Thought they would go for that,' King smiled. 'That will make it harder to get to it now as they must roll the body away. Fuck how many men are on that boat?'

Hawkins's rifle recoiled and this time the rocket tube was slammed upwards and to the right, the force lifting the body up.

'I reckon that the bullet went right up the spout the way it moved,' Bill noted. 'Pity there wasn't a rocket in it. But I will keep an eye on the bloody thing, just in case it's still usable. Hello here comes the army.'

The heavy droning of the powerful Blackhawk helicopter came from a long way off. It took time before it came into sight. Bill could hear Creole talking to them on the radio instructing them where to land, but the pilot ignored his advice and hovered over the ground force before landing in a cloud of dust nearby. The wind swept the dust up over the hidden soldiers and down into the river where it almost obliterated the barge and the boats.

'Fucking wankers,' Hawkins swore. 'Now we can't see a fucking thing. Quick, Jim, get this fucking boat started and out of the range before we are blown out of the water.'

But King was already moving. The motor roared into life and the Italia pushed downstream under full power. She had made only about thirty metres when machine gun bullets slammed into her rear. They could barely see the boats under the now rising dust cloud, but there was someone on the deck of the Bonanza firing the machine gun with one hand. It was a big powerful man roaring with rage, Bull, who had regained consciousness when the Black Hawk landed. As the dust cloud swept over the boat one of his men had helped him onto to his feet.

'Give me the fucking gun, now,' Bull cried in pain and rage.

The man handed him the Browning Mini-machine gun and inserted a loaded magazine. Bull looked towards shore waiting for someone to appear when in the lifting haze he saw the exhausts of the Italia blowing smoke.

'That is the cunt that is shooting us up,' shouted the man who had helped him. Bull was enraged. Why should Wog, his best mate shoot at him? Fuck him, perhaps he wanted all the money.

He raised the gun up with one hand, steadying it against the door frame and roared with glee as the burst of bullets literally walked across the water and slammed into the stern of the Italia before climbing onto the deck.

Hawkins suddenly fell to the floor as the deck table had one of its legs shot off, and another slug scattered the leg of his chair. As he fell, he held tightly onto the rifle to keep it from falling onto the deck and knocking the scope out of alignment. He kicked the chair away and rolled into prone position in one movement. The scope sight came up to his eye and for a split second he had Bull in the centre of the crosshairs before the heavy recoil of the hunting rifle swept him away.

Hawkins pulled the bolt back and slammed another round into the chamber. Again, the cross hairs searched the deck, noting the still and very large form of Bull laying on it before they settled on a man picking up the Mini gun. He died a split second later, on almost the exact instant as the newly arrived SAS force rushed onto the barge and to the moored boats.

Suddenly the river was lit by a mighty explosion that erupted from the barge, a fire ball that shot high in the air, its shock wave travelling across the river and blowing the Italia almost on its side. Hawkins grabbed a rail and hung on grimly the rifle held in his other hand. King was flung against the cruise controls while Bill was slammed against the rails and over the side of the boat, but he managed to grab a rail as he went over. He climbed back onto the rocking boat deck as the shock wave from the explosion wavered, holding his left side, one of his ribs broken.

Dust and smoke hung over the site as King slowly brought the Italia alongside what remained of the barge, the men peering into the smoke and dust, looking for signs of life. There was none, the boats were gone, and the barge was sinking, the mooring area having melted from the heat of the explosion.

'Fuck, what did they have on board those fucking boats?' Bill groaned, clutching his side where the slam against the rail had broken his lower rib.

'Fucking C4,' King said matter of fact. 'It's the sort of stuff you see in movies. But what the fuck were they doing with stuff like that?'

'Terrorists,' Bill informed him. 'Interpol warned us that it could be smuggled into the country for a terrorist operation. I reckon they set it off and took everyone on board with them. I wonder where Creole is. Can't talk to him, I lost the radio.'

Chapter 23
THE COST

It was the Kowanyama police boat that had come alongside the Italia that ferried Bill and Hawkins to shore. Hawkins grabbed the first aid box, leaving King to anchor the boat alone with Suzie, who had come on deck when the shooting was over. She was shivering in fear. They could hear Wog and Broggetti crying out, but they were ignored.

The police party, the helicopter pilots, and the two shore-based men that Creole had setup to handle the bunker were attending several wounded men. None of Creole's people had been killed by the blast, though they were in shock and suffering from deafness. Creole and the two wounded soldiers were sitting up and holding onto their heads, their eyes filled with tears from pain and the salt dust that hung thickly in the still air. The men did the best they could with the Flying Doctor kit from the Italia, but until proper medical help was available the wounded had to endure.

The army pilot suggested that they could evacuate the wounded in the Black Hawk and meet the medivac helicopter somewhere along the route for transfer. They immediately readied the wounded and commenced loading them. Creole was looking better, though he could not hear.

'Fucking bloody idiot. I told the captain not to take his men onto the barge, but he would not listen. He ordered me to provide ground cover while he and his men charged like fucking brainless bulls onto the barge to take the boats. Fuck, this is a disaster, worse than anything that ever happened to us overseas and in Afghanistan in a proper bloody war.'

'Okay, mate,' Bill shouted. 'it's all over. When you can hear, we'll talk. But the wounded men are out of here now.'

'What about you?' Creole asked Bill. 'You should be on the Blackhawk. You are hurt.'

'Only a broken rib. I have had worse. It will have to hold for a while yet. Hawkins strapped it tightly and I can cope, providing I don't laugh and that won't happen any time soon after this shit.'

The Blackhawk lifted into the sky for an hour's flight to rendezvous with the medical team somewhere in the Gulf country wilderness. Bill watched as the helicopter rose above a cloud of salt dust and vanished over the timber line. Only then did he join the other police and the remaining SAS men who were checking out what remained of the barge. The nose of one boat stuck up above the water line, still tied to the barge that was partly submerged, but the other boats and part of the barge had vanished. There was no sign of life. One of the police handed him a phone.

'It's the boss,' he said.

'Bill here.'

'Bill, this is Steve, What the fuck happened?'

'Everything Steve, it was going well until the newly arrived SAS team, led by a brainless captain, charged in without checking the danger. Someone blew him and his men to kingdom come when explosives were set off on one of the boats. The boats and part of the barge are gone, including everyone who was alive or dead on them. We have evacuated the wounded to meet the army medivac team en route. Besides that, we are trying to get all the pieces together.'

'What about Broggetti and Marotsi?'

'Both are on board the Italia under lock and key. We suffered a little damage from machine gun fire, but nothing that will stop her sailing to

Karumba.'

'Machine gun fire, what the fuck are you talking about?'

'Yes boss, machine guns, rockets and C4, they had it all. Thank God we had the army with us, otherwise we would all be dead.'

'Okay Bill, stay with it. I am on my way in the Government jet and should be at Kowanyama sometime after lunch. Inspector Osborne of the Federal Police is with me. I believe a team of army brass and investigators are en route also.'

'Right boss, will keep you informed if anything crops up.'

Bill handed the phone back to the senior constable.

'Need you to come over and have a look at the people in the bunker, sergeant,' he said. 'We are holding a bunch of Asian girls, two Asian men, and two Australian women. Besides you may be interested in what the bunker contains.'

They headed over, Hawkins walking alongside them. Bill noticed that he was carrying his camera, the hunting rifle slung over his shoulder and the big Ruger revolver on his hip. But then again, the camera was never far away when he reflected on it. It was just that he had gotten used to Hawkins taking photos of everything that took his eye.

The concrete bunker was huge, but the inside was well lit by lights powered by solar panels on the roof. The interior was divided into separated bedrooms, a large kitchen and dining section. Inside the dining area were the Asian girls that had been unloaded from the boat, two men and two European women. All were handcuffed. A police sergeant came over and introduced himself as Senior Sergeant Colin Bradley in charge of the Special Response Squad.

'Great to catch up Bill, hell of a mess over there my men tell me. We had our hands full with those people here. Lucky they only had .22 rimfire rifles, but even then, that old bitch managed to put a slug into my chest when we came in. Lucky my vest stopped it.'

Bull's mother was almost as ugly as Bull, thought Bill in silence. She was a huge woman whose life had been one of crime and hardship. Her

244

daughter was a younger copy of her.

Both were subdued, though were asking about Bull and Slime. Bill told them as gently as he could that they were both dead. They broke into tears and cried. Bill felt their pain and understood their anguish, but that was the way crime ends he told himself. The two Asian men could speak only a little English. The girls were young and beautiful, ranging in age between 14 and 17, destined as playthings for sick rich men in Brisbane, Sydney, and Melbourne. They were very frightened. Bill assured them that no harm would come to them. One of the girls spoke a little English and she passed the information to the others.

'What will happen to us,' she asked.

'Not sure, it's a job for the Australian Immigration Department. Only they can decide what to do with you. You are illegals, and the best way of helping yourself is to tell us the truth and tell us why you are here.'

Bradley called out to Bill. He followed him into a tunnel that extended to another part of the bunker complex. He pointed to boxes that were stacked up against a wall.

'Enough drugs to flood the Ice market for months,' he said. 'There is a lab in the next section and believe me someone has been very busy. Another week and it would be on the streets. This alone will save countless young lives.'

'You're right Col, but this is only the tip of the iceberg,' Bill replied. 'There is much more to this. I reckon we have hit the jackpot of organized crime in this country and made a big hit on the international scene as well. Let's get out of here, I need some fresh air. I have a problem breathing with this broken rib.'

'You should have been on the copter with the others, Bill. Just take it easy. By the way, who is the old bloke in the big hat with the camera and the big cowboy gun on his hip? He looks familiar,' Bradley asked indicating Hawkins who was busy photographing the lab contents, the flash lighting up the inside of the bunker.

Bill had gotten so used to having him about like a shadow he had almost forgotten about Hawkins.

'My guardian angel, Col. Come, and I'll introduce you to Vic Hawkins. Without him and his mate Jim King we would all be dead.'

'I have heard some good things about those good old boys. Hawkins is my favourite outdoor writer. They say he can shoot the eyelash off a fly at one hundred metres.'

'No that is fucking bullshit, closer to three hundred metres I reckon,' Bill laughed.

Bill introduced the two men, noticing that they had an instant liking for each other as they talked about fishing and catching barramundi as if the morning's events had never happened. It appeared that Bradley lived for his fishing, and both knew about each other's repudiation, though they had never met. The men walked outside and sat on a bench under old mango trees that partly hid the bunker. Most of the police and the two SAS men were also under the shady place, their voices muted as they talked. Bradley ordered some of his men to provide coffee and food.

'Take what you need from the bunker kitchen,' he said. 'There is plenty of everyone, including the prisoners and the girls. By the way uncuff the Asian girls, but someone keep an eye on them.'

Bill and Hawkins bid farewell to Bradley and walked to the tender. The water about the barge complex was alive with the movement of a million feeding fishes.

'Catfish mostly,' Hawkins said. 'They are coming in for a feed on the tide. A lot of fish would have been killed. It created a great burley trail that is probably a few kilometres downstream by now. There is plenty of flesh and bones to chew on from the fish and men killed in the blast. Nothing last too long in these waters.'

'That will make it hard for forensics,' Bill lamented.

'Probably, but I could never understand why they even bother with cases like this. It appears all clear cut to me, so why risk diver's lives in crocodile infested waters looking for evidence?'

'You're right, but that is the way it is. We must determine what

246

explosives were used, how many people were on the boats, plus of course there is the recovery of remains of the soldiers to think about. They all have families.'

There was no sign of anyone when they tied the tender up alongside the boat.

'Strange, Jim and Suzie should be here,' Bill said, his hand hovering over the pistol he had taken from Broggetti.

'They should be,' Hawkins replied, pulling the big Ruger revolver from its holster and silently sliding onto the deck keeping a low profile.

The rear door was open. Bill led the way in. Hawkins closely shadowed his moves, the revolver cocked and ready. Wordlessly they slipped into the aisle, noting that both prisoner cabin doors were still locked. Bill opened the bow cabin door, the pistol ready and just as quickly closed it. He pushed Hawkins out ahead of him as he applied the safety on the pistol and holstered it.

'What the fuck is going on,' Hawkins asked, somewhat perplexed.

'You don't want to know,' Bill laughed. 'Put your gun away, because while we were on shore working our guts out our old mate decided to celebrate an early Christmas with Suzie by the looks of it.'

'You're fucking joking, this I got to see,' Hawkins exclaimed attempting to push pass Bill, who held him back.

'Later mate, leave them alone. They are both asleep and Jim probably needs it. She is something else, believe me.'

'Believe you, what do you know about her?'

'Look I know, let's leave it at that,' Bill replied, realizing he had said too much.

'No way mate, tell me more. You know the bush code, what happens in the bush stays in the bush.'

'I know, I'll tell you on the condition that you tell me about the death of a certain biker out of Karumba and how the fuck you blokes managed to buy that new Quintrex Top Ender boat and new motor.'

'Will you have me charged if I tell you?'

'No way, it's just that I need to know for myself. The case is closed as far as I am concerned, but it's the fucking intrigue that bothers me. What happened?'

Hawkins pulled a couple of beers out of the fridge and handed one to Bill. He sat down and almost drained the contents of the stubby bottle.

'Fuck, that is good, love to take a couple to the boys on shore, but I suppose they are working, and Colin looks like a bloke that takes no nonsense. Okay, here goes.'

He took another long swallow from the bottle, emptied it and got a couple more from the fridge. He handed one to Bill.

'We left Karumba earlier to photograph the sunrise over the plains on the way home. I noticed a bike rider come up behind the 4WD in the mirror and pulled over a bit to let him pass. When he came alongside, I saw that he had a pistol in his hand. He fired about the same time as I swung the fourbie over to him. He panicked and left the road. The shot must have gone over us. The bike hit a drain and somersaulted several times before it came to a rest. I reversed up and we got out with our guns ready, but they were not needed. His neck was broken. When Jim frisked him, we found a wad of cash and decided that a new boat was in order. That is the truth and in case you are worried about the pistol, it is on the bottom of the Norman River. Jim tossed it in as we passed over the bridge. Never got that sunrise shot either.'

'Hmm, that is about what I thought happened,' Bill said slowly, stroking his chin. 'Andre Jolic, that was the bloke's name, was a professional hit man from Victoria and was hiding in Karumba from the Mafia wars that happened in Melbourne a few years ago. It appears that Bull hired him to revenge the shooting of his mates in the Staaten River. You're lucky to be alive as from all accounts he was very good at what he did.'

'You're dodging the subject, Bill. What the fuck happened between Suzie and you while you were tied up?'

Bill hesitated a little before he talked about the night's event when

248

Suzie looked after him, her raping him, and Slime's intervention.

'You're also lucky to be alive.' Hawkins mused. 'But hell mate, that fucking rape bit is a bit rich. I reckon you were a willing partner if you could get it up.'

'How could I resist?' Bill protested. 'Hey, she told me I was porn star material, and that I was 100% male. But the truth is I felt guilty as fuck about it. I am unsure if I should tell Julie.'

'Well mate, you're a lucky bastard, that is all I can say. I am not talking about you being alive either. But it's up to you if you tell Julie. Personally, I would let the sleeping dog lie, because she won't take it well, if at all. The way I see it you were raped, and I reckon that there is nothing any man could have done with a love expert like Suzie. You were tied up and your cock, not your mind, was in control. It's as simple as that.'

They fried meat for steak sandwiches and noted that the ship's galley was stocked with the best food possible. They cooked enough for the prisoners and the two "root rats" as Hawkins had termed his mate and Suzie. King appeared in the kitchen looking sheepish.

'How the fuck could you?' Hawkins chided. 'While we were working our guts out. Fuck mate, you just can't be trusted when there is a bit of hot pussy about, can you?'

'You're only fucking jealous you missed out, Vic. It's been a long time between pussies for me, believe me. Besides she reckons that I am porn star material.' King paused as the two men burst into uncontrolled laughter.

'What the fuck is wrong with you, blokes?' King asked. 'You know I don't have the smallest cock in the shower room.'

Suzie joined them for lunch, having showered. She looked radiant and happy and as usual smelled good. She doted on King, something that did not escape Bill and he was glad that she got over him so quickly, though he did feel a slight pang of regret. She was a hell of a woman that could keep any man happy, or break his heart, he thought.

Wog and Broggetti were thirsty and hungry and wanted to know what had happened. Both men were stressed and close to panicking. Bill told them they were going to jail, untied them and allowed them to eat and use the toilet before again securing their bonds. The army Blackhawk returned just after lunch and soon took off with the two SAS men that had survived the battle of the Mitchell. Another plane flew over sometime later. A couple of calls revealed that it carried journalists from the Cairns Post and Win TV.

The plane landed on the salt pan, the dust drifting over the river. It reminded Bill to contact Julie and tell her he was alive and well before the press told the world of the events. No doubt they had being alerted to the Mitchell River by all the police and army activity and were looking for a story. Soon after their arrival a helicopter from Kowanyama brought Farrell and Osborne to the strip.

Bill and Hawkins used the tender to meet the newcomers. While Bill was engaged talking to his boss, Hawkins talked to a female reporter who had arrived on the press plane. It appeared that he knew her well, but Bill took little notice of them. The police bosses were tired from the long and rushed journey from Brisbane, and after a briefing they inspected the damage before being transferred to the Italia to meet the prisoners.

The bullet holes in the rear deck and the cabin walls prompted Osborne to ask what happened as all his information had come from Farrell. King handed out a cold beer to everyone while Hawkins readied a late lunch for the visitors. They sat in the comfortable airconditioned lounge, listening in raptures as Bill told them of the morning's battle.

'Had it not been for those two men here, we would not be here today,' he said solemnly. 'We were outgunned and outmanned and the only thing that saved us was their long-range sniper shooting that gave us the edge. If that SAS captain had assessed the situation correctly, he and his men, and others would be alive now. Fuck, I can't believe how stupid he was. He must have thought that civilians were all pussies.'

'Not your fault, Bill,' Farrell said. 'You did everything you possibly could have done. By the way, we do have some good news from all of this. When I received your email with Wog's attachments, we had trusted people go through it. It was one hell of a job, but within two hours after receiving it we had warrants out in dozens of locations around the country and overseas. We are still receiving reports from overseas. Interpol has been raiding some of the places and names we provided, which so far has been highly successful. In this country we have arrested dozens of suspects, raided drug labs and confiscated drugs and illegal guns. It will shut organized crime down for a long time. Moreover, politicians, judges and to our bitter regret, police officers are also involved and are being arrested as we speak.'

He paused as Osborne took over the conversation.

'While your guys were busy this morning a team of crack Federal Police, backed by local police from Normanton and Karumba raided the old prawn farm and apprehended a GBC boat and crew that had drugs and illegal immigrants onboard. They gave up without a fight, so that was one good ending. At the same time our Rapid Response Team raided Blood Creek Station, and what a bonus that was. The raids were a complete surprise, and they were in there before anyone wised up. The report we got from the officer in charge indicates that several drug labs manned by illegal immigrants, and details of networking with distributors and dealers, were found. They also found caches of handguns, automatic weapons, and explosives, though I am not sure of the finer details. In fact, to make a long story short, organized crime in this part of the world has been dealt a deathblow because of your undercover work. A job well done, Bill.'

He shook hands with Bill as did Farrell, before the two men thanked Hawkins and King for their involvement.

'Now we wait,' he said. 'Okay, while we do, let us bring Wog in here and see if he wants to add more on what we already know. Hello, who is this?'

Suzie had come out of the bedroom, after having been asked by Bill to keep out of sight. Both Farrell and Osborne perked up considerably on her appearance. Bill told the officers who she was and how she had helped. He also mentioned that she wanted immunity as she wished to stay in the country.

'Yes, we may be able to recommend her, but that is as far as we can go, as the final say is with the immigration people,' Osborne replied. 'However, I do know some people in the department and will make the recommendation. But folks, we would appreciate it if you left the police interrogation to us.'

They got the hint and closed the door behind them. King and Suzie ferried Hawkins to where their boats were anchored. They were soon hanging out in the current behind the Italia.

King was holding Suzie's hand as they relaxed on the deck.

'Fuck mate, we came all this way for a fish, so we might as well stay on for a week or so. I reckon we need some R&R after this shit.'

'Good call,' Hawkins replied. 'I reckon we should head back to our camp and get the fishing rods out, old mate. But I will ring my wife first, because she will panic when she sees this on the news tonight.'

Farrell and Bill joined them. Hawkins's asked Farrell if they could leave.

'We have been talking about all the scenario today and decided that we are going fishing as soon as you blokes let us go. We need to relax a bit. Even the bloody crocs are going to look friendly after the shit that happened this morning.'

'We are not holding you, on the contrary, you are free to do as you please. If I had the time, I would come along. But I must let the minister know what is going on and head back to Brisbane. Bradley will secure the area until his squad is relieved. He can use this ship as a base. Bill, you, Suzie, and the two prisoners are coming with us to Brisbane. We better move as the pilots are probably sick and tired of waiting. Goodbye gentlemen, and once more I thank you for your help.'

They shook hands with the police officers and got a hug from a teary-eyed Suzie, though she lingered with King longer than Hawkins before they climbed down into their boat. The men told Bill that they would collect his camping gear and ensure that it and his boat would get to back to Karumba. A cheery wave and they were away. Bill watched them go, wishing that he could be as carefree as they were, but there was more work to be done before he could even consider a fishing trip.

The day was coming to an end, it was perfect, a beautiful dry season sunset that promised some great fishing in the coming week. The police helicopter passed overhead, looking like an insect in the blue sky. Hawkins opened the icebox and handed a cold beer to King.

'Fucking good idea to clean out Wog's grog supply, Jim, while the cops were busy with the crims, besides screwing Suzie that is, you horny old prick. But I reckon we need it more than Wog does, or the cops for that matter. Let's grab the rods and toss a few lures about the snags before nightfall. I would love some fresh barra fillets for tea to go with this expensive wine. Pity we couldn't take Suzie with us, she could cook it for us and more. You, a bloody porn star!'

They roared with laughter.

Chapter 24
REWARDS

It was raining, the clouds drifting in from Moreton Bay over the city of Brisbane, miserable stuff that was cold and wet. It made Bill shiver like a dog. It mattered little where he was, the city was getting into his head with its traffic noises, blaring horns, and sirens, but the traffic fumes were the worst. He longed for the dry season sunshine of the Gulf country and Julie. He looked out of the window, hoping for a glimpse of the river but the scudding rain blocked it.

Four weeks had passed since the battle on the Mitchell River. Bill wanted out, he was sick of writing reports and meeting with prosecutors, but he had the satisfaction of knowing that it would send Broggetti and Morossi to prison for life. He wished that they had been aboard the fishing boats when they blew up. It would have saved him a lot of hard work. The chief police prosecutor, a demanding woman, was making sure that no loopholes were present when the case went to court. The days were hectic with appearances on TV and newspaper interviews. The press had much to write and report.

Bill had cursed Hawkins, as graphic pictures of the Mitchell River battle were splashed all over the front pages of major newspapers, including some overseas publications, the day he arrived back in Brisbane. Now he knew why Hawkins had been in such a hurry to meet the lady journalist when she landed. Unbeknown to all, he had handed her a scandisk that contained the digital pictures. Farrell had been furious about it, but as Bill pointed out, Hawkins was a journalist who made a living from photojournalism. Besides the pictures were evidence that the police had followed procedures and protocol always, even though some sources had tried to blame them for the debacle. The phone rang. Bill picked it up and answered.

'Bill, Steve here. We at last have some good news. As you know the Indonesian authorities and Interpol rescued the back packers when the smuggler's boat arrived back at its homeport. They also found $200 million dollars of hard cash, believed to be payment for the next shipment and for laundering purposes. However, they have been busy, and several other girls have been found in various brothels throughout Southeast Asia. Interpol oversees that, and they are continuing their search for others. Some very important people have been arrested over there because of their involvement in the Australian smuggling operation. It will have widespread implications.'

'That is good news indeed, Steve. By the way, I reckon that I will have all my charge sheets and relevant information in order at the end of the day. How is the inquiry going?'

'It is early days yet, and the Mitchell River battle must be sorted out, the blame game is always on the cards. Not that I give a fuck anymore, as retirement is looking good these days. I'll talk to you later Bill, bye.'

Farrell hung up. Bill busied himself and rechecked the reports and charges he had laid against Broggetti and Morossi, ensuring that there were absolutely no loopholes for the two men to escape through. The phone rang; he cursed it but brightened up when he heard Julie's cheerful voice on the other end. How he longed for her and the fresh air and open skies of the Gulf country. The city stank of fuel fumes and the noisy traffic was assaulting his nerves. He wanted out.

'Hi, sweet thing. How are things in Karumba?'

'Oh, still boiling over with talk, theories and rumours. The place is still buzzing from the Mitchell River battle. Dutch tells me that this is going to be his last season. He is going to buy one of Wog's fishing boats and the license, which will be auctioned off after the court is done with them. Do you know a certified skipper interesting in taking over my boat?'

'No, I don't, but I will keep my eyes open. Why don't you take it over, you have always told me that you miss the fishing life?'

'I do honey, but I need a man for the heavy work and the sex. Why, are you offering?'

'That is a hell of a thing to ask a man, darling. I am on the top of my career and will probably make inspector when this is over. It's a big job with a good salary.'

'So, you want me to join you in Brisbane, is that what you want?'

'No, I know you would, but I don't think you would last long in the city. Anyway, let's change the subject, and let me do some thinking on our future when I get this paperwork sorted out. My head is full of shit now. I reckon they will have to extend the Lotus Glen Prison resort to fit all the criminals in that have been arrested in North Queensland alone since the Mitchell debacle. By the way have you heard from Vic?'

'Yes, I have after his TV appearance. He told me that he and Jim have had their pensions suspended because of thousands of dollars' worth of royalties they received from the pictures and the TV appearances. Everyone wants him and Jim on their show. How come you missed out, honey?'

'Not allowed due to departmental policy. Wait until I catch up with those two scoundrels, they owe me a carton of the best wine for their fame. But I reckon I won't even have to ask as they probably have it waiting for me anyway. That is the sort of blokes they are. I'll give Vic a ring when I have the time. Anyway, I must run. I will call you tonight.'

'Another week to go,' Bill moaned, looking out the office window. The enquiries were ongoing and not a day had gone by when someone did not present him with a summons to appear at the Royal Commission that had been set up.

However, he had stood firm; claiming that any evidence he had would be forthcoming at the trial of Broggetti and Morossi and that providing the commission with any evidence would endanger the outcome. They did not like it, but legal opinion backed him, and the collection of and jobs-for-the-boys retired fat cat judges and politicians had no choice but to wait until the trail was over to conclude, not only their findings, but most off all their curiosity. Farrell also proved to be unmoved by their huff and puff, while an impatient media screamed police conspiracy.

The trial commenced and as expected it was long. In between, Julie managed to fly in from the Gulf country to spend a few blissful days with him. While she came down twice to the city during school holidays, there was only time for weekend escapes. The trial judge was unmoved by the pleas of "not guilty" by Broggetti and Marotsi. The jury found both guilty as charged. The judge committed them behind bars for the rest of their natural lives.

Others involved in the case were given long sentences that Bill thought were justified. Overall, he was happy with the outcome and for the first time in months he relaxed a little, entertaining Hawkins and King, who had been important witnesses at the trial of the Mitchell River event.

Bill took the two men to the airport the next day and resisted the urge to get on the plane and get the hell out of the city. There was a message on his desk on his return to the office to meet with Farrell. Before he did, Bill typed out a letter and took it with him. The commissioner looked surprisingly relaxed thought Bill as he entered Farrell's office. For once he was not smoking, though as usual the office smelled to high heaven of stale smoke.

'Bill, great job you did in court. Excellent work. By the way, you are nominated for promotion to inspector. Congratulations my boy. The way you are going you will sit in this chair one day, perhaps after the bloke who will get my job when I retire next year.'

'Sorry Steve, but I don't want it anymore. My heart is no longer in the job, and it is best that I retire from the Police Service.'

'Retire? You are fucking joking, Bill. You are the best I have. The force needs men like you.

Why the sudden change?'

'It's not sudden, Steve, I have been sitting on it for weeks. The Gulf country is in my blood, and I need to get back to it for my sanity. Besides there is Julie, she will come and live here, but she would just pack up one day and go home, or worse still pine away without telling me what is wrong.'

'Bill, I won't stand in your way, but in case you should ever change your mind I will make a strong recommendation that you are rehired in your current status, rather than starting in the ranks again.'

'Thanks Steve, but that is something that is not going to happen. I'm out of here as soon as my time is up on the date of this letter.'

'Accepted, but as they say, wait there is more. The reason I called you in is to have a look at this picture. Is there anything familiar about this boy?'

Farrell handed Bill a photo of a young boy about seven years of age. Bill looked at it, the face vaguely, but strangely familiar.

'That young boy is currently being flown from Jakarta to Darwin. His name is Jason Grant, at least that is what the tattoo on his left arm says. This photo was taken when he was only about four years old, only a few weeks before his abduction. No doubt, it is the same boy. The Indonesian authorities found the boy on a small island. It's the home base of the boat captain of the boat used in the Gulf smuggling operation. From the reports I have from Interpol, the father and the boy were put on the boat by Bull Antinus en route to the Celebes Islands, the plan being to feed them to the sharks somewhere in the Arufura Sea.'

Farrell paused and lit another smoke before continuing the story to his impatient listener.

'Anyway, it appears that the captain and his wife had no children of their own and always wanted a boy, so Jason's life was spared, but his father unfortunately became shark food. The boy can't speak English anymore, but he will soon pick it up. I want you to fly to Cairns tomorrow and meet the incoming Darwin flight the following day. There is a Federal policewoman and the child on board. He will be handed over to you to take the boy to Karumba to his mother on a special chartered flight. It's all arranged. Interested?'

'Of course, I am. Does Julie know?'

'No, she does not. I thought I would leave that up to you.'

'Thanks Steve, I'll clean my desk and get my gear together. But I will be back to see my last days out.'

'Don't worry about that, you have leave and that should cover it. I'll fix it with the personnel department. Though, you will still be required to return on demand for the Royal Commission Inquiry which, now that the court hearings are over, will resume soon. Though from what I hear, the fire has gone out of those old fat cats.'

'Thanks Steve,' Bill replied thankfully. 'Anytime you're in the Gulf let me know, I'll take you out fishing, or whatever else you want to do.'

'You're on, Bill. Me and the missus are going to do the grey nomad bit when I retire. We will buy a 4WD and a caravan and hit the road. Visiting the Gulf country is high on our bucket list. Let me know about the boy and mother reunion. Bye, Bill and have a good trip.'

They shook hands and Bill walked back to his office, feeling elated, but deep in thought.

Chapter 25
HOME BOUND

A stiff southeast breeze blew across the Cairns airport tarmac, carrying with it the smell of the Coral Sea and the Barron River mangrove mud. Bill thought it smelled sweet and fresh after the traffic fumes of Brisbane. Vic Hawkins was waiting for him at the baggage collection area. Bill had called him before leaving Brisbane, telling him to pack a bag for a flight to Karumba – no argument. Hawkins looked fit and well thought Bill as he shook hands, the grip as strong as ever from the sprightly elder.

'Good to see you Bill and welcome back to paradise. I don't know how you can take the big smoke. Jim and I could not wait to get out of Brisbane after the trial. The place is too noisy and stinks of car fumes.'

'Couldn't agree more, mate, but wait I'll grab my bag before someone does it for me. You can't trust anyone these days. What is Jim up too?'

'Nothing much, Bill. Just doing a little prep work on the 4WD and the boat for our forthcoming Gulf country trip.'

'Why don't you take your wife, Vic?'

'Oh, she always used too, but she likes to look after the garden these days and to enjoy the comforts of home. The way my body is ageing I'll be joining her soon, except for the gardening bit. I hate mowing bloody lawns. Tell me what happened to Suzie and those Asian girls?'

'They were all granted asylum, Vic. And some other girls also who were caught up in the cartel's sex trade from previous operations. Suzie got so much media exposure that a model agency picked her up and from what I have seen on the tube she is on track to become one of the country's top models. Good on her, she has the looks, and the body, as you know.'

'That is good to hear, Jim is madly in love with her. They got together during our court case days when we were in Brisbane, but she is not a woman who would want to live in the bush like Jim does and it came to nothing. And there is a huge age difference to consider. But he is over her now and has moved on.'

It was only a short taxi trip to their hotel and after checking in and dropping their bags in their room, the men headed to the lounge bar.

'So, what is so important about me coming to Karumba?' Hawkins asked. 'I have been thinking about it since leaving home this morning. Are you getting married and need a wedding photographer?'

'No, that will happen later if Julie wants me. She once told me that you are the godfather of her son, Jason and that you both were the best of mates.'

'Yep, we were. The missus and I used to take him fishing and did so only a few days before he and his dad vanished in the Mitchell River Delta. We used to spoil him rotten as we never had kids of our own.'

'Do you reckon he would still recognize you if he saw you?'

'Fuck Bill, what the hell are you coming at, he is dead isn't he?'

'No Vic, the Indonesian police found him on an island somewhere near Borneo. It appears that he was adopted by the boat captain who abducted him and his dad. They were supposed to be dumped somewhere in the sea for shark fodder, but the captain took pity on the boy and took him home and raised him as his own.'

'Fuck mate that is the best news I have ever heard. Does Julie know?'

'Not yet, I want to surprise her, but I need someone to positively identify the boy first before I turn up with him at Karumba, and that is why you are here.'

'Take me to him and I will tell you in an instant, Bill.'

'I will, but you will have to wait until the morning flight from Darwin. I thought having you here and along on the trip would help him. It appears he has forgotten his English and he only speaks Indonesian.'

The flight was on time, the passengers spilling into the baggage collection area. Hawkins saw the Federal policewoman and the small boy clinging to her hand before Bill did. He stepped forward to meet them, but Bill held him back.

'Steady mate, let the little fellow get his bearings and see if he recognizes you.'

He waved to the policewoman who acknowledged him with a curt nod and a wide smile. Hawkins kneeled and held out his arms.

'Hello Jason, remember Uncle Vic?'

For an instant, the boy looked startled before he pulled his hand loose from the woman and rushed into the arms of Hawkins.

'Uncle Vic, Uncle Vic,' he cried, tears streaming down his face as the surprised policewoman spoke in astonishment.

'Oh, that is wonderful, he is regaining some English, though he appears to still understand it well enough. That is fantastic as I have only been able to speak Indonesian with him.'

Bill introduced himself and shook hands as Hawkins hugged Jason, speaking to him in a calm voice.

'Looks like a positive identification to me,' said the officer. 'But where is his mother?'

'She doesn't know about Jason yet,' Bill answered. 'She is in Karumba. We have a charter flight waiting to take us there. The old bloke is his godfather. They have been the best of mates since Jason was born. He is a lifelong friend of the family.'

'Well Bill, I am convinced. If you sign these papers for me, I can get going as I have the same plane to board for Canberra. Shit of a place, I'd

262

rather be in Darwin or here in Cairns, but work is work.'

She said farewell and hugged Jason, who appeared more at ease with her now that Hawkins was present and looking after him. He waved to her as she vanished amongst the crowd.

'No English, but I think he is asking for mummy and daddy,' Hawkins said as they walked onto the light aircraft tarmac and boarded the twin-engine Cessna.

Bill noted that Jason had not let go of Hawkins' hand, and that he had accepted Bill as a mate of his. Bill was happy that he was at ease with him because now would come the hard part, a fresh relationship with Julie and Jason. As he knew she was working and would not leave school until it was time, Bill had phoned Sergeant Jack Simpson earlier and informed him of the developments.

'Can you ensure that she will be at the airport, Jack?' he requested.

Simpson had been delighted at the news.

'Don't worry Bill, she will be there. In handcuffs if I have too. See you when you get here, mate. And welcome home.'

'Home, what do you mean by that?'

'Mate, everyone in the police service knows of your resignation, the departmental email reported it this morning. But I have not told Julie as I reckon you would be coming home to surprise her. She will be surprised all right. Must go, duty calls. See you after lunch, Bill.'

The flight over the Gulf country savannah appeared endless, but at last the pilot pointed the nose down to the tiny settlement that resembled flotsam on the point of the Norman River and its meeting with the great Gulf of Carpentaria. The plane landed with a couple of bumps, taxied along the tarmac and parked in front of the low buildings of the airport.

Hawkins said something about it being good to be back in the Gulf country, but Bill hardly heard him, being more interested in the police car that had pulled up near the terminal building. He saw Simpson get out and open the door for Julie, the sight of her bringing him alive. But now his attention was drawn to Jason who had also seen her. En route, he had been told by Hawkins that they would see mummy soon. He hoped that Jason would recognize Julie when he saw her and that the woman who had adopted him was not imprinted in his mind.

But Jason was looking through the window, waving madly and crying "mummy, mummy" as the pilot taxied and shut down the engines. Someone walked up and opened the door for the passengers. Hawkins hung on tightly to Jason who was struggling to get out and pointing and talking in what the men perceived to be Indonesian.

Bill stepped out first onto the tarmac and waved to Julie and Simpson before turning and helped Jason down the steps. There was strangled cry from Julie. She ran towards the plane as Bill let the child go. The two met halfway, Jason crying loudly "mummy, mummy." Julie was calling his name repeatedly, her eyes filled with tears as she hugged and planted wet kisses on his face. Bill knew his own eyes were wet with tears. Hawkins also had damp eyes, which surprised Bill as during the time he had known him he had rarely shown any emotion.

They walked over to Julie and her reunited child – no one knowing what to say, just being content to leave them in the joy of being together again. Simpson came over and wordlessly shook hands with the two men, his eyes glistening.

'Mates, this is what makes being a copper so worthwhile,' he said in a choked voice. 'As long as I live, I will never forget this moment.'

Hawkins hunkered beside Julie and Jason, hugging both, his head between theirs.

'Come along Julie, before you flood the runway with your tears,' he said. 'Hey, little Jason, didn't I tell you I would take you home to your mummy.'

In reply, the child gave him a hug as Julie was supported by Bill, her legs and body shaking.

'My God Bill, why didn't you warn me about this,' she uttered, tears streaming down her face.

'I'll tell you later why, but I really wanted to surprise you. Besides I wasn't sure it was Jason until he and Vic met in the Cairns terminal this morning. He has forgotten his English because he has been living in Indonesia since he was abducted.'

'Oh Bill, is he okay?'

'He sure is as he was adopted by a childless couple and from all accounts loved as their own son. But come, we must get you both home.'

Simpson dropped them off at home, the boy clinging tightly to Julie during the brief drive. She turned to Bill and Hawkins.

'Thank you both for bringing my son home,' she said with a touch of sadness in her voice. 'But what about Alex?'

'Sorry Julie, he is gone and won't be coming back,' Bill answered gently. 'I'll tell you the full story later when Jason is asleep.'

Jason has heard his father's name and he suddenly grabbed Julie's hand.

'Daddy, mummy, daddy?' he asked in English before lapsing into the Indonesian language.

Julie comforted him before looking into his eyes.

'I'm sorry Jason, but daddy won't be coming home anymore. He went to heaven a long time ago and is now with Jesus.'

She stood up, grabbed Bill's hand and placed it into Jason's.

'Bill is your daddy now. He will look after you and take you fishing like daddy used too. Uncle Vic will also take you, won't you Uncle Vic?'

'I sure will, little man, what say we go and catch some fish tomorrow, you, me and Bill so that we can get to know each other again.'

The boy nodded his head vigorously, a big smile on his face. Bill knew that he had been accepted by the child and that becoming part of the family was a reality. Later they had a late lunch on the veranda, watching an ebbing tide and the sun kissing the Gulf waters before it vanished below the horizon. It was a beautiful, serene scene. For the first time in months Bill felt as if a huge weight had been lifted from his shoulders.

'I have resigned from the police service,' he suddenly blurted, looking at Julie. There was dead silence. Julie looked at him as if she had misunderstood.

'You have, but what are you going to do now?'

'Well, to tell the truth I know this rich widow with a barra fishing boat and a ready-made family. I am going to marry her and go fishing. That is what I am going to do.'

Julie kicked away her chair and rushed over and embraced Bill in a bearlike hug.

'Oh, you are a wonderful man, of course I'll marry you and of course we will go fishing.'

'Well, let me be the first to congratulate you both,' Hawkins smiled. 'I reckon this was going to happen sooner or later anyway. I'll take your wedding photos – free of charge.'

'You bloody old prick, you better or I'll have you jailed,' Bill threatened him. 'I reckon that you should be good for a carton of champagne as well seeing you made a packet from those battle photos and the story.'

'It's on the way, folk,' Hawkins replied with a laugh. 'Jim should just about be here. He left the Tablelands early this morning and is towing our new boat up with his new 4WD. Yep, we both spent up big since we last saw you guys.'

'That reminds me, where is my boat,' asked Bill, turning to Julie.

'It's under the house silly. It's a wonder you did not see it. I towed it home when the police brought Wog's and your boat in. Harry serviced and cleaned it when it got back. The Crown is auctioning Wog's boat next week and the GBC boats and other assets if anyone is interested.'

'You know I just might be,' Hawkins mused slowly, stroking his chin. 'providing the price is right. I reckon that I could spend the rest of my life floating about the Gulf in the Italia. Hell, even my old lady might join me. That would enable me to see you guys occasionally and make sure you don't stuff the fishing up with those blasted nets. However, I will need more money, a lot more, to buy that boat. You know, Bill, I just happen to know about a heavily defended farming venture growing "grass." The raid would make a good story. Interested Bill, before your resignation comes through?'

'Vic, you know what you can do, pass it to Simpson, but leave me out of it. I retired when I left Brisbane. You will just have to do with the boat you have.'

'You're right, Bill, probably safer that way. Besides, I am getting too old for that sort of shit anyway.'

About the Author

Dick Eussen has lived in the Australian tropics since 1959, where he has spent a lifetime working in the bush, on cattle stations, and living in remote mining communities. He also owned and operated a tour operation out of Port Douglas into the Daintree Rainforest for over a decade. He is Australia's premier and one of the most published freelance outdoor writer/photographers in the country. His first magazine piece was published in 1957.

He currently freelances for a dozen magazines and submits articles and photographs to photography, fishing, hunting and shooting, camping, 4WD, boating and quad bike adventures, bush lore, and northern history to national magazines. He is the author of seven factual books on fishing, hunting and camping along the Savannah Way - Cairns to Broome. Dick and his wife Eileen live at Mareeba from where they take regular bush trips to ensure that his many readers are kept informed on the tropical lifestyle when they head north.